A SKELETON IN BONE CREEK

A NASH RUNNING BEAR MYSTERY — #1

BAER CHARLTON

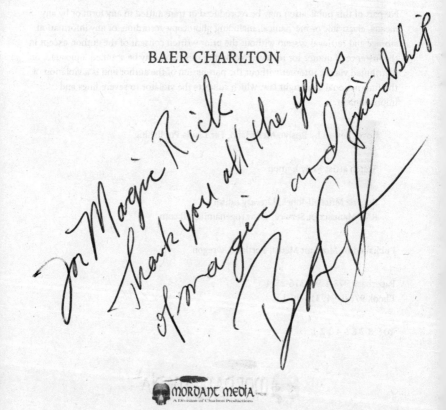

For Magic Rick
Thank you all the years
Homagic and friendship

MORDANT MEDIA
A Division of Charlton Productions

Cover design by Roslyn McFarland, Far Lands Publishing

Sketch artist Kelly Eamon

Rogena Mitchell-Jones, Literary Editor
RMJ Manuscript Service, www.rogenamitchell.com

Published by Mordant Media, Portland, Oregon

Paperback 978-1-949316-25-4
Ebook 978-1-949316-26-1

10 9 8 7 6 5 4 3 2 1

MORDANT MEDIA ™©®
A Division of Charlton Productions

CONTENTS

Powder

1
BRASH BEGINNINGS

NASH ADJUSTED THE SIDE MIRRORS.

"Stupidest car a special agent could get caught in."

She adjusted the rearview mirror. It had been pointing straight at her. She grumped at the reflected image her wife graciously referred to as rustically handsome. She smiled to ensure there wasn't something left from lunch on the airplane. *At least she had straight pearly white teeth*. And then she adjusted the mirror to look at the empty lot behind her.

Nash found the lights, air conditioning, and radio controls. Everything worked. After closing her eyes, she took a deep breath, and while holding her eyes closed, she pushed the start button. The car's seven hundred horses rumbled to life. She changed the temperature and chose a new channel to listen to. She turned on the headlights and opened her eyes. The daylight was too bright to see if the headlights worked. It didn't matter.

Pushing the button to open the trunk, she hit the left turn signal and climbed out of the red Challenger. Ignoring her bags, she walked around the car, checking the vehicle's condition and if the turn signal was working. She leaned into the trunk, assessing the state of the spare tire and jack. Returning to the open door, she changed the turn signal.

She picked up her bags and walked around the front and back to the trunk. Her two years at Langley training new special agents and CIA operatives about knowing everything about a strange car had saved lives. She knew only one agent who had died from a bomb when he finally used his turn signal. Tiny details matter.

She closed the trunk and stepped to where she had told the rental agent to stand and not move. The bored young man had behaved while he absently reamed his ears with his keys. He held out the clipboard with the paperwork for her to sign.

Nash looked at the silver Toyota with a bashed-in door and the white Nissan with a sad look on its front end. "It must have been a hard month." She scrawled her signature and pulled the papers apart, taking her pink copy.

"They sold off almost everything when the pandemic hit. Now they can't buy more than a few hundred cars at a time because of the chips. The big cities get their stock first, but it's still slim pickings. You're lucky we had this. The guy rented it in Reno, drove to San Francisco to have an affair, and died of a heart attack yesterday." He cocked his smirk to one side and rolled his eyes the other way.

He pointed at the fire-engine-red modern-day muscle car. "It came off the exotics lot. It's not even supposed to be here. It's not your standard horsepower car. This is the seven-hundred-horse Hell Cat. So I recommend you keep your foot out of it until you get used to it."

Nash folded the paper and turned to the car with her new respect. "I'll bear that in mind."

She had some issues to work out in the next three hundred and seventy miles. Three hours of Bay Area freeways and then three hours of winding backroads into an area of small minds and the past. Two hundred miles of county road, but a mind running at freeway speed. Saving the man's rubber was not one of them.

Two hundred years before, the pioneers might have called it the unknown. But Nash knew its history, and none of it was pleasant.

The rental agent watched as the bright red car fishtailed out of the lot and onto the highway leading north. He turned and shook his head, hoping the car would return in one piece. The federal government didn't have an exemplary history.

2
COULD BE WORSE

THE YELLOW SWIRL pattern of the Formica counter dimly reflected the tacky plastic lampshades made to look like stained glass. The bright light of the naked bulbs bathed every six feet of the counter in the hope it would pass for cheerful instead of pathetic.

Nash slowly scrolled through the file on her phone using her left thumb. Leaving D.C. had been less than pleasant. And she knew it was her own fault. She never worked well with others.

She had been late coming to the meeting about the fresh case out west. Her pants had barely dusted the seat when she spotted the words *Bone Creek* and the misspelled Harden County. She stood to walk out.

"Where do you think you're going, Bear?" The deputy director didn't like the show of disrespect. The agent had been late and was now walking out on his presentation.

She turned from pulling her leather jacket over her starched white shirt. She considered correcting him for the umpteenth time about her last name but bit her tongue. "Airport, sir. You can text me the file."

He shook his head and squinted. "Nobody said you were getting this one." He pointed out the freshly scrubbed face floating above the cheap gray suit all newbies wore. "It's al-Faragi's turn up to bat."

She glanced at the young Black woman in the dark gray hijab, fresh from the body farm. Nash wondered if the young woman had learned to stop fainting or throwing up yet. "Not to be disrespectful, sir... but..." She turned on the young woman. "Al-Faragi, do you know where Harden County is?"

The diminutive agent stumbled and swallowed twice as her eyes tracked to the deputy director.

"He's not asking the question. Nor does he know the answer. Do you know the answer?"

Her voice was shy and low. "California?"

Nash pointed at the CA on the board. "Good guess. North or south?"

She looked at the front of the room. "Um...?"

Nash squared her body toward the deputy director, but she faced the young Black woman as she walked to the dry-erase board. "Thanks for playing, but it was a trick question. It's not in California, but the infamous Independent State of Jefferson." She wiped *Harden* off the board and wrote Harkin.

Turning back to the junior agent, she continued. "The ratio of illicit guns to rednecks to blacks is forty-seven thousand, to six thousand, to one." She turned to the deputy director. "The Latino population of the area is fourteen percent because of the small amount of ranching and the larger money crop of weed. The First Nation population is and has been for the past eighty years, about nine percent. There are two people of Asian heritage, and they're not having any more children, but the food is decent. If you send al-Faragi, she will be dead by Wednesday. Only one agent knows where Bone Creek is and why this needs to be managed locally instead of the usual federal agents sweeping in and creating a total cluster..."

The deputy director squinted and pointed at al-Faragi. "At least take a team…"

Nash furled her lips and shook her head. "If she comes with me, she'll only be sucking air until Saturday. I need someone here to research information, as I might need it." She turned on the junior agent. "You have until I land in San Francisco to find out why people call it Bone Creek and where it runs from and to. Otherwise, I'll use Mable." She turned as most of the older agents smirked. Mable was a legend in the basement. She remembered more than most computers could find. You just needed to get past the concept of her being eligible to retire during the Clinton administration. When Ruth Bader Ginsburg became a Justice, her only comment was *good to see the kid made it.*

At the door, she turned and looked at al-Faragi in her dark charcoal-gray hijab. "You didn't stand a chance. It might have almost been fair if the deputy hadn't misspelled Harkin County. It's up in the corner of California. Stand at Sacramento and point at the corner where Nevada, Idaho, and California come together. Your wrist will be in Harkin, the largest town in Harkin County. The heel of your thumb will be in the warm waters of Bone Creek." She gave the deputy director a hard, knowing look.

Nash twitched as the cell phone vibrated in her hand. She looked at the dialog box and poked the accept button with her thumb.

Her voice was quiet as she was aware of the surrounding diner. "Hey, princess…"

The voice was tired. "You left again. We were supposed to have counseling tonight."

Nash glanced at her watch. It would be midnight in D.C. "You're up late."

"It's just as easy to throw up at night as during the day. You're avoiding the issue."

"I figured the counseling was off with you in the hospital for the chemo. Besides, this case is where only I can go."

"Home."

Nash rocked in the understanding of her wife. The woman had connections running deep in D.C. "You spoke to Prentice."

"He wasn't happy with you."

Nash took a small bite of whatever she forgot she ordered. "He's a big boy. He needs to get over himself."

Mina sighed. "He's your boss. You need to get over yourself."

A part of Nash flared. She changed the subject. "So the chemo is worse this time?"

A floof of pillows accompanied the tired voice as Mina fell back. "It's changed. This is more targeted. The docs warned me it could be rougher, but they need to get in front of the tumor and shrink it before they can operate. Zabriskie is looking for at least an eighty percent reduction before they open my head."

Nash never knew what to say when the conversation reached the squishy parts. It was hard enough to admit she was in love with Mina for the first year, and then it took them another two years to get around to talking about marriage. With the brain tumor, their never-easygoing relationship was strained even more. Both understood the nature of the storm they both had married.

Mina, the more intuitive of the two, sensed the quiet. "Look, I'm going to try to sleep. We'll talk when you get back."

Nash cleared her throat. "It's just a skeleton someone found. It shouldn't take exceptionally long." She neglected to mention it was in a creek people called Bone Creek for a good reason.

The phone cleared before she could thumb the red phone icon. It wasn't anything, but it irritated Nash. It was as if she were being dismissed.

The report replaced the phone app as she dug another fork-full of food from the plate. Her gaze crossed the sheriff's name as the fork approached her mouth.

"Oh, great…" The fork settled to the plate, and she pushed the plate away. "As if this wouldn't be awkward enough… Thomas f-ing Brady? Sheriff?" She grabbed her coffee as she read on. "You would think being the quarterback, team captain, and Homecoming king had been enough."

The waitress in the pink uniform with a white apron appeared. "Ready for some pie?" She peered at the remaining full plate of food. "Was something wrong with the chicken fried steak?"

Nash rolled her eyes up. "Oh, that was what it was? I thought I had ordered a steak. You know, cows, red meat, honest food…?"

The young woman snorted. "Not in corporate America. I think you'd have to go hunt one of them down around here. If it don't come out of the freezer and into the frier, the Tucker brothers don't know what to do with it." The young woman narrowed her eyes as her left hip cocked from the weight shift. "You look familiar. Where you from?"

"Harkin County. Why?"

"The reservation?"

"I grew up more near it than on it…" Nash leaned back. The young woman looked familiar somehow. Twin braids pulled back into a black Dutch rope bun bracketed the solid black eyes.

"You know Oscar Brown. Everyone called him—"

Nash snorted softly as her smile pulled back to one side. "Three Toes. Best kicker the high school ever had. We were in sports together and in the Spanish club."

The girl glowed. "The team won the state championship down in Sacramento. You all went to a city park and had ice cream. They took a photo of the team for the paper. That photo is in a gold stand-up frame on our mantel. Three Toes was my daddy."

Nash glowed with the memories. "Small world. How's your daddy doing?"

The girl's lips turned hard. "He was hunting a few years ago. Some city slicker thought the orange jacket and hat looked like a deer. The idiot was hunting with an AR-15."

Nash's eyes narrowed as she shook her head. "He never stood a chance. AR-15s have no place other than on a battlefield. I'm sorry. He was a good man."

The young woman slumped her weight hard onto her right hip as she leaned her left hip against the counter. "It's really been hard on my mom."

Nash thought but couldn't remember Three Toes ever dating anybody. She shook her head and stuck out her hand. "I'm sorry, I'm Nash Running Bear, and I don't remember Toes ever dating."

The waitress shook. "I'm Tracy. My mother was Norma Garcia. Her father was the county hydrographer. Mom was a few years older than dad. I'm twenty-six..."

Nash leaned back. Her mouth was half open.

Tracy's lips furled as she nodded gently. "Yeah, I was born about the time you were seniors at the State Championships. The folks got married the next summer."

"You seem okay with it."

Tracy rolled her eyes to one side. "I have a daughter of my own. Her daddy is in prison now for growing pot. It's funny, really. If he had just grown pot, he'd have been popped out when they made it legal. But he had an automatic pistol on him when they busted the farm. So he's in for the gun more than the pot."

Nash cocked her head. "Sorry."

Tracy harrumphed softly. "For him being out of my life. Trust me when I say it's a blessing. I get the best daughter. My mom has a granddaughter who thinks the world of her nana, and we don't have to put up with his shenanigans or his friends."

"So I take it you never married?"

"Nope. I'm a Brown through and through. Right down to only three on the left foot. Mom is Latino. I'm just Brown." Her smile glowed. "Now, how about some apple pie? On me."

Nash felt the tenuous connection that the girl didn't want to lose quite yet. "Sure. One slice of pie won't ruin this body." She dusted her fingertips down over her muscular body.

Tracy cleared the plate and returned with pie and more coffee. "You back here visiting family?"

Nash closed one eye as she thought. "Work. But I'll stay with

9

my sister and Uncle."

The young waitress smirked knowingly. "Your uncle... or Uncle?"

Nash chuckled. "Everybody's uncle."

Tracy pointed back and forth. "So... Uncle and your sister are...?"

Nash closed one eye and shook her head as she thought about her younger sister and the man who was old when she was in high school. "Just a living arrangement. He has a teepee out behind the barn or something."

"What kind of work would bring you back to Harkin?"

"Nothing pleasant." She cut the tip of the pie off and shoveled it into her mouth. Her face lit up, and she nodded.

"Right?" Tracy smiled. "Nothing pleasant ever happens up Harkin way. The other day, a hunter found a skeleton up in Bone Creek."

Nash put her fingertip to her nose as she chewed. She nodded.

"You're law?"

Nash swallowed. "FBI. But I'm not sure why I'm here."

Tracy's face lit up as she waved her hand excitedly over her head. "I'll take '*I think I know* for a thousand, Alex.'"

Nash chuckled. "I'll bite."

"They think it's the Air Force guy who went missing last year up here. Nobody was supposed to know, but a military ring was on the finger." She rolled her eyes to one side. "Or so I've heard."

Later, Nash sat in the car, looking at the text message from Special Newbie al-Faragi. She had found no water named Bone Creek, but she had found the correct spelling of *buena agua*, Spanish for good water. The creek came from a confined aquifer or artesian well. It wandered for a few miles, in and out of reservation land, and then disappeared back into the ground.

She texted her back. "Okay, you can help."

It was after midnight in D.C., but her phone vibrated instantly. The text read, "Thank you. Muna."

3
HOMECOMING

THE HOUSE WAS dark except for a dim light deep past the front room. Probably the light over the dining table. Nash thought about her sister. Teachers are notorious for being early risers, so it would be logical to expect Daisy to turn in early, even though midnight wasn't early for Nash.

Nash popped the trunk and grabbed her two bags. She thought about the house. It had been the parents' home until cancer had taken the mother. Their father had given his life to the Northern Pacific Railway. Literally. His body had gotten trapped between couplings, and he survived for the twenty minutes to say goodbye over an early cell phone with a crappy connection.

Nash was at Camp Gonsalves in Okinawa, Japan. They tried to call, but the cell contract didn't allow for international calls. She got a letter from her mother three weeks later. It was the first lesson about Nash having a life and there being life if she hadn't left home.

As she strode up the front walk of cracked and chipped concrete, heat-burned crabgrass, and lots of dirt, she thought of the book she had to read in college.

"Fuck you, Thomas Wolfe. I'm home again."

"Not hardly, Secret Squirrel."

Nash started and stopped. Her first reaction was to drop the bags and draw her weapon. But the voice was ground into her being from her time in diapers. The shadow on the porch moved the rocker and stood. The man seemed less of a giant than he had when she was growing up.

"Good way to get your head blown off, Uncle."

The grizzled older man stepped to the railing. "Not hardly. You have bad habits, squirrel. You snapped down your weapon as you left the car."

Despite being the town drunk, she had always hated how he knew things. "Did not," she lied. She marched up the three steps and held her shoulder forward for the obligatory hug.

He reached out his left arm as he turned around to face the door. "Yes, you did. And you have both hands full. I would have thought they would have beat that out of you at Langley."

She looked at him with a bored look from long suffering. "Goofball. Langley is CIA. FBI is Quantico. What are you doing up so late... or home so early?" She didn't smell alcohol on his breath but wondered if he hadn't been down to the Short Branch or the Golden State.

"I heard you were headed this way." He opened the front door.

"Bullshit. I only found out this morning. And I didn't talk to anybody about coming."

He rested his hand on her upper back. "Yeah. I know. That's why I made up the couch."

The small lamp on the side table shined softly on the pillow and sheets. Her old blue robe lay on the back of the couch.

She looked at him. "What about my room?"

He shrugged with his shoulder and face. "Daisy's monster quilting machine takes up a lot of space. But all those tubs of cloth take up more. She also has her computer in there."

She thought about the living arrangements when her mother was still alive. Uncle had always been around, but she couldn't remember where he had slept.

"What about you?"

He wandered into the kitchen and turned on the light. "What about me?"

"Where do you sleep?"

He stood looking at the food in the refrigerator. "Same place I always did. The teepee out back."

She gave him a stern look as she reached past him and grabbed a chicken leg off a plate. He snorted softly. "I wouldn't if I were you. She fried that rooster up before the weekend."

She watched him as she bit off a chunk.

He watched as she slowly chewed.

She leaned over, toed the lid to the dented trash can, and spit. "Gad, that is nasty."

"Yeah, it wasn't any good the night she fried it up, either. I tried to tell her not to cook a yard rooster, but try to tell your sister anything…"

"Like what?" The subject of their chuckling stood in the archway, her arms crossed and eyes narrowed. She was trying for an angry look, but the Hello Kitty bathrobe didn't carry the attitude.

Uncle rolled his face toward Nash. "Uh oh. Time for me to be in bed. Talk in the sunshine." He bobbed his head at Daisy and stepped out the back door.

Nash leaned against the counter. "Hello, Daisy."

The woman slowly drew a breath through her nose and let it out. She turned around and walked back up the hall. "Uncle made up the couch for you. I get up in four hours."

Nash's hands rose from her sides as she softly had a conversation with herself. "Hello, Nash. Long time no see, Nash. Good to have you home, Nash. How was your trip? What are you doing here? How long are you planning to stay this time?"

Nash sighed and glanced at her dive watch. The dots and lines glowed against the black face and body. It was after midnight. Talking to Three Toes' daughter had been nice but also reminded her of how small the sizable area of California could be. Tracy might

13

as well have lived in Harkin for all the separation the fifty miles had been on her knowledge of the local goings on.

Nash turned off the kitchen light as she stepped from the kitchen into the living room. She looked at the deer heads on the wall. There were five stuffed fish scattered between them. Her father's pride and joy hung over the archway to the hall. A badger with three points on each antler. The deer heads were roadkill. The fish had come from the fish market in Sacramento. Her father had a few books on taxidermy, but with the fish, he learned more about making molds and casting fiberglass. The painting had come with books from the library. The brass plaques were wood he had carved and then brass leafed.

In true fisherman style, every one of them lied.

The forty-pound rainbow trout he cast from a Chinook salmon. The Neolithic brook trout was his best mold of a fish and was a bloated sturgeon. He had blown a tire coming back from Sacramento. The ice melted, and the rotten fish ballooned into the grotesque. Years later, he would taste sturgeon and grump about how his sturgeon was better when not eaten.

Sitting on the couch, she pulled off her boots. The FBI preferred their female agents to wear sensible low heels. She got the foot doctor to write a prescription for Wellington boots that were like the boon docker boots she was used to in the Marine Corps. When she and Mina got dressed up, she would pull on her nice pair of cowboy boots. Nothing fancy, just comfortable, and didn't embarrass her wife.

She pulled her cell phone out, thumbed in a text of a single purple heart, and sent it to her wife. Over the years of her constantly on the road with special investigations, their long texts and conversations had shrunk to the shorthand of two common souls. She placed the phone on the side table near where her head would be. Pulling her holstered weapon from her belt, she laid it next to her phone.

She stood and finished undressing. Removing her bra, she

pulled the T-shirt back on. Pulling on the threadbare robe, she drew up a large section to her nose. After her mother died, Nash wouldn't let Daisy wash it. It still smelled like her mother had always smelled—somewhere between her lye soap and the squaw tea she washed her hair in.

She let the robe drop and padded toward the bathroom.

SITTING ON THE COUCH, SHE GATHERED HER THOUGHTS. The house smells, the light, the feel of the braided rug they had always had, now under her feet. Everything was still in place. She knew it was her that had changed, but the feeling of her fitting here was so right, yet...

She pulled the small chain on the lamp. The darkness was instant. And as sudden as the dark was, so was the eerie light in her mind. She froze. The fog or mist hung in wispy tendrils along the creek bed. The trees never grew thick, only shot up for a few years, reaching out like skeletons, searching for a grip in the sky against the draw from the mud and rotting lime water.

She sensed the person next to her. She knew the moonlit night. It was Homecoming, and they had skipped the dance. The small party was downstream at the pillars. The remnants of the old bridge. Two pillars still stood on each side of the creek that only threatened to be a small river. The crossing was where the county road and the lumber wagons crossed. It had been the place for teens to bring beers and to party for as long as anyone could remember.

But this night, Nash and Thomas had not felt like drinking. They had walked upstream into the night talking. Then they stopped, and as they kissed, they heard voices.

She could feel the braided rug under her feet. But her knees were damp. Her hand could feel the rough bark of the scraggly sapling. In the mist, there was a form of two people. The voices were guttural and indistinct. The moonlight cast only enough light through the trees to provide a crude zoetrope between the trees of the movement. An arm raised. Then disappearing. Cleaving of the mass. And the sound of something large falling into the water. And silence.

Nash jerked back to the living room. The dark was almost complete. The soft glow of yellow light washed from the alarm clock and across the side table as it illuminated her weapon and phone. From where she sat, she could see the tiny reddish light on the bottom of the refrigerator, letting one know it was on.

No creek. No mist. There was no full moon. But she could still smell the lime of Bone Creek. She drew her hands up to her nose. She could smell the pine bark. It was the same as twice before.

She fumbled about and pulled the small chain. The small light filled the room. Nash looked at her hands and knees. They were dirty. The herd of butterflies beat their wings against the inside of her chest. Her heart raced, and she couldn't seem to catch her breath. Her eyes were fixated on her hands.

She had never had a panic attack for five years in the Marine Corps. She had never taken after her mother, the woman who saw things.

Daisy had told Nash that their mother had sat down at the table with the phone. She had asked Daisy to make some squaw tea with black willow to calm her nerves. When the railroad called, their mother had been sitting and staring out the glass door for almost an hour. She had talked to her husband for the last time and said goodbye. Afterward, she calmly got up and put the teacup in the sink, saying she was tired and was going to take a nap. She saw things.

Nash didn't know if she saw things or not. She never talked about it with her mother or anyone else.

Now. It all rushed back.

She shook her eyes closed. She was not that woman who saw things. Nothing had come of the night up Bone Creek. Nothing had come from the things she thought she had seen or dreamed. It wasn't her. She was not her mother.

Her hands rose to her face. She slapped them down on the couch and stood. Walking to the kitchen sink, she washed her hands. Grabbing the washrag, she bent to wash her knees. There was nothing there.

There was nothing there. She was *NOT* her mother.

She returned to the couch and leaned down into the sheets and blankets. The pillow formed around her head as it had for so many years. She didn't remember if her feet found their way under the covers. She was tired.

4

POWDER

NASH WOKE to the tiny tinkle of a spoon slowly scraping against a bowl. Her left eye cracked open. It was pitch black. What the...?

She rolled over and immediately regretted doing so. The kitchen and dining table were ablaze with light. She flipped back to face the couch. The rough weave of the Indian blanket upholstery her mother had done when they were little still hadn't softened or worn. Nash felt she could still smell every dog they had. Butch the Labrador to the small fluff dog her mother had at the end, without exception, slept on the couch.

Nash snuck a peek at her watch. Doing the math, she realized she would already be at work in D.C. The three hours meant nothing. The deputy director would want a situation report.

She rolled back over as her bladder reminded her of the coffee she had consumed less than six hours before. Daisy glanced up as the blue robe circled in the air and came to rest on her sister's retreating shoulders.

Nash started the slow-to-warm shower before she sat. She studied the wall. It was the same pale blue her mother had painted it after she delivered Daisy. She worried about the fumes and being pregnant. Nash stared at the towels. Thankfully, they were a pleasant yellow instead of the flowered towels she had grown up with.

She glanced at her watch, pulled her T-shirt off, and stepped into the shower. As she pulled out the rubber band and unbraided her hair, she thought about the memory she had seen during the night. But, according to the preliminary report, the remains were near the pillars. Thomas had explicitly noted them the same way one would say they found a body seven feet west of the First and Elm Streets post on the northwest corner. It was a landmark you could find with Google Earth or an auto club road map.

She washed her hip-length black hair with whatever was perched on the tub's edge. If it worked for Daisy, it would work for Nash.

She thought about what Tracy had said that wasn't in the report. She knew they had converted McClellan Air Force Base shortly after she transferred from the Marine Corps to the FBI. So the nearest base would be Travis unless the guy had been a Secret Squirrel down at the former base for the SR-71. Now retired, but who knew what progeny it had spawned besides the B-1 and B-17?

She turned off the water and started twisting her hair to wring it out. In her younger days, she would leave it and let the air dry it. But with time and a specific look to uphold, she started pulling the sections into her signature tight braid. In D.C., she split the time between a braid and a braided tight bun. She hated how short she had to keep it in the Marine Corps. Now nobody complained if it didn't impede her from doing her job.

She pulled the braid up through her T-shirt and pulled on her panties. After her sister left, she would go through her pack and change. The robe was on the hook of the door. She hesitated and left it. She regretted her decision the moment she turned the corner.

Her sister had already gone. Uncle sat quietly, waiting.

"I figured you remembered the chicken from last night."

Nash blinked.

Uncle smirked. "Yeah. Her coffee is worse."

Nash sagged against the side of the refrigerator. "Why do I feel I'm going to hate this investigation?"

"I have coffee out in the teepee... or we can go to town."

Nash's eyes closed slowly, and she rolled back along the fridge. "I'll get dressed."

Uncle cleared his throat. "I hope you brought jeans and some proper shit boots."

She glanced back. Her eyes narrowed. "Why?"

His face and body never moved, but it seemed as if he had shrugged. "I saw what the county guys looked like when they returned to town. They were swamp sludge from head to toe."

She thought about the double indigo jeans Mina had bought for her. They were the perfect look for poking around the shops in Falls Church on weekends or a few days in the Adirondacks, but they were nothing like the jeans of her youth. They also cost Mina a few hundred.

"I'll go shopping if I need to."

THEY STEPPED OUT ONTO THE FRONT PORCH. NASH HAD never thought about how large the area was. The round table could fit at least six people without their elbows knocking. The timbers didn't have the thin hollow sound most porches did. She slowly took it all in.

Uncle snorted with a smirk. "Just now noticing the porch?"

She snuck a quick look back at him. "I just never noticed how solid and large it was."

"Pine Nut... er... your dad and I hauled all this back from the yard where they rebuilt the flat cars. This was six-inch-thick car decking beat all to hell, only used the pretty stuff and threw what was left in a heap to maybe burn later. It's probably still at least a good five inches thick."

"But it's not beat up."

Uncle squinted out through the fields. "Now. Your dad bought a two-foot block of pumice. He would push it around the porch every night after work to sand it down. The old navy ships called them holy stones. They used them to sand off all the blood after a battle. It got rid of the hell of war."

He stepped down to the front yard. "We'll take my truck. Give you time to get acquainted with your new partner."

"I don't have a partner."

He stuck his finger and thumb in his mouth. The whistle was loud and throaty. He turned and smiled. "Now you do. Meet Powder."

She snorted and looked around dramatically at nothing.

The dog was a lightning flash of dark gray and white as it turned the corner. Uncle turned and pointed at Nash on the porch.

The dog made a broad curve around the man and went straight up the stairs. Or straight over the stairs. The dog didn't seem to have legs, just a jet propelling it over the land. He circled Nash three times and was back at the man's side, looking up.

Uncle peered back at Nash. "Kneel or sit on the edge. She needs to smell your breath."

"My breath?"

Uncle raised one eyebrow. "You took a shower this morning. She can't smell you. You just smell like your sister if you use her soap. She thinks you're Daisy."

"And that matters... how?"

Uncle turned and looked out across the fields and into the forest. "Your sister doesn't work. She doesn't like animals and doesn't understand how you do." He peered back over his shoulder and waved his hand down. "Just sit."

Rolling her eyes, she sat.

The dog's nose was still pointed across the fields. Uncle flicked his hand. The dog ignored him. He snapped his fingers. The dog looked up and begrudgingly stood and walked back to the stairs. Slowly, she made sure all four paws touched each stair tread.

Circling twice, she finally sat next to Nash.

"Look at her and talk to her. Just don't touch her. She's not a petting dog. She just works."

Nash turned her head. "Bullshit. All dogs want to be petted." She looked at the mass of the strange-coated dog. The brownish, dark gray, and white patches belonged to another kind of dog. The size and coat looked more like a sheep or cow dog. But the face was the strangest. The muzzle was the wider of a hound, but the color looked like it had stuck its nose in the fan at ground zero of a shock wave of white paint or flour.

"What kind of dog is this?"

Uncle chuckled as he watched the field. "The father was a huntin' dog. The bitch was a cow dog. Most came out looking like a regular cow dog. But Powder kinda got the full cluster of their mating."

"Interesting markings on her face. It gives her a scared look."

"Yup. Looks ain't everything. She's anything but scared."

The dog sat, ignoring Nash. Her nose hadn't twitched or moved. Nash turned toward Uncle. "I'm getting kind of hungry."

Uncle held his hand out low in a stop motion.

Nash peered out at the empty field that seemed to hold the man's attention. There was a flash from the sky and a large brown bird lifted from the ground. An animal, almost the size of the bird, hung from the talons.

Uncle turned with a smile on his face. "That eagle has been cleaning them ground squirrels out of the field for the last week. I think she or he or they have chicks."

He looked at Nash. She glanced at Powder and shrugged.

"Well, Powder... truck?"

The dog stood and made her way down the stairs. It was as if she had suddenly gotten ten years older than the pup who had run around the corner minutes before.

Uncle scratched at the base of his ponytail. "Guess she's still thinking about it. She must have smelled a lot of your sister on you."

Nash gave him a side-eye as they walked. "I washed my hair."

THE TRUCK WAS A LOT NEWER THAN NASH FEARED IT would be. The dog sat between them and only looked straight ahead.

"It was Daisy's shampoo, wasn't it?"

Nash glared at the dog. "Honestly. This has gone on long enough. The dog just doesn't like me, and I'm okay with that. My pet squirrel never really liked me either, even after I'd saved its life. I don't have to sit in a drum circle with every animal and sing Kumbaya."

Uncle eased the truck into the parking lot. "You need to rinse your hair with sage and squaw tea. It will get rid of the white man smell your sister likes so much. And Kumbaya is a dumb song. It has nothing to do with nature and animals. It's something the white man made up to teach his children to sing around a campfire. Better to tell stories about how the world came to be." He rolled down the window and opened his door. He turned off the truck and smiled. "Pancake day."

Nash slid out but looked at Powder. "What about...?"

Uncle closed the door. "She has the window if she needs to do anything."

As they got close to the door, Nash's pocket dinged. Uncle glared. "I'll get you coffee. Don't let it get cold."

Nash narrow-eyed the man's back as she stopped to pull out her phone.

She read the text and hit the button to return the call.

"Al-Faragi." The voice sounded more self-assured than she knew the young woman was.

"It's Nash. Reach out to Travis Air Force Base. They lost a young airman last year up here hunting or something. Find out if they ever found the body. If they haven't, we'll probably need dental records and anything on the bones. Bone Creek is anything if not effective. The lime and alkali strip the bones of anything that might have given us DNA."

"The autopsy said it was..."

Nash cut her off. "I saw that. But I've got a hunch there is still something there. Nobody goes soaking in Bone Creek for longer than a half-hour. It's warm, but not that warm. The pH heals cuts and scrapes, but only if you can stand the pain. But it's great for overworked muscles, which is why the athletes are always down there after big games. But the tissue is gone if the body is there for more than a week. After more than a month, lime can start filling in breaks and cracks. I need to see the bones, but I think there's something there."

The deep voice behind her gave Nash a start. "People are going to think you're talking to the spirits or something."

Nash glowered. "I gotta go. Get me the information."

She put her phone in her pocket before she turned. "Sheriff."

Thomas Brady stood well over six feet, and the years had only thickened him in kind ways. His blond hair had a touch of winter next to the ears. But his face could still set the ladies' hearts racing and get him re-elected.

He reached out and opened the door. "Agent."

She narrowed her eyes as she walked in. Uncle was in the booth halfway down the windows. His face was passive as he searched the tableau of Nash being followed by the sheriff.

She slid into the booth across from him and took up her coffee mug. It was tepid but still good. She sensed the presence of the tall man. She kept sipping her coffee.

"Is this a private powwow, or is it open...?"

Nash didn't look up. "Did the insensitive white man talk come with the job, or was it from just staying in the small town?"

Thomas stood with his mouth cracked. He knew anything he said at this time would just escalate the situation. He turned and walked to the other end of the restaurant.

Nash looked up and then fished her phone out.

The text was a simple purple heart and the word *up*.

Nash texted a rainbow and a purple heart back. She turned the phone face down on the table.

Uncle grumped, "Wife?"

Nash nodded as she glanced at her watch. "She's about seven hours behind where she would normally be when she was working." She noticed his narrowing eyes. She realized there were parts of the world he had no privy to. "Chemo... again."

"Breast?"

Nash shook her head behind her mug as she sucked the last of the now-cold coffee and then put it down at the edge of the table for a refill.

She studied the conundrum-who-walks-like-a-man. "That was eleven years ago before we started dating. She's Irish and Chinese mix. The Irish never contributed much to the chest department, so there wasn't much to remove. She has more help with dresses now than she did before. But this one is a tumor at the base of her brain."

She looked out the window as a battered truck rattled down the street. It was comfortingly homey in a strangely perverse way. It had filled her childhood—battered trucks, Indians with no horses, and cowboys with no cattle—just groves of marijuana.

Uncle nodded and looked up at the bottle-blonde waitress. "Usual, Katy."

Nash glimpsed at the young girl, barely old enough to be her daughter. "Same."

As the waitress finished pouring fresh coffee and left, Uncle looked back at Nash. "I only knew you were married. About two years ago, Daisy let slip it was to another woman. A lot doesn't filter between the trees from the outside world."

"And it never gets to the last stool at the bar of the Golden State?"

His face hardened. The wrinkles became more chiseled and less fluid.

Nash grimaced and hung her head. "I'm sorry. That was cruel. You didn't deserve that."

His voice sounded less like the wind through the forest and more like rocks tumbling in the spring runoff.

"When you're in Washington, D.C., where do you work?"

"The old field office on Fourth Street. Why?"

"That's a building. Where do you work?"

"The Office of Special Field Investigations. It's on the fourth floor. My desk is the one that looks like it was in a fight between a bison and a Chevy truck, and the rockslide won."

He didn't blink. "My stool has a heart with an arrow carved into it with a boy scout pocketknife. The four initials SS and SS came later with a can opener. I made the stool from a fine New Jersey maple. Hard as hell and great in a bar fight. It doesn't have any padding like the ones the white guys sit on. My ass is as hard as an old fence post. On the underside of the seat are the words *Semper Fi*. Never forget that there is a lot you never knew and don't care enough to find out now. Not everyone works in an office."

The tinkling voice seemed to be dialed up well past just perky. "Okay now. Two mudslides, wild pigs, and a heart attack in the middle. Y'all need anything else?" She placed the two platters on the table.

Uncle looked up and smiled calmly. "Put the sheriff's bill on my tab. He was treated poorly this morning. And he's going to be experiencing worse before the week is out."

The girl tightened her lips over her teeth and sucked as she spun. "Sure thing, Uncle."

5

THAW

UNCLE NUDGED his elbow against Nash's. Leaning in, he pushed his chin toward the sheriff sitting alone in the last booth. "Sheriff sits alone more than anyone else in here. He's an ass, but he won the election—maybe because of his football days, his time served in the desert, or because he was the only man running. Nonetheless, he is the sheriff. Go make nice, or you're on your own for clothes."

Nash hung her head and then gave him a side-eye.

The blond waitress, Katy, looked back at the sheriff and then down shyly. "He ain't never have nobody sit with him. He has the prettiest wife, and I've never seen her come eat with him." She looked up, blushing. "Okay, I've said too much. I'm going to go in the back and open a big can of hush up."

Uncle drooped one eye and opened the other. "I'll go take Powder down the street to my office. You can pick her up later. Make sure you don't smell like your sister."

Nash watched him leave. The man walked in peace with the world. It didn't seem to matter whether it was because he had a pickled brain or was just old.

Nash rolled her head and watched the sheriff. His left thumb hadn't stopped its slow death scroll of his phone. She focused. It wasn't the same scrolling as Mina scanning through the news of the day. The people going through their Facebook or emails stop occasionally. His scrolling was slow and methodical. He was looking for something, but she didn't know what.

Her sliding into the booth startled him. He jerked and put his phone away. His face was the same when they got caught with the beers behind the gym. They were seventeen and seniors. The world was theirs to command... until the janitor caught them.

"Going through your Tinder account? I'm not sure Cindy Lou would approve."

The thick neck above the collar glowed with extra heat. "There's a lot of things Cindy no longer approves of. Tinder isn't one of them. Besides, the Tinder in these parts is breeding stock or marijuana. I have less than an acre, so both are not on my radar."

Nash squirmed. "Let's start over..."

"We can't." He waved his coffee mug in the air. "We have a lifetime of history. Good and bad. It is who we are. Maybe if they had sent some guy from the city instead of you..."

She looked up at the waitress and turned the other coffee mug over. "They tried. She graduated from Quantico last spring. She's up for a single but would need at least a double if not a team with this."

Thomas's eyes narrowed under his wrinkled forehead. "Why? Is she that bad?"

"Nope. She's quite good, really. But I don't think she would get the same reception."

"Because she's not a local?"

"No. Because she's Black. And very good-looking. Halle Berry kind of good looks. The kind of good-looking to make middle-aged white women wish they were young, fit, and Black, kind of looks."

He held up his hand. "Okay, okay. I get the picture."

She leaned her head over to one side. "The kind of looks that would leave you with a dead Black woman in a hijab by tomorrow.

So they sent the local Indian lesbian, who wouldn't be a threat to the cowboys around here."

The sheriff spat half of his mouthful back into his mug. He grabbed the paper napkin and started wiping his shirt.

"Looks like we both need a change of clothes."

Thomas froze and looked in question at Nash.

"Uncle said the original investigators came back from Bone Creek muddy from head to foot. He said I'd want at least knee-highs, if not full-bib waders. From your shirt, I'm reassessing and might go with a full dry suit and helmet."

The sheriff smirked and took her napkin to finish the wiping. "I had some usual splattering, but Taylor stepped on a submerged limb. The limb gave way, and he went full face-plant. But we have jumpsuits and deep waders."

"So this is the boggy area upstream from the pillars?"

He frowned and twitched his head. "No. This is downstream about two hundred yards. There's a dogleg that becomes a large flat back bay. We think the body got caught in the eddies. Didn't you guys get my report?"

She fished out her phone and found the report. She found the notation and turned the phone for him to read.

"Says fifty yards upstream..."

He slowly thumbed through the report. Frowning, he turned the phone around.

She read the location. It wasn't the location she thought she had read. She looked up. Thomas had his head cocked with his jaw in the other direction.

"Maybe you read it in the middle of the night and thought..."

She snapped the phone shut and stuck it in her pocket. "Yeah, maybe that's it." She frowned. *But the placement was so vivid...*

He pulled his things together. "Maybe we need to swing by the office and grab some gear. Then we can go look and see what you think. It's been what... twenty years since you were here last?"

"Three."

29

"Three?"

She stood. "Twenty-three years since I was here last."

"Weren't you here for your mom's funeral?"

Nash furled her lips. "Topeka. Missing money at a bank. We're talking real money, not computer shenanigans. They had bricks of cash disappearing from their vault. We were there for three weeks before we figured out the camera in the vault turned off when you shut the door. They figured the light went off, so the camera should also."

Thomas's mouth pulled slowly to one side. "Let me guess. The light didn't go out."

She drew her eyes tight as she leaned her head. "I had Quantico overnight four cameras directly to the police station. And four more to my room at the hotel. The ones I got were infrared. Not outstanding quality, but they also sent me a text message when there was movement, so I knew when something was happening.

"For three nights, I slept like a baby. On the fourth, my phone blew up at three in the morning. You couldn't determine who the two were on playback, but they talked. The cameras the police got were just dumb cameras. No sound, no fancy stuff. But the cameras I installed looked the same but had great microphones."

The sheriff looked at the bill and laid down a twenty. His face was incredulous. "They talked?"

Nash snorted softly. "Never stopped. And they used each other's names. Real genius material. We were standing in the basement utility closet doorway when they got back with two footballs of hundred-dollar bills."

Thomas and Nash were laughing as they pushed out of the diner door. "I understand the bank manager, but where was the basement?"

She looked at him as they got to his SUV. "Police station. The lieutenant had been doing some spring cleaning and found the access tunnel running right under the bank vault. They put a lift under one large terrazzo tile, and, boom, they had a door. The security was all in the big 1927 Miller Safe door."

As they climbed in, he looked over. "So I'm assuming the light did go off, but there was enough for your cameras to work."

She swung her head once. "Just like a Frigidaire. The door had a switch to kill all the electricity into the vault. Saves money. Or so they thought."

"But the two guys knew about it and wore night goggles?"

She snorted as the sheriff nosed the SUV out of the lot. "Nope. They had a light in the crawl tunnel. There was plenty of light to see the pallet of money and where to touch and where not to touch. We got great videos."

"But you missed your mother's send-off."

"We dusted her ashes the next summer. She liked Shasta, so we hired a guy with a Maule to slowly fly us over the top with the door off. Daisy hated it. I was always curious about the California Highway Patrol and their Maules. Turns out, they're weather wimps."

Thomas laughed. "Doors closed and heat on. I could have told you that. Those guys fly over the interstates for five and six hours. And it's cold up there."

"Yeah, we found out."

As they slowly cruised through the middle of town, Nash thought about the town she remembered growing up in. She hadn't remembered so much empty space between stores. Only the center three blocks were full of stores. Harkin was smaller than she remembered.

As they broke free of the population, ranches appeared among the sparse trees. There was more low brush than anything with what one would call a trunk.

Nash watched the brush. In an open area with no trees, she spotted what she wanted. "Pull over here."

Thomas slowed. "Here?"

Nash jerked her hand back over her shoulder. "No... back there

31

a hundred yards. You do remember what a hundred yards are, don't you?"

He backed up and pulled off the road. She opened her door and swung out. He followed her.

"You do remember this is rattler breeding season, don't you?"

She waved behind her. "Keep your pants on, Sheriff."

She bent over a sage bush. Grabbing one stalk, she pulled up, stripping a wad of leaves into her hand. Stepping to a smaller and scrawnier bush, she repeated the stripping with her other hand.

She straightened and rubbed the two handfuls of leaves together in her hands. Finally, she reached back, grabbed her thick braid, and massaged the leaves into her hair, rubbing her head and neck.

"You know you just guaranteed Powder to go schizoid."

Nash walked back and stood in the sheriff's face. "No. With the power of the squaw Tea and the Sage, she won't be able to smell Daisy's soap."

He watched her face for the joke. He broke out in a braying jackass laugh when he realized she was serious. "You have no idea what that dog can smell or do."

Her eyes narrowed. Her growl was as thick and barky as an old, gnarled oak tree. "Truck. Now."

He turned and headed back to the truck. "I'm just saying…"

She pulled her braid around to her nose. "Dammit."

6

MUD

Nash stood knee-deep in more slurry than mud. She held her hands on her hips and swung around, contemplating the yellow cords running from stake to stake. Sectioning the large flat pool into a grid of ten-foot squares.

"I don't remember it ever getting muddy like this." She looked down the creek where Thomas had been going over the survey notes. "Is this normal?"

She realized what she thought was the sheriff bending over was only a large stump. "Thomas?"

The weak voice came from off to her left. "Yeah... I'm okay."

The tall mud pile walked out from the small back bay caused by the eddies eating away the walls and into a small, depressed flat. Even his signature blond hair was now dappled with greenish-white mud.

Nash's forehead frowned as she laughed. "Did you decide the day was over and to go swimming without me?"

He looked back at the boggy area. "Nah. I was looking at where they had noted more possible bones, but I didn't see any." He glanced at Nash, standing in mud to her knees, as his neck turned red. "But I lost a bet." His mouth snarled as he turned toward his SUV. The swearing was mumbled and almost inaudible.

Nash continued her query but louder. "There is a lot of loose mud or slurry... What happened this year that was so different from when we were kids?"

She watched him pull off the shoulder straps and let the bib waders fall. He stepped out of them and peeled himself out of the jumpsuit. Even from a distance, she could tell the twenty pounds he had put on since high school hadn't gone to his waist. He hadn't turned into the type of person to go home, crack a beer, and lay in front of the TV until bedtime.

She looked back toward the creek. The ground around the banks was hard pan for the first several feet. Then there was a stunted undergrowth of dry land fescue and dry land alfalfa. Neither one was good enough for grazing. The scrub brush started about twenty feet away from any area which could become a bog, overflow, or wandering stream. The stunted pines and catalpa trees didn't start for another forty yards. It was all the same as she remembered, except for the prolific amount of mud. And floating mud.

Thomas stood twenty feet from the mud. He wore a T-shirt and jeans. "You were asking about the mud... we don't know. It started about five years ago. The dirt around here has clay but mostly decomposed granite and broken-down volcanic rock. The mud should be just watery dirt, but this..." He looked around. "Is more like floating silts. The college guys up from UC Davis and Chico think it came with the water from wherever this all starts. They took a lot of samples, but you know how those eggheads are... They just forgot about telling us what they found... if anything."

She looked about at the mud. "You mentioned someone saw or found something to make them note a possibility of more bones. Did you ever think about bringing up a floating X-ray?"

His eyes opened. "They have those?"

Nash hung her head, muttering, as she slogged her way out of the mud. "I'm stranded in the middle of nowhere. Please send rescue as soon as this message in a bottle, tied to a messenger pigeon, reaches civilization." She bobbed her head once. "Yes, X-rays... Well, sort of. They're called magnetometers. They read the density of what is below them. It's how we sort of X-ray an area of ground to determine where bodies are buried at suspected body dumps."

She looked at the sheriff's bare feet. They hadn't seen sunshine in decades. She remembered he used to be as tan as she was naturally. Besides the blond hair, which got lighter in the summer, the two could have passed for family—and just as close.

She got to the bank and brought her one foot up and onto the bank. Without thinking, she stuck her hand out. It hung in the air for a second before she looked up. She waved her hand for help.

She could see he was chewing on something as he stared at her. Ignoring the hand.

"You slept with my wife."

Nash's hand dropped. "Really? This is about something that happened twenty-some years ago?" She stepped back into the stream and jumped onto the bank on her side. Flipping her legs over her in a roll, she cocked them and stood from a fighting crouch. She moved into his face. "You need to get your facts right. You two were dating when she came over to have sex with me instead. She found out it wasn't her thing and went back to the team. If you still have a problem with that night, you need to take it up with your wife."

His face was stone. "I did. And I made a stupid bet and lost. And that's her car just pulling up behind me."

The sound of the car stopped. The sound of the window hummed menacingly. "Anybody ready for lunch?"

The door opened. Nash turned her head. Cindy Lou could probably still fit her cheer squad uniform and do all the same gymnastics. It was as if time had stopped for her twenty-three years before. Only the rest of the world got older and fatter.

Nash watched her pull the picnic basket out of the trunk.

35

Turning back, Nash watched Thomas clenching and unclenching his jaw until it was white.

Nash rolled her eyes as she patted him on the side. "Get over yourself. You're still married to the queen of the prom we snuck out of. And she didn't turn into a heifer at the state fair."

He turned. "Hey, honey, I was just leaving. You two have fun."

Cindy smirked at Nash. She looked at the mud all below the knees. "I told him you wouldn't get messy and wallow in the mud. He said it was in your nature as a Jar Head."

Nash lowered her eyelids as she evaluated her old friend. "Let me think about this a moment. Who was first in line for the greased pig catch at the county fair? Who raised pigs? Who raised goats and two steers? And for your information, I was a Shore Patrol in Japan. No mud, no nasty swims through muck, and few fistfights. Great food and a bit of interesting sake."

Cindy's eyebrow went up. "For some reason, the rumors were about you wading through swamps and cutting your way through jungles."

"Maybe those stories sounded good to those wrestling wild, long necks down at the Golden State. But other than getting sweaty with a sandbag or speed bag, I liked to keep it clean. It was safer, and I came home in one piece."

Thomas hung his head as he looked for a graceful exit. "Well, I'll leave you to it. Nobody will disturb you two while Otis has the road blocked."

Cindy tinkled a giggle. "Yeah, old Otis was watching his eyelids for pinholes when I drove by."

Nash unsnapped the straps on her waders and let them fall. "Look, I don't understand what this bet was, but I sure don't need to have you leave. The three of us can enjoy lunch like civilized adults. You two can work out on your own time whatever is going on."

Cindy smirked. "Besides, I brought bathing suits for all of us, just in case you went face down in the mud."

Nash gave her a mock face of horror. "And ruin my makeup?" But, regaining her seriousness, she turned to the sheriff. "In all the gear you brought here, are there any containers we can take samples of the mud?"

He walked back. "Why? It's just mud."

Nash pointed at the back bay. "The semi-solid muck over there is close to mud." She turned and pointed to where she had just been standing in the water. "Look at my waders. The mud was floating around my knees, and there was a strange floating slurry below, but the creek bottom was firm—no mud." She turned back with a frown. "Mud is one thing, but this...? This is something else entirely."

Cindy frowned. "Do you think it's toxic?"

Nash turned toward Thomas for the answer. "How often do you come to soak?"

Cindy glanced at her husband. "We're up here more nights than not. There are a handful of couples from the old days who come, barbecue, and soak. We built out an area upstream with benches and everything." She laid her hand on her husband's arm. "When some of them go more than a few days, you can see it when they bend over or walk."

Nash leaned in, examining Cindy's forehead. Her mouth furled as she twitched her head to the side. "And I don't see any signs of a third eye growing... How about cancers?"

Cindy looked at Thomas. The silence was thick as he stuck his hands in his pockets and drew his arms in hard.

Nash's eyes narrowed. "What?"

Cindy leaned into him. "We lost Harold this last winter."

Thomas's voice was thick as he watched Nash's feet. "I don't think it was the water. I think it was more the bottle of vodka under the seat of his truck..."

Cindy nodded. "And in the flowerpot, under the couch, in the nightstand, the freezer, behind the flour he never cooked with..." Her smile was sad. "We loved him like an older brother, and he never drank with the rest of us. He always said someone needs to drive. We never saw him as anything but sober... until the end. We cleaned the house out. The final was in the hospital. The DTs didn't help, but it ended his suffering."

"What kind of cancer?"

Thomas looked up. His eyes looked more like a basset hound than the man an hour ago. "Liver, pancreas, kidney... You name it, his guts were a train wreck and must have burned something awful."

Nash nodded. "Yeah, not the water. Sorry about losing a friend. It's never easy."

He drew his head back with one eye closed and pursed his lips as he softly shook it off. "Thanks." He looked back at the SUV. "I have zip-lock evidence bags. Would those work?"

She bent to pull the waders back on. "Let's see. Make out the forms before I fill them. How about something to scoop with or a cup? I'll have to capture the stuff floating at ankle depth with another bag and then stick it in a clean bag."

He turned. "I'll get my waders and the bags." He retreated to the official SUV.

Nash snorted and called after him. "Forget the waders. I'm not trusting you near the back bay again. Your years of running the obstacle courses ended the day we graduated high school."

Cindy snickered. "You don't know, do you?"

"What?"

"He was first in his class at boot camp in San Diego. They tried to get him to try out for SEALs, but he doesn't like to swim."

Nash watched the man pulling gear from the SUV. "He was navy?"

"Helicopters. He started OCS over in Chico and then transferred to San Diego."

Nash frowned. "They make good money. What's he doing here?"

Cindy's face wound up as she looked over at her husband. "Short story is after he made captain, he was in the middle of his third deployment to the sand. The rocket hit his ship as he was walking away. The shrapnel… well, you'll see when we go soak. He's moving slowly today, so the pain is up. His back cracked in seven places. So he took the eighty percent, and we came home about when the old sheriff was retiring."

Nash's smile pulled to one side. "Hard to beat a hometown war hero in a dogfight."

Cindy snorted softly. "Once he put up the first campaign poster, all the others came down from windows and off the lawns. Nobody would run against him. They still won't."

Thomas returned carrying a cooler with a box of bags and a sharpie. He looked at the two quiet women. "What?"

Nash just shook her head as she leaned forward and scrutinized the bags. "Nothing. Just nothing but girl talk. Oh… good thing they're gallon-sized." She tapped the foam cooler. "Good choice." She looked up. "You didn't want it back, did you?"

He lowered one eye and growled. "I've dealt with the federal government before. I'll be throwing a party if they even hint at replacing it."

Nash opened the box of bags and pulled one out. "Well, let's get this party started. I'll get the mid-level drift sample while the one with the most legible handwriting marks the other bags." She looked back as she walked to the edge of the creek. "Figure out some way to get the other samples without scooping it with your boot."

She stepped into the stream and missed seeing the wooden spoon he had pulled out of his back pocket.

Cindy leaned over and looked closely. "Is that the spoon I told you I lost just before Christmas?"

Thomas chuckled as his chin tingled from the red growing below. "No, it's the wooden spoon to remind me to get you a complete set or something... to replace the one you lost last year." His eyes grew enormous as he watched Nash instead of looking at his wife.

7

THINGS REMAIN THE SAME

"Who let Pocahontas crash the party?"

Nash didn't move. Her eyes rose to lock on Cindy's. She could see her own slow burn was a snail's crawl behind the blonde's.

Thomas beat them both to the punch. "Same person who let the asshole come. And now I get to choose which one stays. Which one do you think is better looking, more intelligent to talk to, and we ought to keep around?"

The blustering man in an oversized cowboy hat pulled himself up by the large belt buckle with a Chevy bowtie. He smiled and glowed at everyone.

Thomas put down the long spatula. "You're pretty sure of yourself, eh, Darrel?"

"I'm more liked than anything coming off the reservation."

Cindy straightened and turned. "Care to put it to a vote, Darrel?"

Nash sensed things getting out of hand fast. She held up her hands. "Hey, no harm, no foul. I've been gone longer than I lived here. I can leave."

Without looking, Thomas pointed his finger out at her. "Stay out of this, Nash. This is about those who built this pool, those who were invited, and those who just assumed they were welcome."

Cindy pulled on Nash's arm. "Only builders get to vote. Thumbs up and thumbs down. We just get to watch."

Thomas held his hand up with his thumb to the side. "Builders... the vote is on Darrel. And vote."

Nine thumbs pointed down.

The man fumed and threw his can of beer on the ground. "That's just bullshit. She don't even live here anymore."

The redhead with the prophet's beard waved his fingers. "Bye-bye, Darrel. And remember, it's a no-wake zone. So keep it slow driving out of here. Don't want to wake up Otis."

As the man spun a doughnut in the dirt and left recklessly, Thomas held his hand out with the thumb to the side. "And now for welcoming Nash back to our slice of heaven."

Several fingers floated in the air, along with calls that Thomas was burning the burgers.

Cindy turned with a lazy smile and looked at Nash as she gave her a side hug. "You really need to come back more often. It helps clean out the swamp. And if you need a place to stay instead of the bible house, we have a spare bedroom."

"I feel bad about Darrel."

Cindy shrugged. "He always was a jerk. Now we know he's a bigoted jerk."

"Yeah, but you guys live with him. As soon as we figure out this case, I'm gone. Back to D.C."

Thomas leaned over with a burger on a plate. "To be honest, the only time we see him is out here. He never brings more than a single beer, but before the night is done, he has sucked at least six and a couple of burgers. He's a leach. And he wasn't a good ball player either. Tonight was a good thing. So enjoy the buffalo burger and visit. We don't soak before the sun goes down."

THE ORIGINAL SOAKING CREW HAD BUILT COFFER DAMS to create work areas. They made two arched concrete walls and benches that, if they met at the ends, would create a circle the size of a modest living room. The seating could comfortably seat twelve. Or if the entire team showed up like on the Fourth of July, twenty-eight. Year-round, the water was a consistent ninety-eight degrees.

The golden light didn't hide the spider webs of torn flesh and highways of cadaver stitch marks from military surgery. Nash had seen her share of what a field surgery and a delicate scar look like from a caring surgeon who takes their time to leave the fewest markings. The range of scars, in her experience, was the spread ranging from testosterone to estrogen. The display on Thomas's back ran the gambit.

"Who did the first work?"

He turned around and looked at Nash and Cindy, sitting neck-deep, shoulder to shoulder. The ticking of the seconds was as audible as the spinning of his mental tires trying to gain traction and only creating a burning of rubber.

Cindy rolled her eyes. "It's not a gotcha question, genius. She's asking about your back. Where or who took the shrapnel out of your back?"

The snorting laugh from the other bench sounded like a moose fart.

Cindy leaned close to Nash. "They served together. Buck played defensive tackle for USC and even got drafted to play for the Denver Broncos. He gave up on his career because of the war and his sense of duty to his country. His left knee, which he had been babying and hiding, ended his time of active duty. The IED only hurried it along."

"The captain got the best of the best the Green Zone offered back then. The proper hospital with the big tents and thick walls didn't go in for another year."

The sheriff glared at the larger man in the gathering gloom. He turned back to Nash as he slowly sunk into the water. "Like the mouth said. They stabilized me in Baghdad and then lifted me to Turkey. There, they found more metal to take out and then started putting in their own." His head sunk below the water.

Cindy quietly took over. "From Turkey, they moved him to Germany for the next year. Eventually, he spent another year and seven more surgeries in Bethesda."

Nash drew a line in the air. "Those would be the fine scars."

Cindy dropped her chin as she looked upward. "Who are we kidding? They left the worst scars and railroad tracks. Bethesda only has the name but no reputation for fine work. For that, he was out here in San Francisco."

Nash smirked. "Kind of like the ten-gallon hats with no cattle."

Buck laughed. "But they have the bull."

Cindy laughed back. "And the truck to haul it all."

Everyone laughed as Buck turned red. Nash now knew who owned the largest truck with the dual rear-end. Her eyebrows raised, but she said nothing.

Cindy filled it all in. "Buck likes the cowboy look but is deathly allergic to getting trampled again. When he was ten, his 4-H project steer spooked in the ring when he was showing. His back looks worse than Thomas's, but he's sensitive about it. That's why he's wearing the T-shirt. I've only seen his back once in twenty years. But as for the truck, he and his two uncles rebuild hydraulic rams. He has a five-ton trailer that I've seen him max out with two rams off earth movers." Her finger rose like a periscope and circled. "Year in and year out, he makes more than the rest of us combined."

"I guess I missed a lot, living out on the reservation."

Cindy snorted softly as Thomas's head surfaced. "Not really. Just the politics, bullying, and the usual small-town bullshit."

Nash's voice was low. "You two seemed to do all right."

Cindy gave her a hard look. "I wanted to quit the cheer squad more days than not. Thomas told me if I quit cheer, he wouldn't play. I don't know if we were arguing about us, saving the school, or just practicing for marriage. We did more ass-kicking than encouraging. We still do. I think that's why I hit on you."

"Your heart wasn't really into it."

The blond shrugged her one shoulder. "It was fun, but it wasn't something real. But it was also what he and I were. Just fun. Year after year. I wanted to know something real."

"Did it work?"

She furled her upper lip as she shrugged carefully. "Not really. He was mad, and we ended with plenty of loose ends. Then school was over, and life got complicated. The next thing I know, it's six years later, and I'm looking for a room near the VA in San Francisco. When I saw him in the bed, face down, and his back all torn up, I realized it didn't get any more real than that moment. I don't think he knew who was sitting in the room every day until the second week. They had backed down the drugs. He still couldn't see who it was, but he said if I was reading a story, then to read it aloud. So I did."

"Do you remember what you were reading?"

Cindy giggled. "I was deep into the *Bell Jar*."

Nash's eyes got enormous. "No! You. Didn't."

She shook her head. "Luckily, I had picked up another book at the Goodwill. Mitchener's *The Drifters*. But, two weeks later, I introduced him to the *Bell Jar*."

"What did he think?"

"It wasn't as silly or light at Catcher in the Rye. It's very depressing. I don't think we finished it. I know I'm not going back to find out."

"Catcher in the Rye?"

"No. That's just about an Incel who should have been shot instead of getting laid." She rolled her head instead of her eyes. "I can't believe they thought either book was suitable for coming-of-age teens."

Thomas turned at the snippet of the conversation. He frowned. "Bell Jar or Catcher?"

Nash laughed. "No. The Drifters."

Buck growled from the dark. "Hey now. Don't you be bad-mouthing my bible."

Cindy laughed and stood. "Uh oh. We've just drifted downstream to religion. Time to get the sheriff to bed."

Nash held up her finger before she realized nobody could see it. "Just a minute." She sunk under the water and untied her braid. In the slow, lazy current, she fingered her long hair out in the moving water to wash it.

Surfacing, she stood in bright light. Someone had turned on a couple of camp lanterns so everyone could see.

Thomas pointed toward the stairs. "Smart move. Powder will appreciate the effort if you don't smell like a decomposing body."

Nash wrung out her hair. "Speaking of which, where did the bones go?"

Thomas grabbed some towels from the large stack and handed her one. "We sent them down to Sacramento. But as soon as the FBI called, they took them to San Francisco, where I can't get access. As usual, the feds locked me out of my own investigation."

Nash could see the scowl on his face. It was the same as he got when a play he didn't call went wrong.

As Cindy and Nash stood on the other side of the SUV to change, Nash thought aloud. "I guess I get to head down to San Francisco for a few days." Without thinking, she looked up. "Want to come and have a girl's weekend in the city?"

Cindy looked at her with only one eye open.

Nash replayed the words in her head. "Oh." She blushed and smiled. "That certainly didn't come out the way I meant it."

Cindy glanced back through the windows of the SUV. "Separate beds?"

Nash glanced back and watched the woman. "Separate rooms even."

Cindy laughed and pulled on her pants. "Ha. You haven't seen the price of hotels in the city, have you? Uncle Sam would have a stroke if we got two rooms." She looked over. "But yes. I think I'd like that."

"You think Thomas would be okay with it?"

She pulled her T-shirt down over her braless top. "He's done a lot of growing up since high school. I think if you get past his resenting the FBI being here to watch over his shoulder, you'll find out he turned out much better than his father."

"I don't remember much about his father. Only his mom."

"Her always being home? Or the drinking?"

Nash's mouth turned into hard rolls. "Kind of both. I don't remember either of them coming to watch him play any sports."

Cindy grimaced and nodded. "They didn't."

8

CITY SLICKER

THE LARGE WHITE marble edifice was one of the first buildings to be built after the 1906 earthquake and fire. What was once the First Bank of Italy moved closer to uptown when it changed its name to the Bank of America. The building languished for a while until the army didn't like the navy hanging around their Presidio, so the navy took the building over for the duration of the Great War.

By the time they realized they needed to number the wars, the building had gone through many hands until it ended up as a forgotten adjunct of J. Edgar Hoover and his gang.

Most who drove past the building on the backside of the University of California at San Francisco never realized it wasn't part of the law school or the medical school. But a few adjunct professors of the two schools had day jobs in the expansive building behind the large walled compound.

Nash rumbled the Challenger in under the large portico and stopped. The guard passively watched as the door of the bright red muscle car swung open. As the woman emerged with her signature orange-tinted aviator glasses and long thick braid, the man smiled to show a large picket fence of ivory.

He stood from behind his podium desk. "Be still, my racing

heart. Super Special Agent Running Bear in a red-hot Hellcat. And here I always imagined you as a Mustang girl."

She smiled. "Hello, Randy Andy. Keep talking this trash, and I'll be forced to have you hauled up for nasty talk and a spanking. Either that or you've confused me for my wife and her little pony car. How have you been?"

The older gentleman slowly wagged his head. "Just counting my days until retirement. You?"

She smirked as she wagged her head. "You won't be retiring anytime soon. You have all those grandbabies to put through school."

As Cindy rounded the car, he fished out his phone and pulled up a photo. "Number five just got her grand champion this past weekend down in San Diego." He held out the phone for the two women to see. The dog was jet black and stood proudly next to the trophy.

Cindy leaned in closer to see. "What kind of horse is that?"

Nash smiled and snorted softly. "Andy, here, breeds black English mastiffs." She looked at the man. "Andy, this is the Harkin County Sheriff's Office representative, Cindy Brady."

The man tipped his two fingers to his forehead. "Pleased to meet you, miss."

Nash barked a soft laugh. "Not hardly, Andy. Cindy here is Sheriff Brady's wife and ass-kicker."

"Well, in that case. I'm very pleased to meet you. I have one of those myself. Going on forty-six years and counting on every finger and toe we have." He turned back to Nash as he saw a van pulling through the gate. "Did you have something to drop off or just stopped to schmooze?"

"I need a lock bin cart."

He held up his finger at the van driver as he stepped to one side. "I'll have that for you in just one second. Go ahead and open your trunk."

He returned, pushing a cart with a lockable lid. They loaded the evidence bags into the cavity and closed the lid. He handed her the lock and watched the van as she reset the code and locked the cart.

"There you go, Andy. Now, where do you want me to park? We'll be here for a while."

He waved at the parking lot. "Anywhere in the blue area. I'll have your cart right here."

The car rumbled to life, and Nash nosed it toward the parking.

"And the locking cart is because…"

Nash eased the car into a slot. "Chain of possession. He can guard the cart, but only I can touch the bags. When we get to the lab, they will sign the bags and forms, and then it's theirs to protect." She looked over as she got out of the car. "I doubt there would be a problem with mud… but you never know. So you cover all the bases."

THE MAN WITH GRAYING BLACK HAIR ON ONE SIDE, AND snow white on the other, stood looking in the top drawer of the filing cabinet. Beneath the white lab coat, he shifted his weight from the right prosthetic leg to the left. The shift allowed him to reach farther to pull a file from the cabinet to his left.

The white cabinets were white with bits of wear on the edges. They always struck him to be more fitting in the butcher shop of his youth.

He looked up at the white wall behind the bank of cabinets.

"Chrysanthemum nauseosus, or rabbitbrush, with just a hint of Ephedra nevadensis, more rudely called squaw tea." He looked back down into the file drawer. "I approve of your new hair rinse, Running Bear."

Cindy's eyes narrowed as she turned to Nash. Her voice was barely louder than the air movement in the morgue. "He couldn't have smelled…"

Nash rolled her eyes, pushing her eyebrows up. She smirked.

"When Thomas walks into the house with a bouquet of roses, can you smell them?"

"Of course. But he would have to do so first."

Nash frowned and glared at the blond. "We'll talk about it later. But if he comes in smelling of having been somewhere…"

"Like stopping in for a quick drink at the Golden State? Sure. He reeks of bad beer and cigar smoke."

Nash ground her head around. "I thought California was a no-smoking in public buildings state?"

Cindy softly snorted as her head rocked back. "Cliff owns the Golden State. He also loves cigars. So he also licensed it as a cigar bar. He probably sells almost as many as he smokes. But your point." She pointed at the man, now closing the file drawer as he turned on his two metal legs.

Nash raised her voice so her former teacher could hear. "Your mind and nose acclimate to persistent surrounding smells, even noxious fumes. Your mind ignores them after about five minutes. If you introduce an unfamiliar smell to the environment, you can smell it, no matter how subtle. As a case in point, we can smell a skunk fight from several miles away on a soft summer breeze."

Cindy winced. "Yes, we can."

The man nodded. "Bravo. Or, in your case, brava. You really weren't sleeping in class."

Nash swished her finger back and forth. "Mike, meet Cindy Brady. Cindy, this is Mike Sidebottom. And if he starts eating a hoagie sandwich and offers you a bite, know it is eighty-seven percent garlic."

The man rolled on one foot and turned toward his desk. "Hmm, I seem to remember you ate at least half of that sandwich."

"You had the courtesy of roasting the garlic. And the ham was Jarmon."

He dropped the files on the desk and turned to walk to the wall of large drawers. On the way, he toggled on the two X-ray viewing light screens.

"Harkin County has an interesting geographic anomaly. And it has regurgitated an interesting body of evidence."

Nash followed and veered off toward the tables. "Buena Aqua springs from the basalt rock bed, runs for about two miles, and disappears back into the earth among the lava field from Shasta. The many hot springs along the way produce warm stretches of lime-enriched water."

Mike glanced over his shoulder. "You did your homework. I'm impressed."

"I cheat. I was born a half mile from the basalt field and spent a lot of time soaking in those hot pools when I was growing up." She glanced at Cindy. "In fact, we were soaking in one night before last."

The man pulled the long drawer out and shifted the tray onto the moving gurney. He frowned in confusion as he waved his finger at Nash and Cindy.

Nash's one eye closed. "Cindy represents the Sheriff of Harkin County. This means anything you derogatorily say about Harkin, she will share with the sheriff in their bed when she gets home and elsewhere about the county over the next week. So tread nice."

His face brightened. "Good. Because I seem to remember meeting a tall Asian woman the last time I was in Washington. Brilliant conversationalist and extremely knowledgeable about the inner workings of the Beltway."

"Mina. Like the bird. My wife."

He smiled. "Just checking. There were rumors…"

"Nope. She's still alive and very much missing the poisoning, back-stabbing, and toe-stepping of the cocktail parties."

"How is she doing…? If I may ask."

"In the fourth round of chemo, but fighting hard. I just spoke to her this morning. She sounded weak, but was due for a platelet infusion, iron, and a sip of whiskey."

"Good. I approve of the whiskey therapy." He pulled the large envelope from the tray and drew out the X-rays. Slapping them up on the light panels, he continued to lecture.

"The limewater, along with the arsenic, does an excellent job stripping the meat from the bones. But then, because the skeleton remained soaking, the lime also deposited on the calcium." He pointed along the ribcage. "The deposit forms a fuzzy shell around the bone, like here on the ribs."

He lifted one rib from the mass and pointed to the cut end. "As you can see, the bone is the darker yellow tan. The lime is the white shell. Loosely judging from what we know of the chemical makeup of the water, I would put the time of emersion at fourteen months. This would account for the body mass's putrefaction, the skeleton's fine stripping, and then the layering of the lime."

Nash closed one eye. "So around last May."

He furled his lips and sucked a juicy but crisp chirp. "More like April."

Cindy snorted as her eyes remained transfixed. "Before or after lunch?"

The man smiled at the innocent question and the old sarcastic joke. "Probably before." His eyes grew large as the two women looked at him. "We can only assume because there was nothing in the stomach."

Cindy groaned at the joke she had unknowingly stepped into. "No stomach, either."

Nash cleared her throat. "Any guesses as to the cause of death?"

Mike raised his one finger as he wheels around and walks to the light screen. "That would be over here."

He spread his hand as he waved it over the X-ray films. Film after film. "As you can see, we shot film of the entire skeleton. We can guess this young man broke this toe about five years ago. He probably played baseball, as this fracture of the arm is quite common. But I didn't see the usual markers one gathers from football."

Nash closed her eyes as she thought. "So more of a loner as opposed to a bonhomie."

"It's not my job to do the profiling, but I would say it would be consistent with your conjecture."

Cindy turned to Nash. "Would that mean a quieter introvert type willing to be a team player, but not a more physical guy who's ready to storm the beaches with the gang sort?"

Nash cocked her head with a question on her face.

The blond stuck her finger out in the air as she cocked her hip. "Air force instead of a marine."

Nash raised her eyebrows as she turned back to Mike, whose hand had stopped over the last group of films. "And true to Lesson Plan 101, you have left the best for last."

He pointed out the small spider web on the back of the skull. The center was a large chicken egg of fractures, with the spider web working its way out from the center. "If this is the worst injury, I would conjecture it is not the cause of death. But..." His finger circled the X-ray of the cervical spine and neck. "Neither is the hyoid bone crushed." He looked at Cindy. "Which is the tiny bone here, and easily crushed when strangled." His index finger stroked his throat around his Adam's apple.

Nash leaned into the one X-ray. "Would a blow like this at least knock them out?" She turned to look at her former teacher. "And could this have been from them falling backward and striking their head? I mean... if we're ruling out strangulation..."

Mike's mouth furled up into a thoughtful smile. "We haven't run ballistic analysis yet, but my guess is no. Once we get the lime layer off, I think we will do more matching to blunt force object than fall trajectory."

Cindy narrowed her eyes. "Murder more than accident...?"

Mike smiled. "The correct comparison is murder versus mayhem. But you get the point."

Nash waved her hand at the X-rays. "I don't think so. There's no evidence of a stabbing at all."

9
DEEPER IN

THE LESSER HIGHWAY off the freeway opened to the more pastoral landscapes of alfalfa, grains, and cows spotted with the occasional building. The car rumbled with each slight grade. A counter beat to the disco and techno music playing quietly on the radio.

Cindy raised her seat back. "If I thought I had a chance with Thomas, I'd ask for one of these cars. Just the seats make it worthwhile."

Nash gave her a motherly glance.

"What?" The blond ran her hands over the soft leather. "The leather is softer than any saddle we rode, and run back and laid out... the sex could be..." She stared over at the thunderstorm brewing in Nash's face. "Oh..."

Nash narrowed her eyes to razor slits and glanced over. "Oh...?" She returned to driving. "... And that was supposed to mean... what?"

Cindy gazed out her window for help. "I wasn't thinking. I mean, with your wife... well, the cancer..."

"We've messed around. It's not like cancer is contagious."

Cindy squinted down at her thumb, picking at the side of her other hand. She needed to sand the callus down or go back to wearing gloves. Her head bobbed up as she looked around. "So why are they having us bring the mud back up here to Davis?"

Nash gazed over her shoulder as they passed an extensive herd of cows. Three men on horses, and two kids on quad-tracks were slowly moving them. A dusty gray streak raced along the fence line. She thought about Powder and how Uncle was sure the dog would be helpful. She wasn't so sure. Although, the morning they left, the dog did come over and sit next to her while she had her coffee and watched the sky lighten.

"The university up here is mostly agricultural. Some smaller schools within the agriculture umbrella, like forestry, soils, and ecosystems, are better at analyzing. The FBI has some great labs, but we can't do great work in all the fields, so we farm out a lot to the best labs who do the work." She glanced over at Cindy, still fixated on the road ahead.

Nash continued... testing. "Plus, they have the aliens from Area 51, and they do the best sequencing of cow DNA if other UFOs irradiated it. But only when the cheerleader isn't listening to the history lesson."

Nothing.

Nash went back to driving.

NASH LOOKED AT HER PHONE AGAIN AND THEN PULLED up to the parking attendant kiosk.

She flashed her badge. "I have a secured delivery for the Ecology Forensic Laboratory."

The young woman smiled as she grabbed a preprinted map off a clipboard. She highlighted a route and marked the lab. "I don't know how good your GPS is..."

Nash pulled her dark glasses to the middle of her nose and peered over the tops of the mirrored lenses. "It's a rental..."

The young woman smirked in knowing. "Umm huh... I heard all seven hundred horses as you came of the drive. My dad has the same mid-life crisis. And the junk GPS; you're going to need this map if you've never been there before."

She leaned in close as she pointed. "You go back out to the main road. Turn left and then left again on this road. It's unmarked, but it will take you back here behind the cow barns. You want to go around to the back of the technology labs building and pull up to the loading dock. I'll call ahead. Will you need a security cart?"

Nash leaned back some as she scrutinized the young woman.

The guard and student stood smiling. "It's my major. And whatever you're bringing, I might have my hands in it this afternoon."

Nash snorted softly with a smile. "No making pat-a-cakes."

The young woman turned serious before finally smiling. "Well, look at Ms. FBI getting all serious and spoiling the best part of the job."

THE LAB WAS SMALL BUT ONLY BY COSTCO STANDARDS. The bald, dwarfish man led them to an area set aside for security. Nash kept picturing the man as a Santa elf or a leprechaun. The tie-dye T-shirt didn't help underscore the seriousness of the lab. Neither did the strains of Pink Floyd coming from the boombox duct taped to the wall.

"When San Fran-psycho called, we cleared out our pot farm, and steam cleaned the lab to sterilize and prepare it for your mud. Mandy will be out this afternoon and will start the cataloging. The psychos have already pulled samples and are running them through their mass spectrometer.

"I'll pull samples and start them through our digital atomic spectrometer for a more detailed analysis. We're not the whizbang labs you see on TV, so don't expect a full analysis after lunch. It doesn't happen like that. But we should have something in a few days. Do we have your contact information?"

Nash pulled out one of her cards. "Nash, like the car they supposedly conceived me in."

The man produced one of his cards and wrote Mandy under his name. "The number is the one on the desk. Anyone near will pick up. Otherwise, leave any kind of message."

Cindy leaned over Nash's shoulder to make sure it didn't read Rumpelstiltskin. "Pi? What kind of name is Pi?"

The man's mouth pulled back to one side—tired of explaining his name. "My parents were mathematicians. It's short for Phillip. I was born on the fourteenth of March, which is better than my sister got. She was born on the twelfth of January and named after the Fibonacci sequence."

Nash lowered one eyelid. "Fibby?"

The man smiled evilly. "Only when I teased her. No. Her name is Golden Rule Farman, but she goes by Goldy. Mom loved Goldy Hawn growing up. My sister has the same laugh, just more of an Elvira sense of humor."

Nash gave Cindy a sharp look to back down. Turning back to Pi. "So who will I hear from first? The old tried-and-true, or the new whizbang steeped in cow shit?"

Pi ignored the dig. "Mine will make a light pass and spit out a gross analysis in about an hour. But the next pass takes hours as it breaks the various samples down to the atomic level. Actually... only elemental. But I understand you have three distinct kinds of mud?"

She nodded. "Sedimentary from five locations just because the texture felt different as I walked in it. I broke them out by location and the water patterns, like in the stream, eddies, a quasi-back bay, and the walls of the stream. Then there was something weird going on in the calm water at the back of the bay. There was a whole floating layer of mud on the surface, then some water, and another layer floating at half the depth. Better to bring you all the samples now instead of having to go back and get more."

Pi closed his eyes. "Which brings us up to about a dozen samples, all total?"

Nash nodded. "Sorry for the work."

Pi pushed his lower lip out. "No. No, we're good. This is cleaner and easier than the tubs-full we get from mobile autopsies. Those can run in the hundreds. There is never a single cow down… they usually have five or twenty before they call."

Nash rolled her eyes. "I don't want to know. Call me when you get anything." She turned Cindy around and marched her out the door.

TRACY REFILLED THE COFFEE MUGS.

Nash watched her from the corner of the booth. The young woman's smile at seeing Nash walk in had faded when Cindy followed her. When they had sat, she had simply nodded. When she took their orders, she had been nothing but business. Nash let it go. In the country, small-town politics always bled past county lines.

Cindy pushed her coffee mug in thoughtful circles. Finally, she looked up at the silence.

Nash waited for a three-count. "What?"

"You invited me down to San Francisco. We deliver the mud and then bring it back up to the college. And now we're going home. This is your job? What am I doing here?"

Nash leaned back into the corner. "What did you think was going to happen?"

The woman squirmed slightly and gazed at her mug. "I don't know…"

Nash sighed lightly. "You thought I was going to take advantage of you at the hotel? The name of that ship is history, and it sailed twenty years ago. You're married, I'm married, and I don't think either of us has the energy to do stupid anymore."

Cindy frowned in denial as her head shook. "No…" She looked up. "It's just a long drive…"

"What? To talk. Catch up on what's been going on the last twenty years in Harkin? Find out a little more about you two? You didn't like the Italian dinner last night? What is it, Cindy?"

The blond tipped up both of her hands from the table. "No. Dinner was great. In fact, better than great. It was the best lasagna I've ever had. The conversation was pleasant…" She pushed the mug out of her way. "I don't know… maybe it's me. I haven't been out of Harkin since the pandemic. First, it was all a big nothing-burger, and then people started dying. And then you don't leave your house because you're afraid the mask you ordered online doesn't work, but you need to go buy food because nobody would deliver, and the pantry is empty. And then they have shots, so you get them, but so many didn't… so more died. And the next thing you know, it's been two years, and you're just shaking from one day to the next, just hoping you get through."

She sat quietly. Her lips furled as she stared at the table, blinking.

Nash took a slow breath through her nose. "I guess, in a perverse way, I dodged that bullet. The division never gets the luxury of a day or week off. We just put on our masks and kept at it. Most of us were in the field more often than not. And the few left in the office felt like they were just working from home anyway, except you still put on your suit."

Cindy looked up. "The Special Investigations; does it keep you traveling?"

Nash's eyes got enormous as she rolled them to one side. "Sometimes too much. Other times, not enough. But yeah. We take the cases which don't fit into straightforward jurisdictions. If it's a bank robbery in Harkin, you're less than a hundred miles away from three other states. So San Francisco would handle it. Same for a kidnapping."

"But bones found in the creek...?"

Nash turned to sit straight in the booth. Her elbows cocked on the table as she clasped her hands under her chin. "Special circumstances. Bones, not a body, so nothing to autopsy. Miles to state lines. And the topper... bones in a natural setting."

The blonde's eyes narrowed. "And the mud?"

"Collateral interest. I always investigate anything unusual about a crime scene. It may be nothing, and then again..." Her arm twitched to her pocket. She pulled out her phone. She held it up and thumbed the screen. "Running Bear."

The voice on the phone was light but business. "Hi. Nash. Muna al-Faragi. I just got a message from San Francisco. But they want you to call a Pie?"

"Yeah, he's a forensic squint out at the college they farmed some evidence to. Did they say anything else?"

"Just a minute. I have it here." Nash could hear papers shuffling. "It's an extensive list of chemicals. If I had time, I would have looked them up, but I guess this Pie is waiting to hear from you."

"No problem." She started scooting out of the booth but put her hand to stop Cindy. "I have his card in the car. I'll call him now." She hung up. "I'll be back in a few minutes."

She started the car and waited for the Bluetooth pairing.

The female voice sounded like it was in a tin can, on speakerphone, or in a toilet stall. "Lab."

"Special Agent Nash Running Bear calling for Phillip Quantum."

The girl giggled. "Hi, Agent Nash. This is Mandy. Sorry for laughing. I've just never heard anyone use his entire name. Anywho... Pi is down in the mud pond trying to get one of your samples to float. Well, I think two of your samples. The mid-level floater is intriguing, but we may have at least a partial answer. He just wants to reproduce it in the pool. The other—the surface floater—wants to get radiated in the grow lights to see what algae the buoyancy regulator is. Did you take temperatures of the water where you pulled the samples?"

Nash swore silently. "No. We didn't have a thermometer, but I can get it for you tonight or tomorrow. You want it in Fahrenheit or Celsius?"

"It doesn't matter. We can always convert it. We have smart phones to do the grunt work. Oh, just a minute, I can see Pi coming through the airlock."

Nash could hear the explosive air exhaust from the sealed door. "The FBI agent is on the phone."

The man grunted as if lifting a heavy weight. "I'll be right with you, Nash. I need to get out of this barrier suit."

Nash watched Cindy through the windows. Whoever she was texting had her face frowning and red. The sounds through the car's speakers didn't help the dialogue.

The sound of a metal stool scrapping on concrete accompanied the sound of rustling paper.

The man sounded out of breath. "Psycho got some hard hits in their initial Spectro analysis and had some questions."

Nash nodded in the dark car. "Shoot."

There was a quiet pause. "Is that a shoot as in damn, or an affirmation to continue?"

Nash felt a need to bang her head on the steering wheel. "Yes. Continue."

"Ah, good. There were high concentrations of what they think were acetone and latent traces of ether. Which begs the question of what industrial manufacturing is in the area? Or, worse, is a drug lab."

"What nature of manufacturing?" Nash thought about what Cindy had said about Buck Crawford soaking in the creek.

"My guess would be like machine shops, but then it wouldn't explain the ether. And acetone is regulated, so any quantity would be on record."

Nash saw Cindy get up from the table. She bent like she was leaving a tip or money for the bill.

"Pi, let me look into that. I'll get back to you." She snapped off the connection as Cindy pushed through the glass door.

As Cindy slipped into the car, Nash watched without a word.

Cindy snapped the seat belt and looked up. "What?"

"I was going to get the bill. It's a travel expense."

"I took care of her."

Nash watched Tracy through the window. The young woman picked up the money and the bill. She stared at the bill and then the money. She gazed out the window at the red car.

Nash kept watching the girl. "Did you leave her a tip?"

"Why...?" The chill of her voice frosted Nash's memories of old attitudes about the Native Americans on the reservation and how they supposedly got fat checks from the government. She never remembered any government checks, just the slights and insults.

Nash climbed out of the car and walked back into the restaurant. She pulled a twenty out of her wallet and shoved it in the young woman's hand. No words were necessary.

10

WRONG NUMBERS

NASH PULLED ON THE THICK, rough wood door and stuck her head in the bar. It was low and subdued, but redneck country was what the music was about. The aged wood everywhere had darkened with smoke, beer, and time. The smoke was clear, but the wood held the smell of spilled beer, spit beer, and thrown beer. Not to mention the aged after-scent of puke. She had never been in or wanted to go into the Golden State. It was the cowboy bar. The beer hall where the Paiutes drank was home or the community center where they ran the stick games. Being buried deep in the reservation meant no more than the rare cowboy would venture in. And the tribe generally respected them as friends.

She stepped in and let the door gently swing shut against her back. Only the man standing behind the bar, slowly polishing a glass, was more than a dark lump in the dim light.

The man hardly moved his head, but the nod was toward the darker shadow in the dark corner of the bar.

Uncle sat hunched over the bar, seemingly asleep or passed out. As Nash approached, the dog rose from the floor. She came and sniffed at Nash's leg and then her hand as she leaned down.

The growl resounded off the bar. "At least you didn't pick up any city smells from your time in the big city."

Nash pulled out a stool and settled down as she glanced over at the thin book he was reading in the dim light. "You know. When a horse becomes as ornery as you, they usually put them down. What are you reading?"

The bartender eased closer. "What can I get you, Agent?"

Nash studied the man and thought. She weighed the two inches of dark liquid in the rocks glass in front of Uncle. Nodding at the glass. "I'll have the same."

Uncle growled as he looked at the bartender. "You won't like it."

"It can't be any worse than I've had before."

The bartender furled and then fluttered his lips. "It's your money."

She watched as he pulled an unmarked bottle from the refrigerator and poured the glass half-full. He scooped a single ice cube from the bin and dropped it in. He pulled a clear bottle out of the well, measured some clear liquid into the glass, and then stirred it.

She leaned over and frowned at the book. Uncle pulled the book closed with his fingers in his place. The cover read *Quantum Physics of the Departed*. "Satisfied?"

She shrugged and raised the glass. The bartender stood watching. She spat the drink back into the glass and glared at Uncle.

He picked up a tattered business card, stuck it in the book, and closed it. Setting it face down, he took a sip of his drink and looked over. "What did you expect?"

MANDY FROWNED AT THE GRAPH ON THE SCREEN. SHE rubbed her eyes at the late night and squinted at the screen again. She hit the save and print buttons. The paper spit out from the printer, and she pulled the three sheets.

Still reading the printout, she wandered down to the other end of the extensive lab. "Hey, Pi...?"

She continued at the grunt from the bunny suit bent inside the isolation chamber. "I think we have a problem here."

The bunny suit turned on the stool. The muffled voice was barely understandable from experience. "Did San Fran-psycho send more data?"

She shuffled back to the second page. "It looks like we have car parts here, too." She looked up. "Well, transmission fluid and brake fluid, at least. But there's some glycol in here as well."

His face wrinkled into a dark mass scrunch as the man thought. "Sounds like we have multiple dumps. It could be a convenient spot for more than one person, or we have an aggregate dumper. But being so rural, I wouldn't rule out multiple toxic dumpers. We should have the complete data from our analysis the day after tomorrow."

She glanced at her wristwatch. "I'm out of here. Tomorrow I'll start running the spectrograph on the minerals of the mud. That mid-level floater has me curious about the possible presence of rhyolite and schist. There aren't any deposits in the area, but it might give us a picture of the underground river source."

He snorted. "I don't think that's what killed the airman, but it would be nice to help with geological mapping. I've seen several Ph.D. theses based on more specious theories."

───────────

"WHAT DID YOU THINK I'VE BEEN DRINKING ALL THESE years?"

The bartender leaned in. "Now, would you like something a little stronger than iced squaw tea? I've got some huckleberry bark and roasted dandelion root."

Nash's eyes slowly narrowed at the man. "What kind of scotch do you have that's fit for a human?"

The man smiled. "Fiddich. Eighteen-year-old."

Her one eyebrow raised. "Double, neat, in a bucket."

The man's face slowly slid open to the first smile she had seen out of him. The silver-capped front tooth reminded her of whom he was. She had watched that quiet smile stand in front of the quarterback for three years. If the smile was broad, she knew the kid in front of him was about to have his helmet taken. If the smile was slight, at least one, if not two, would wind up on the ground under the center as the quarterback ran over him. She was sure there were still some cleat scars to this day.

The rocks glass was half-full. The man had a small smile. "Have you figured it out yet?"

She sipped. "You were the center for Thomas." She glanced at the head of mostly silver-gray hair. "The hair threw me off."

Uncle rumbled. "Six tours in the sandbox will age a man."

The man drooped one eye as he shrugged his head to one side. "Eight, but who's counting? Either way, it was nine long years."

"Why so many?" She sipped and then studied the glass.

"I poured it from my personal bottle in the freezer. It kind of consolidates it."

She hummed through another sip. Putting the glass down, she looked at him again. "Why so much time?"

The man glanced at Uncle.

Uncle shrugged his face. "Tell her. She's going to find out, anyway. She's nosey that way."

Nash didn't move. Her eyes narrowed.

Uncle groused. "Oh hell. The man was CIA. Happy now?"

Nash's eyes open only a bit. "They have a football team?"

"Xǔduō." Many. The man's Mandarin was more War School than Beijing.

She smiled. "Nice try, but I hope your Pashto or Dari is better than your Mandarin. But then, my wife is Cantonese, so we only speak Hong Kong Street trash."

"I've never met her, so I merely guessed. I can get us into

trouble in a restaurant, but I can't find the toilet. All six Middle Eastern languages were easier than trying to fit in on Trenaman Square."

Nash grimaced. "Yeah, it's the lack of glasses and the size seventeen shoes." She stuck her hand out. "Nash... if you didn't remember."

"Ben. Ben Bulpit. Taylor was my dad. When he passed, I quit Uncle Sam and came home to care for the bar and mom."

Uncle snorted softly.

"You hush, old man. It's a better cover than you being a rummy and driving home straight as a nun."

Nash's eyes ping-ponged back and forth at the two. There was more there than was being said.

Uncle drained his glass. "Drink up. You're taking me home, and your sister is already asleep."

"Where's your truck?"

"Shop. It needed a new muffler bearing or something that costs a few hundred more than it should." He jerked his finger at her glass.

———————

Uncle ran his hand along the leather seat. "Government fixed you up pretty nice."

Powder stood with her front paws on the center console as she watched the street ahead.

"I think she likes your smell now."

"What makes you say that?" She glanced at the side of the dog's head.

"Her paws are on your side of the console."

"So who does Ben really work for?"

"DEA. Same as me."

She leaned forward and contemplated the man she only knew as a man with no job, no place to be, and yet everywhere people were.

She remembered him at every game the school played. If it was away, he was at the bar. If the white church was having a picnic, he was there. But she rarely remembered him at a stick game or ceremony on the reservation.

She slammed on the brakes. Powder surged forward but only took one step. She gave Nash a hard look and then looked at the man without a seat belt, crumpled against the dashboard.

Powder calmly eased back but placed the paw on Nash's thigh. Nash blinked once as she watched Uncle collect himself. Her voice was calm and quiet. "You know better. Now put your seat belt on."

The man grumbled back into the seat and fished for the belt. "I also know better than to let someone else drive." The belt clicked. "Okay. It's on. We can go now."

Nash turned in her seat. Her arm rested on Powder's back, kneading her fingers into the neck fur. "Not until you tell me whose uncle you really are."

He stared out the window. She waited him out. He finally turned and looked at her and nodded down the road.

She raised her eyebrows and her chin. "Whose?"

"You aren't going to like it."

"Try me. Before I sic Powder on you."

The dog gawped at her as if to ask why Nash was putting her in the middle.

"Nobody's."

Nash reached for the button and turned the car off. "Explain."

"Here?"

"It's as good a place as any. And I'm in a mood already. So spill…"

"At least let me roll the window down."

Nash held up her finger. "Depends on what you say. Start at the beginning. Are you even from here?"

He shook his head. "No. I knew your dad. We served in the first sandbox together. He talked about Harkin like it was the garden of almost Eden."

"Are you even Paiute?"

"Close, but no cigar. My mother was maybe Muskogee or Okefenokee, and my dad was Plains. He didn't talk much, but there were stories of him growing up on the Navajo reservation and down in the Sonoran territories. So take your pick, Apache, Navajo, or Hopi. The only language other than English I ever heard him speak was Athabaskan."

"So a more convincing argument for Apache and Navajo. They mingled."

His eyebrow raised as he nodded in admiration. "Your dad and I were the only First Nation. So we hit it off. But after the sandpile, I side-slipped Uncle Sam to the DEA, and when the area came up, I jumped at it."

Nash turned on the power and lowered both windows. Powder sensed they weren't leaving and laid down on the console. "Why would they send a... excuse me... two DEA agents to Harkin?"

He nodded. "Bruce came later. We recruited him to do the family business and keep his ears open. But back when it started, we were looking for pot farms. After a while, we realized the farms needed more water, like over in the Green Triangle."

"But you stayed..."

"We knew there was money flowing through Harkin. We just didn't know how and why. So what had started as a few years became decades. People think in months and years, but governments think of decades and generations. Pot became legal, but the farms and money are still going."

Nash leaned forward with her arms folded over the steering wheel as she thought. "Now what?"

"The skeleton might be our best lead yet. What did you learn in San Francisco?"

She pushed the start button, and the Hemi rumbled to life. "We don't talk about ongoing investigations with strangers."

11
OTHER DREAMS

NASH ROLLED over on the couch. She picked up her phone. The time read three forty-two. She sat up until her foot felt fur. Adjusting, she moved to put her feet on the braided rug.

When did we let the dog in the house?

She reached down. The head floated up only slightly. She smoothed along the crown and fondled one ear. The head lowered back to the floor with a grunt.

Nash rose and padded toward the bathroom before her sleeping sister, the human tornado, woke up and locked the bathroom door for twenty-eight minutes. If her sister was anything, she was predictable.

The cold seat stunned her into the same dream she had had before. They were at the creek. The distant figure in the steam or fog raised their arm and struck something. It collapsed. In a second, it was over. As she jumped from the beeping in the other room, her vision returned to the darkness of the bathroom. *Daisy.*

She flushed and ran her hands through the cold tap water. The light flared on.

"Oh."

Nash turned. "Just finished. All yours."

As Daisy closed the door, Nash stuck her foot out, stopping it. "What time does your alarm go off?"

"Four ten. Same as always. Why?"

Nash stuttered her head. "No reason. Just wondering what time it is."

As she walked down the hall and heard the lock click, she remembered their years of growing up. The door always got locked. *Good morning to you, too, Daisy.*

In the dark, she could hear her phone whistle once. It was the ringtone for her wife. She had recorded a Mynah bird wolf-whistling at a roadside amusement. They had laughed for two hundred miles across the desert afterward. Every time she said she was going to turn it into a ringtone for her, it was ten more miles of laughter.

She grabbed the phone. The face was a number four frowny face.

She thumbed the dial button.

At the sound of connecting, she hummed. "Not even a neutral five. What happened? Are you at chemo?"

"Yeah. But they aren't going to do it today. My neutrophils are only four sixty-eight. They're supposed to be at least twenty-six hundred. They're running a couple of other tests while I'm here. So I'm having some tea and waiting. I think I'd rather have some scotch instead."

Powder nudged at Nash's leg. Nash looked down and then out the glass door. "You want to go out?"

"Are you back home?"

Nash fumbled with the lock on the door. "Sorry. No. I was talking to the dog. I'm still in California."

"Is *dog* a euphemism for something else?"

Nash pulled the door open and waited for an alarm to go off. As the dog stepped out into the backyard, Nash remembered where she was and what person her sister was. A locked door was one thing, but a security system was aliens coming down to take her for a joyride. "No, she's a Queensland heeler. You might have heard people calling them cattle dogs. Her name is Powder."

"How big of a dog?" Nash could hear the exhaustion in her voice.

Nash tried to see the shadow moving about in the dark. "You know that brown and white dog down the block? I think they call it *Major*."

"The guy drives a Mercedes, and she drives a land yacht? Yeah."

"About the same size. I think I'm supposed to bring her home if today works out."

"What happens today?"

"The sheriff and I are going to go for a walk with Uncle. I think there is more here than just some old bones. But you sound tired. If they aren't going to do the chemo today, why not just go back to bed?"

"I have an appointment I've been putting off. Three of the four people are in town. I need to ambush them. They think they are having a secret luncheon." Nash could hear her put her hand over the phone while conversing with someone. "Sorry. The other tests are back. She will give me some iron, and we'll test again tomorrow. She also said a dog would be excellent therapy for me."

"I think me coming home and handcuffing you to the bed would be better therapy."

"Let's start with the dog first."

Nash snorted. "I love you, too, princess."

The last was more of a tired whisper. "Not as much as I miss you."

Powder walked out of the dark and stood looking at Nash.

"What? It was my wife."

Powder turned and looked back out into the dark and the trees walling the back of the property.

"What are you looking at?"

Powder looked back and then took a few steps and stopped. Still looking out at the fading black.

73

Nash narrowed her eyes. She knew Daisy would come flying from the bathroom like a tornado any minute. She didn't want to be in the way. "Let me get my pants and shoes." *And my gun.*

Nash walked across the grass into the dark. The treetops were now darker than the sky behind them, but underneath was darker still. "Powder." Even though she felt as if she was whispering, her voice echoed back from the trees. "Powder."

The dog came from behind and rubbed past her leg. She startled and then followed the lighter blur deeper into the dark.

Nash fought the nagging urge to draw her weapon. A dim light, no brighter than a yellow nightlight, shone through the trees. Powder kept walking but was slow enough to keep Nash only a few feet behind her.

As they approached the structure, Nash realized the nightlight was more like a cracked open door. She had once seen a smaller version of the low round tent. But this yurt was almost thirty feet across.

Powder nosed open the door and went in. The darker shadow near the door moved.

"I was wondering when Powder would get hungry. Ready for some breakfast?"

She leaned over and smelled the large mug of strong coffee. "Got more of that?"

"Always." Uncle rose. "Come on into my teepee."

"Yurt."

He clutched at his chest as he turned around. "I'm yurt you said that."

Nash rolled her eyes.

The inside was an open plan. The small light was on the man's desk. As he moved to the small kitchen area, Uncle set his mug on the dining table. He turned on an overhead light. It wasn't bright but illuminated everything else in the living area.

"A little larger than you imagined?" He held out a mug. "Cream and sugar are on the table."

Nash moved around the living spaces. It was all open, but there were definite areas; office, dining, relaxing, sleeping, and a wall. She pointed. Bathroom?

He held out his hand. As she stuck her head in the small room, lights under the cabinet lit red. *Battle lights.*

"How do you like your eggs? Scrambled or over easy?"

She walked back toward the dining area. "However, the cook wants to cook them. I like the battle lights."

He stood cracking eggs into the pan. "That way, it doesn't wake you up or destroy the purple in your eyes." He glanced over. "I saw it on a sub and liked it." He pointed at the overhead light. "This is only eleven watts. But you can see everything. And what you can't see won't hurt you, anyway."

Nash ran her finger along the edge of a bookshelf near the door. "And dust...?"

Uncle glanced back. "Your people, as well as mine, lived long, healthy lives with dirt floors, no vacuum cleaners, or dust chickens. But if you feel better, there's a broom around here somewhere." He peeked at her face over his shoulder. "I think I used it right before the pandemic."

He bent to open the oven. Removing the heavy pan, he pulled out the racks and slid the bacon onto a plate. Reaching back into the oven, he drew out a pan of biscuits and turned them upside down on another plate.

The eggs went into a bowl, and he placed them all on the table. "Got enough coffee?"

They sat eating quietly. Powder came back in and laid down next to Nash. Uncle couldn't see the dog, but he smirked.

"What?"

"She took to you since you stopped using your sister's city froufrou juice in your hair. Maybe your wife likes it, but she'll like what the squaw tea does instead."

Nash grumped. With radiation and chemo, hair could be an especially touchy subject.

"How did Powder know you were awake and making breakfast?"

The man paused the fork at his mouth. "The same way she knew to stay with you last night instead of coming back here. You have a lot more to offer her than sitting with me in a bar."

"Like what?"

He chewed and then sipped his coffee. "We'll see out at the creek today."

Nash bristled inside. "What makes you think I'm going to the creek today?"

Uncle broke a piece of bacon in half and stuck one in his mouth. "My guess is those smart guys down in San Francisco haven't any definitive answers yet."

She shook her head as she chewed.

"Did they hazard any guesses?"

She looked at him hard.

He shrugged his face and went back to eating. "I didn't ask for the nuclear launch codes. And I wondered if they had X-rayed the skull yet?"

Her fork stopped at the last bite of eggs. "There's a fracture pattern on the back of the skull. He didn't presume to conjecture."

Uncle nodded as he chewed on the last of the bacon. Taking his coffee, he leaned the chair back on the hind legs. "But shallow enough for the lime deposits to cover it up."

She put down her fork and dabbed at her lips as her eyes narrowed. "You saw it?"

He rolled his eyes and looked out the door.

"Wasn't the scene secured?"

He snorted as he rocked forward and stood. Taking the coffeepot, he refilled their mugs. "Old bones found in the creek with half of Harkin County traipsing in and out of there all summer long? What was to secure? Besides, more white folk are afraid to touch old bones than can fit in the township of Harkin. Hell, even old Otis didn't want to touch the skeleton, and I've seen him clean up a lot of roadkill. A dead body is one thing, but one without its clothes on gives them the heebie-jeebies."

"So you were the one who hauled it out of the water?"

"Out of the water, into the truck, into the mortuary, back out to the truck, and drove it down to San Francisco. I got more time with that lad than his mother."

She jerked at the sex. "How do you know it was male?"

He looked hard-faced at her. Finally, he quietly put his mug down. "Did your mother ever talk about having visions?"

"What do you mean? Dreams?"

"More. Sometimes she would just touch something and freeze. Her eyes were there, but her sight wasn't. She would see things."

"Things...?"

"Sometimes, it was about what was going to happen. But also, sometimes, what had happened already, where it came from, or who it belonged to. That sort of thing."

"Why would she talk about it to me?"

"Same reason she talked to me. The day I came to Harkin, she brushed my arm in the grocery store. She turned and called me Uncle. And then she asked when I had gotten into town and if I had figured out where to stay yet."

Nash narrowed her eyes, trying to remember when she was first aware of him. It was hazy.

"She invited me to come out to dinner. It was just the three of you. Afterward, we sat out in the backyard and talked. She brought me out here and told me I could pitch my teepee or build a Hogan, whichever I wanted. I had never mentioned I was Navajo; she just knew."

"And you have this second sight also?"

His head twitched to one side. "We're all different. My grandmother used to have long visions. She called them Spirit walks. Sometimes she would sit in a trance for hours. But when she was through, she knew long stories about people, events, or places. Not just in her time, but deep in the past, or what would come." He sighed. "Me, I just know. One instant, I don't, and the next, I do."

He watched her.

She realized the silence had wrapped around her, picking at her thumb in her lap. She leaned over in embarrassment and stroked her hand down Powder's head and back. "It's like a dream, but I'm awake. I just see things happening. They don't make sense, but sometimes I see them a few times."

"Just see?"

She shook her head. "More. Like I can feel the warm water of the creek. It's night. I know I'm with Thomas Brady, and we have skipped out on prom. But in the distance, through the rising steam, there's a shadow of a large man, and he hits something. I can't hear it, but I feel the impact. I don't know how. We're not close. But I just know... it's a killing blow."

Uncle looks down at the floor to one side. "When was your first vision?"

"The Monday before last. I was stepping into my morning shower if it matters. Why?"

"Because they didn't find the skeleton until Thursday."

Her face drained of blood.

12

A WALK IN THE FOREST

UNCLE POINTED UPSTREAM along the small creek. "The artesian spring is about fifty yards up there. Unless you want to go boulder hopping, we can just wander down this way. The hot springs add to the volume as it wanders down the way."

"And we are doing... what exactly?"

Uncle sighed. He looked around at the trees, rocks, and water. "For you city people, we Indigenous Peoples call this walking in the forest. It's like you going to a large area to walk around invasive grasses brought over from what you call the old country. Except, ours comes naturally, and we don't have to mow it."

Nash squinted over her mirrored sunglasses. "Do we need to drug test you?"

"No, ma'am. I know what all the drugs are and how to use them." He started strolling along the water.

Powder wandered back and forth as they walked. To any onlooker, the three would simply appear to be a couple out for a walk with their dog. For Uncle and Powder, it was anything but a simple walk in the woods.

For Nash, she wasn't sure what kind of walk it was, but she did see purpose in the way Uncle was walking. Even with his hands in his pockets—projecting an air of casual aloofness.

Powder stopped and sat near a stunted tree about thirty feet from the water. On one of the dead branches, the pine needles had a spray of orange paint.

Uncle stopped and fingered the paint. The needles crumbled in his hand. "I marked this about a year ago. She triggered in the same way." He turned toward Nash. "Do you know how to mark a GPS spot?"

She pulled out her smartphone. Opening her GPS app, she let it orient and then marked it. The app would send her a text message as to the coordinates.

She looked up. "Okay, I marked it. What do you think it is?"

Uncle started walking, and Powder resumed her darting here and there. "A body." He looked back over his shoulder. "Well, what remains of a body. The question is more about being buried or in the creek. The creek is small there, so I'm guessing buried. You'll see what I mean in a few minutes."

Powder sat at the edge of the creek. There was a slight drop in the creek's elevation, and the water tumbled down a face of rocks. Thus, creating a turbulent pool at the bottom.

Nash and Uncle bracketed the dog.

Looking at the turbulent water, Nash turned to Uncle. "What do you think?"

He shrugged his face and eyebrows. "My guess is the skeleton is a matched set to the one in San Francisco." He pointed at the dog. "She was about a year old when she first brought me here. I didn't know what to make of it yet. But after the skeleton turned up, I started thinking about these spots. And this isn't all of them."

"But how do you know she's triggering on bodies? Maybe she just likes the feel of this grass on her butt?"

Uncle stepped back to the pine tree twelve feet from the water. There were three dots of orange paint in the cracks of the bark. He drew his finger along the trunk below the dots. "This was a line about two years ago. It's grown over now. But the line is the creek."

"And the three dots?"

"It was the third time she had triggered in this spot."

Nash squinted at the man. "How many of these spots are you going to show me?"

"I'll show you number seven... but I need to see a man about something I asked him to make me. Are you ready for lunch?"

Nash looked at her watch. "A little early, isn't it?"

"We need to run down the road a piece. And Tracy doesn't come on shift until eleven."

THE MACHINE SHOP LOOKED MORE LIKE A BLACKSMITH'S shop, with some large machines in the shadows. When they pulled up, the man was enough of a stereotype to make Nash laugh.

She pointed at the man just inside the wide doors. "The guy is straight out of Hollywood general casting."

The man stood well over six and a half feet tall. His body would make a football coach cry, and the other team run away. The sleeveless shirt made his leg-sized arms look larger than the rippling bulges were already. Nash was certain the large hammer was something the movies took a mold off to cast Thor's hammer. The worn and sweat-stained, full-length leather apron finished the picture.

The red metal in his hand resounded with each blow of the hammer.

The man looked out. Seeing Uncle, he stuck the metal back in the fire.

He shed the gloves and laid them on the anvil. "I was expecting you this morning."

"It was a wonderful day, so we went for a hike." Uncle randomly waved his finger around in the air. "Jake, Nash. Nash, Jake."

Nash nodded as she noted the man did not extend his hand.

The giant turned and walked to the wall near the door. What he brought back looked like an extra-long pitchfork bent into a rake for digging clams. The tines were an inch apart and hooked back toward a user's feet. The whole rake was about two-feet wide.

"I think this is what you were talking about, but everything would fall through unless you're raking those large Pismo clams. So I built you this." He showed them a screen of half-inch squares. "When you want the finer screen, you just slide it on like this and rake." He raked the concrete floor. "The three inches of tines will still cut through the streambed, but the screen will catch most of what you're looking for."

Uncle pulled something out of his pocket and flipped it onto the screen. One end poked through the screen, but the bent metal in the middle stopped it from going through. "Perfect."

"Wheel weights? That's what you're fishing for? Hell, I've got hundreds of pounds of them in the back. You can have all you want."

Uncle smiled. "I appreciate the offer, but it's the catching that is important this time. That and the location."

"Well, I'm glad you like it. Just keep liking it come elk season."

Uncle smiled. "Not a chance. You're my good luck charm. Without you, I just go sit, glass the hillside, and come back with a hangover. At least with you, there's meat to freeze."

UNCLE STOOD IN THE WATER, CAUTIOUSLY DRAGGING HIS rake along the bottom. He pulled the rake up and removed the few twigs from the screen.

Nash sat leaning against an old high stump. Powder was at the edge of the water, watching Uncle. She looked back at Nash.

Nash shrugged. "I don't know Powder. He thinks there's something down there. You've known him longer than I have. If you have a better idea, you tell him."

Powder came back to her and licked at her face. Nash pushed her away as she giggled. "Go play dead stuff with Uncle."

Powder moved back to the edge of the water but was six feet upstream of Uncle. She sat and watched Uncle, then looked back at Nash.

Nash watched Powder watch Uncle and then glance back at her. She furled her lips, weighing whether she wanted to buy into the notion of the dog being right. Or Uncle being right about what he was looking for. "Hey, Uncle?"

The man looked up.

"You're off your mark."

He frowned. Confused.

Nash pointed at Powder. "She's been trying to get your attention since she moved. Either get with the program or go sit on your stool. The big dog is running the show... or so I've been told."

Uncle watched the dog as he sloshed his way into deeper water. "Here?" He stuck the rake in the water.

The dog nervously danced her front paws as she moved them upstream a few inches. Uncle adjusted and pulled the rake. His head twitched as he looked back over his shoulder at Nash. "I think I've got something."

Nash pointed at the small pile of sticks and rocks on the side of the creek. "It better be more productive than the pile you already have."

Uncle pulled up the rake. Glancing at the screen, he looked up. "Better bring some of those extra-large evidence bags of yours."

Nash rose and brought back a handful of gallon-sized zipper bags. "What've you got?"

"I don't want to move. Bring them out."

Shit. Walking back to the bright red car, she popped the trunk and pulled out the box of evidence bags. Returning, Nash leaned against the stump and removed her shoes and socks. She thought about rolling up her pant legs but looked at Uncle mid-thigh in the water. She removed her wallet and pistol, eased into the water, and waded out.

"What is it?"

He held up three long wheel weights the size of a middle finger. "The wheel weights were what I was expecting." He held them out and dropped them into the bag Nash held out. "But I also got a bonus." He held up the screened rake. Nestled in among the expected bits of twigs and slime was the dull white of bone.

Nash opened another bag and reached into the rake. She pulled out the skeleton of a partial left hand. "The skeleton you found last week...?"

He gave her a stern look. "Both hands were there."

They both swore at the same time. "Shit."

Nash pushed her chin out at the water.

"Yes, Master." Uncle reached the rake out as he watched Powder. The next raking produced five more weights.

The three sat on the grass. Four legs hung over into the warm water. Nash stopped picking at her thumb and looked up at the water in the early evening light. "When I was a kid, the water was so magical. Fairies and wood nymphs came out at night to bathe in the warm waters."

Uncle nodded, a shrug on his face. "They still do. They just grew up and became adult humans. But they still come to capture their youth as the wee folk dancing in the forest."

She glanced over. "Brady and friends."

His head bobbed like an oil pump. "Et al."

Nash furled her lips in thought. "What do you make of the haul? What you expected?"

He glanced back at the stack of evidence bags. "The wheel weights were what I expected. But the bones...? Bonus."

She waved her hand at the water. "The rest of the skeleton out there...?"

"I suppose."

"And if tomorrow we haul in two more hands?"

"I guess then we keep on digging."

She closed one eye and looked at him. "I think it's called dredging. But the wheel weights...?"

He nodded in twitches as he slowly looked up. "I found the first one lodged in the ribcage of the first skeleton. I figured it didn't just land there or get washed down the creek in the spring."

Nash frowned. "I don't remember. Does the water level change with the seasons?"

Uncle shook his head. "Nope. Confined aquifers aren't affected by the seasons. And if they are, it's minor."

"So the wheel weights...?"

"I thought about it for a couple of days. You have a body in the warm water. It's not hot enough to cook it, but it is warm enough to cause it to rot faster. With rot, you get internal gasses; with the gas, you get a floater. But a floater is bound to be seen. So you need to weigh the body down."

"How much weight?"

He stuck his finger out. "And there is the point." He looked over. "I did some digging. Scuba divers use about ten-per-cent of their weight. But if it's warm and they aren't using wet suits, they deduct about six pounds. And if you're in freshwater, you can take off another couple of pounds for the lack of buoyancy. So a guy of, say, a hundred and eighty pounds is going to use eighteen pounds, less six, less two or ten pounds."

"But when the body bloats..."

"Then you use the Chicago Shoe System."

"Chicago Shoe System?"

He smiled. "Add more concrete."

She looked back at the heap of bags. "And we figured somewhere close to twenty pounds of weights..." She looked back at him. "So what? You just push the body down and lay the weights on them?"

Uncle took a deep sigh. "I was thinking more about stuffing the pants and shirt with them. By the time the clothes are rotting off, so is the body. And then it all just becomes part of the creek bottom in the deep pools."

"So you think there's more out there in the deeper part of the pool?"

His head rose, and he looked at the sky as he took a deep breath through his nose. "Let me ask you this. We just spent only about two hours dragging the bottom of fewer than twenty feet of the creek that runs for two miles. We have one full skeleton and a hand…"

"Reasonably suspicious…"

"At this point, would the FBI consider it suspicious enough to suspect a serial killer?"

"As the Field Officer of Special Investigations, even by the book, I would lean more toward a summation of let's see what tomorrow turns up. But, for now," she looked at and petted Powder. "I think we're all hungry."

"Until tomorrow, then." He stood and put his hand down to help her up.

13

WRONG WAY

NASH TURNED out onto the highway. Breakfast with Uncle hadn't been as insightful as it had been comfortable. The bison steaks were from his friend, as were the multi-colored eggs. The bread he finally admitted to buying at the Safeway in town. He had no idea who made it, nor did he care. It was just bread.

During dinner the night before, San Francisco had called with an update. When she mentioned the new hand, he had strongly suggested she bring it all down. He also wanted to show her something he didn't want to share over the phone.

So road trip it was.

The siren whooped once. She looked at the flashing red and blues in her rearview mirror. *Damn.*

Pulling over, she shut the muscle car down and waited.

Brady strolled up alongside the car. She watched him in the side mirror. His right hand rested heavy on his sidearm. She didn't have to look at his face to know he was mad. He wouldn't be the first local law enforcement she had crossed or skirted. The chilly morning, and him wearing the puffy uniform jacket, wouldn't have improved his attitude.

"Nash..."

She kept looking along the road. "Thomas…"

"You violated my crime scene yesterday. You took evidence outside the chain of possession. And you were aided by a civilian."

She raised her eyebrows and leaned her head to look over her aviator sunglasses. "Those are some tall accusations, Sheriff. Do you have proof?"

His left hand raised to his hip. "I want whatever it was you removed from the creek."

She sighed and channeled herself into the people she had spent two months with down in Mississippi the previous year. "Why, shoot, Sheriff. It tweren't nothing but water. The jug is still in the trunk." She leaned forward and pushed the trunk release. "If you want it so badly, you can help yourself to it. I thought it might help my ague, but it tasted nasty. I just forgot to throw it out."

He glanced back at the raised trunk lid. He wanted to see what was in the trunk, but she had called his bluff. He knew now he wouldn't find anything else in the trunk. But he had to look.

He pointed at her. "Wait here."

He bent into the trunk. The gallon jug of water was in one corner. There was nothing else. He raised the carpet under the floorboard to look at the kiddy car spare tire. *Nobody gives you a real tire anymore.* He pulled at a few other sections of the carpet trunk liner. The jug of water sat in accusation. He didn't know what she was pulling, but he knew Nash was at least one step ahead of him. He jerked the jug of water out of the trunk and left the lid up.

He returned to his SUV, climbed in, and made a U-turn.

Nash stepped out of her car. Watching Thomas storm back down the main drag of town, she quietly closed the lid. Obviously, twenty years of maturing hadn't fixed the man's hotheadedness. And making him the last word in local law enforcement hadn't helped.

She pulled over behind the battered truck ten miles farther down the road. Uncle climbed out.

"Did he take the water?"

Nash smiled as she pushed the trunk release and climbed out. "He did. But he wasn't happy about it not being what he expected."

Uncle grumped a smile. "Kind of makes you wonder who knows what around here. Did he ask about the rake?"

She helped pull the heavy bags from the tattered toolbox. "I don't think his information was as complete as he wanted me to think he had. Or what he would've liked to have. He just knew we were down fishing in what he would like to think is his private fishing hole."

Uncle dumped the last two bags in her trunk. As she closed the lid, he turned to her. "I wouldn't stop until you get at least past Chico."

"I've got a full tank. I'll grab fuel and a bite somewhere near Vacaville. You keep your head down. He knows you're somehow connected here. He just doesn't know what or how. Let Powder guide you."

Uncle chuckled. "Now you understand what I've known for a couple of years. You sure you don't want to take her with you?"

Nash patted his chest. "I'm only headed for the big scary city with violence on every street corner and a boogieman in every doorway. Why would I need any help? You're the one staying around here. Just watch your back."

He held her door open. "You too, Agent. And drive careful. The highway boys love to ticket the red car."

She gave him a knowing smirk. They both knew what he really meant. The Indigenous are also people of a darker skin. A color that many in law enforcement don't equivocate in difference.

MIKE LOOKED UP AS NASH PUSHED THE CART INTO THE lab. He slowly rose. "I didn't expect you before tomorrow..." He frowned at the evidence bags of wheel weights and the one with the skeleton hand on top. "Did a tire repair place offer to lend you a hand?"

Nash winced at the gallows' humor. "Have you identified my full skeleton yet? Because I'm afraid this is the tip of a bony iceberg."

The man held up the evidence bag with the hand. "Where was this left?"

Nash narrowed her one eye. The man wasn't going to give up the terrible puns. "We don't have a full picture, but this came from the same side of the same pool. But then, we only had bare-bones information to work from."

The man studied the skeleton hand as his face morphed into a static cringe. "A six…"

"What's a six?"

"Your pun." He glanced up at her. "You don't practice much, do you?" He turned back to one of the lab tables.

She watched him bend over his work. "When was your last period?"

Distracted, he glanced over his shoulder at her. "Period?"

"Menstrual cycle."

He froze. His head ground around and dragged his body with it. His mouth opened and froze at the sight of her face.

"You see… you don't have one. You don't have tits, either. And as if that weren't enough, you're white. So, you see, you're one of the boys. You get to laugh and joke, and the rest of the locker room follows along. No matter how inappropriate it gets. It's just us boys. Except it's not. There are women now. And they are trying to survive long enough for you guys to slow down just long enough to see us. And more importantly, to hear us, and maybe understand us. But if being one of the locker room kids takes a practiced sense of humor, well…" She pointed at the hand. "Then let's talk about the hand with no penis to masturbate."

The man blushed. "I'm—"

"Can it. It's not you. You just caught the end of my rope. I've got another swinging dick who makes you look like a two-year-old smearing your poop on the bathroom wall. What makes it worse is he's the sheriff in a one-horse town. I'm not sure how he fits into all this, but he is a piece of the puzzle. I just can't figure out if he's an edge piece or the final one in the center."

A thought flashed across the man's face. His finger rose cautiously. "And the blond who was with you last time..."

"The wife."

"And you and her..."

"Were a fling in high school. Your point?"

His face extended in horror. He shuddered as he turned back to the workbench. "Oh, you are so screwed. I'll stick to the lab work, thank you very much."

He fiddled the skeleton hand out of the bag. Taking up a small circular saw bit, he mounted it into the rotary tool. Slipping on safety goggles, he cut through the bone of a finger. Slicing off a small disk of the bone, he placed the disk under a photomicroscope. The image showed up on the computer monitor. The quarter-inch bone was now twelve inches across in living color.

Mike pointed at the thin layer of white.

Grabbing a computer stylus pen, he touched each side of the layer on the screen. Turning to his keyboard and mouse, he called up another image. Splitting the screen, he took the two halves of bone and put them together to form an almost whole. The two layers were markedly different.

Pointing at the thicker layer. "This is your first friend. I figured he was in the water for about fifteen months. This is your new friend..."

She smiled. "Lefty..."

He gave her a side-eye. Her smile appeared relaxed. He cleared his throat. "Lefty went in the water about six months ago."

Her mouth tightened. "We have..."

"Technically, not until you bring me the third. When are you planning to dredge more?"

She looked around the lab. The evidence of many cases lies in heaps here and there. Files lay stacked on some. Notes on others. Some with only a series of multi-colored sticky notes. For the first time, Nash realized how busy the seemingly empty lab was.

"Why?"

The man sighed as he leaned back against the workbench. "How much lab work do you remember?"

Nash thought back on her time at Quantico. "I put in my time... and then some. I wasn't exactly the fair-hair man-child they were eager to get out in the field. The labs were a suitable place to bury someone like me." She looked around. "I'm guessing by the rough notes and stacks, you've been understaffed for a while."

"Four years." He looked up. His face was tired from the bureaucracy. "Every quarter, I have sent another request for staff. Every quarter, I get..."

"Shafted?"

He nodded.

"Well, girlfriend, welcome to the club of the eternally shafted." She unbuttoned her shirt sleeve and rolled it up. "Where do you want me to start?"

"When are you due..."

"Back in the field? You forget I'm a Special Agent of Special Investigations in the Special Operations division. We are always in the field working on our special Secret Squirrel shit twenty-four seven. Sometimes it looks like I'm going for a swim dredging for bodies, and sometimes it looks like I'm riding your ass to get the lab work done right." She shrugged one eye as she tilted her head. "And knowing my boss, he's just glad I'm not hanging out in D.C."

He hesitated for only a moment and then nodded. Pointing out the piles with files on them, "These need to be coded and filed. Most of them are resolved. If so, they must also be boxed and sent down to the basement." Pointing at the piles with notes here and there. "These... Crap. These need to be pulled together and typed up. Only then can they get coded and filed." He peeked up with a pleading face. "What do you prefer?"

She smiled. "Let's work it like the young golden boys do. Fast and easy stuff first."

He spun on the fore-pad of his mechanical leg. The traditional prosthetic swung around in a small semi-circle. "I like how you think. I forgot how linear you were in your triage at school."

Nash's pocket buzzed.

The man moved through the lab. "Only if it is work, Special Agent."

Nash chuckled and then looked at the screen. She did the fast calculations for the time zones. Agent Muna was logging late hours.

"What do you have, Muna?"

"This is Agent al-Faragi... oh. You..."

"Caller ID. It's been two days. Where have you been?"

The young woman flustered. "It was the weekend."

Nash drove it home. "What the heck is a weekend?" As the woman tried to recover, Nash called loudly across the lab. "Hey, Mike. D.C. has something called weekends. Imagine that."

"Lucky bastards."

Nash brought the phone back to her mouth. "We're in the middle of a shit storm here. If you don't want to have me requisition you to come help, you better have some better news."

"I found your skeleton."

Nash looked at the wall of body lockers at the far end of the long laboratory. "I know. It's right here in drawer seventeen."

"No. I know who it is."

Nash bluffed. "It's an airman from Travis Air Base. Went missing last summer."

The young woman gathered her guts. "No. That was Nilesh Desai. He went AWOL last September. Your skeleton is a National Guard airman who went missing in March of last year. He was a student at Sierra College in Grass Valley, California."

Nash hummed. "Mmm, not all that far from Harkin. Who reported him missing?"

"He was staying in a boardinghouse. A Ms. Henrietta Miller runs it. I can text this all to your phone."

Nash walked over toward Mike. He looked up as she switched the phone to speakerphone. "So you say his name was Nilesh Desai?"

"No, that is the other one who went missing just this past September. Your skeleton is Curtis Ghoulish. He was an airman at Castle Air Force Base in Merced, California. I'll send all that. In fact, I'll send you both files. Who knows what might turn up?"

Mike held up the bone hand.

Nash rolled her eyes. "Great. Thanks, Muna. Excellent job on this. We'll sort through this and see what we're left with."

The tinny voice sounded chastised. "Enjoy all that California sunshine. We're in the second day of drizzle here."

"Naturally. I'll check in with you in a couple of days. I'll go chase down what I can about both men." She ended the call and slipped the phone into her pocket.

Both looked at the left hand. "Nilesh?"

UP IN THE AIR

NASH LOOKED DOWN along the workbench. The black soapstone shone in the afternoon sun. The way the top had soaked in the mineral oil gave her a sense of how long the laboratory had been shorthanded. At Quantico, she knew of at least three treatments of the lab's workbenches she had applied herself. She enjoyed the shine before she washed the top down with alcohol to remove the residue.

"It looks nice."

She turned and smiled at her former teacher. "Thanks, Mike. It was the least I could do for you."

He grumped a chesty snort. "Yeah, like the three days of sorting, finishing, and filing were nothing..."

She grimaced. "I filed a report with the deputy director about how shorthanded you have been. The second busiest laboratory in the west shouldn't have to farm out work they could do here with a staff."

He rolled his eyes. "I bet he yawned when you told him I needed three techs."

"Six. Six and a secretary."

The man laughed. "They have never staffed this lab to that level.

Even Steven in L.A. only has three with three part-time assistant technicians he steals from other parts of the labs…"

"Well, you never had to process so many skeletons before."

He turned on his titanium leg. "Speaking of which…" He pulled the drawer out. Lifting the skull, he walked it over to the exam bench and placed it under the camera. He adjusted the focus. The shallow, crushed area filled the large monitor.

Nash stood behind him. "Wow. That cleaned up nicely."

"Now I have to figure out what matches this shape."

"It looks like a goose egg. But would it have killed him?"

Mike shook his head. "Probably not." He typed on the keyboard and chose one of the thumbnail photos. Dragging it to the primary display, it filled the area. "This is inside. We took a snake in through the optical port. The interior telegraphs the dent, but the posterior cranial fossa is intact. A killing blow usually will shatter the fossa." Pointing to the screen. "But this… would incapacitate the guy. If he wasn't dead, he would probably wake up vomiting."

Nash leaned in. "More than a mild concussion." She turned. "Any guesses on the blunt object?"

He twitched his head to one side. "Not even a clue." He returned to the exterior view. "We get the same spider with a pipe or bat, but the dent is more of a trench or furrow. A hammer leaves a straight wall with the center punched and is the shape of the head. When the killer uses the claw, they usually hit once and then leave it there. Usually, vomit is found at the site or close by."

"I remember the class. The sight of the hammer sticking out is upsetting."

Mike held up his finger. "I think you got an A in the class."

"Of course I did; it was a great class." She looked back at the image. "Petrified goose egg?"

Mike stuck out his lower lip in thought. "I froze an egg and used it in a sock."

"Did it work?"

Shaking his head. "Right shape, but didn't deliver enough kinetic energy. This weighed more than a frozen egg."

Nash waved her hand around the laboratory. "Well, now you have time to figure it out."

The man looked down at the bench and then back up at the taller woman. "Go find me the rest of Mr. Nilesh Desai. If that's who our lefty is."

As Nash found out, Castle Air Base had decommissioned as an active military base in the mid-nineties. Now it was a mixed bag of many groups. The Air National Guard was little more than an office in the back of a hanger, with most of a small Cessna 152 parked in a space meant to garage a DC-3. The small plane looked more like a toy, and the secretary in the office wasn't any more professional.

They attached Nilesh Desai to the Air National Guard while he was at Fresno State college and was now learning the fine art of air traffic control. Or was until he didn't show up for his fall classes. Students ditch classes, blow off school, or just stop going. Schools are used to their enrollment shrinking. It's because of expensive education and the nature of not-quite-mature students. The school never gave a second thought to a missing student. The National Guard student signed up for the classes, and they got paid.

The missing person report had come from the empty apartment three months in arrears on the rent. Even the post office didn't file a report or make a note of a mailbox jammed full of bills. The utilities, credit card, car, and school had simply turned the bills over to a collection company that kept calling a disconnected number. Eventually, they even sold the debt to an offshore company with the same luck. Even at ten cents on the dollar, the effort is no longer worth the effort.

The last charge on his credit card was at a gas station in Harkin

County. Thirty-eight dollars and seventeen cents. Fuel, coffee, and a burrito.

Nash shuffled through the bills and missing person report on her laptop. Pausing, she looked at the half-eaten chicken burrito in her left hand. She peered over the top of the laptop at the farmland across the road from the roadside café.

In the middle of the half-grassy field, a farmer on a small tractor slowly dragged a large array of steel disks. The ground behind him turned over in large clumps. Somewhere she had heard the term green manure. They grow the grass for a few months and then turn it back into the dirt to break down and become compost. After the last harvest in September or October, they plant the grass and leave it. In the late summer, they turn it. The time schedule is in seasons or years.

She thought about her wife's day planner—always open on the buffet. Unless they had guests over. And then they would sanitize the condo as if there were no other important events. Her days had always been jam-packed. On their first real dinner date, Mina had turned off her phone. At the car, she had turned it back on. It showed eleven missed calls during the two hours. She had explained the lack of calls was because little happened on Saturday night. Nash found out about Sunday night the following weekend. Everyone in Washington, D.C., seemed to be panicking about the next day. The next day was only another Monday.

Nash realized it had been a long time since they had had guests over. True guests. Friends. Just a relaxing evening among friends. Too long.

She scrolled back through the credit card bills. There was one bill she had only glanced at. She didn't remember when she had last seen a phone bill with numbers called. She looked at the header of the bill. It was a pay-as-you-go phone.

One of the area code numbers she recognized as Harkin County. She pulled her phone out and dialed. Her thumb paused over the green phone icon. It was her personal phone. It would show up on any caller ID system.

She looked around the small café. The only other person was the bored waitress sitting at the end of the counter. Picking up the laptop, Nash approached her with her own phone held out in supplication.

"Hi. I hate to bother you, but I need to check this phone number, and my battery is so low that it can't even rent a bar. Is there a phone I can use?"

The waitress nodded and wiped the screen she was scrolling through. "Sure. Here, use mine."

Nash dialed the number off the bill.

"Harkin County Sheriff's Office. This is Deputy Otis Greely."

She hit the red phone icon. Gently handing the phone back. "Thanks. Sorta what I thought. Do you have any pie?"

As she sat back down at her table, Nash looked back at the field with the farmer plowing. The farmer was out of sight. The only evidence of the farmer recently having been there was the darker, damper dirt clods. Evidence. The turned land would be the lasting evidence of the discs slicing through the earth and rendering shallow cuts.

The huckleberry rhubarb pie was less than fresh, but it reminded Nash of kinder times.

She looked across the plowed field as the late sun warmed and softened the day. She rolled on the bench as she reached into her pants pocket to fish out the vibrating phone. Her eyes rose in calculation of the time zone difference as she answered.

"I don't know if this is a late night or you're home early."

Mina laughed warmly. "I was with the big agriculture boys for dinner. One of them whipped out a cigar before dessert had arrived. So I told him if we were showing our ugly side, I might as well join him. So I pulled off my Raquel Welch wig and told him it was getting close to my chemo time, so let's cut to the chase. We hammered two weeks of horseshit into about forty minutes. If it holds past next week, I think we have a solid move forward. And how was your day, dear?"

Nash chuckled. She liked the wig. It was one of the best uses of ten thousand dollars she could think of. "I think that wig and its sisters got paid for tonight. But for me, just baby steps and an interesting insight."

"One you can talk about?"

Nash forked off a tiny nibble of the pie. "Once I figure out how it fits."

There was silence on the other end. Nash looked at the phone. The connection was still active. "Mina...?"

The voice was soft. Nash realized her wife had called from their bed. "What are you eating?"

Nash looked at the pie and over at the waitress, still busy with her own phone. "Three-day-old huckleberry rhubarb pie. I was fantasizing about it being fresh out of the oven."

"You don't bake."

Nash snickered. "And you don't cook."

The sigh was soft. "That's what we have people for."

"I'd rather be home and cooking for you."

"How close?"

Nash knew she was asking for a timeline. She looked back at the freshly plowed field. "I have a lot of dirt to turn over. We think we may have a serial. Also, there are some strange chemicals in the water which shouldn't be there... ever."

"Industrial waste?" Nash could hear her wife's interest perk up. They were now in her expertise and lobbying forte.

Nash slowly shook her head. "Easy tiger. In an exceptional year, the biggest industry in the area doesn't make enough to twitch your alarm clock. Everything in the county is family owned. I think the biggest employer is the California Department of Transportation. All eight people and two snowplows. I told you eleven years ago; you married a country bumpkin."

"Yes, but you're my handsome country bumpkin super-agent." The voice was getting wispy. The battery was dead.

Nash resolved to let Mina go for the night. "I love you dearly, but I can tell you need to sleep. Dream of me fighting crime in my leather chaps and cape."

"I love you too. Stay safe. But no capes."

The phone clicked dead in Nash's ear. Not for the first time, she wasn't where her heart wanted her to be. And, it had nothing to do with the vow of 'in sickness and health.'

15
WHAT'S LEFT?

NASH STROLLED into the sheriff's office with Powder weaving a zigzag course behind. Nash almost rolled her eyes as the dog briefly sniffed the seat edge of every plastic chair in the lobby.

The large man rose behind the desk. Nash remembered his graceful coif of hair as black and smelling of the same Aqua Velva wafting from the boys' locker room on Friday afternoons. Many of the boys only took showers at school. She knew some families on the reservation barely had running water for the kitchen. The sight of a small shed in the backyard was still common after the twentieth century.

The man's hair was all but total snow. But she also remembered the denim jeans. Even as a young man, he wore the baggier jeans most would associate with farmers. Even the narrow side tool pocket hung with weight from an unseen tool. The jeans were as if one cut the bib off a pair of bib overalls.

"How can we help you, miss?"

Nash smiled at remembering the whispered calls as the old sheriff's car drove slowly down along the creek. "Deputy Greeley, if I remember right."

The man squinted at her. Forcing his eyes to see better as he tried to recall the face. "I'm afraid you have me at a disadvantage…"

She held out her hand. "Nash Running Bear. Well, Special Agent Running Bear, now."

His still attractive face frowned tightly. "I don't shake. I remember your mama… and you have a sister still about here…"

Nash lowered her hand. "Yes. Daisy. She's a teacher down in Taylor."

The man absently dismissed the information with his hand through the air. "What can I do for you, Agent?"

Nash's eyes narrowed as she felt Powder leaning against her leg. "Is the sheriff in yet?"

"Was."

She tipped her head slightly. "Well, deputy, do you know where I might find him?"

"What about?"

Powder growled quietly. She rested her fingertips on the dog's head.

Otis leaned forward and growled back at the sight of the dog. "Animals aren't allowed in here."

Nash growled back. "She's a federally approved working K-9. But if I find the sheriff, I'll take it up with him." She turned to leave. "Right after I check in with my supervisor about bringing out a squad to search for the sheriff."

The deputy flustered. "He's up at the café having breakfast."

She turned back with her fingertips still on Powder's head. "Now, see. Was that so hard? Which café?"

He jerked his thumb north. "Golden State."

She rolled her eyes under her slowly blinking eyelids. "Golden State's a bar. And a piss poor one too."

The man growled as he resettled into his desk chair. "Café in the morning."

Nash stood looking at the desk. She knew she wouldn't get any more information from the man. She turned and pushed the door. "Come on, Powder. I guess it's Golden State for breakfast."

NASH LEFT THE WINDOW HALF DOWN ON BOTH SIDES. She gave Powder a stern look as she opened the door. "Behave yourself, and we'll go for a long walk later."

Nash was expecting the bar to be dimly lit and seedy. Instead, it reminded her of several small eateries in and around the greater D.C. area. Excessively lit to make them appear cheery.

The sheriff sat at one end of the bar, reading a newspaper and sipping coffee. It could have been in any café across America.

She sat two stools over. The bartender stepped up. She nodded toward Thomas. "I'll have the same."

The man rolled his eyes as he turned. "Okay, but I'm getting low on the squirrel and might have to substitute skunk."

Nash clamped down one eye as the man looked back. "Yeah, no. Not a big fan of squirrel. I'll just go with the skunk."

The man chuckled lightly as he moved down the bar to place the order.

Thomas fluffed his newspaper and turned it over. "The skunk is from back east somewhere. Should have gone with the squirrel."

Nash glanced down the bar. "As long as it isn't from New York City or Coney Island. Their skunk always smells funny."

The sheriff turned the page and smoothed out the newspaper. "Been a long week."

Nash looked down at where her coffee should be by now. "And getting longer. Is the service always this slow?"

"Nope. Just for the tourists." He looked across the bar. "Hey, can we show a little consideration for the hardworking federal agent here? A little coffee, maybe?"

The man sauntered back with a mug of coffee and set it on the bar. His face said growl, but his voice was statically deadpan. "Anything else you'll be needing?"

Nash held his stare. "Cream and sugar. I like my coffee like I like my women—lightly tanned and sweet."

Thomas pushed the creamer and sugar holder halfway. "Don't worry, Paul. Law enforcement can share."

The man's face turned foul as he understood Nash's reference to women. He turned and walked back to the other end of the bar.

Nash shrugged as she glanced over at the sheriff. "I guess it means he'll now spit in my eggs."

"Nah. The cook already took care of the spitting the minute you walked in. This town isn't much on catering to tourists."

She sipped on the coffee. "Don't people still come up here to hunt and fish?"

"Not so much hunt food as they hunt targets. There are three unofficial gun ranges within five miles of here. Then there's old Jake Ferguson's range. Skeet, pistol, rifle, and a Sacramento manhole cover hanging up the canyon at the one-mile mark."

She looked over with a raised eyebrow. "Ever hit it?"

He scrunched up his one cheek as he shook his head. "Only rifle I have is dad's old 30-30 lever action. Great for hunting deer you plan to sneak up on in the brush, but anything past a city block, you'll need a reservation for a chip shot out of the rough."

Nash scrunched up her face. "I think you mixed up the two sports."

"And that'll tell you how much I know outside football. But seriously..." He fluffed the newspaper as he turned it over. "Some not-so-humorous dudes come up here from the cities to dial in weapons I don't want to know about."

"Isn't that kind of your job?"

"Nope. Says so on my truck. To keep the peace. So I peacefully avoid situations which could cause arguments requiring backup."

"Backup? You have backup?"

Thomas rolled his eyes. "Glen, Judy, Pete, or Otis. Take your pick."

"I just experienced Otis. Isn't he getting a bit old for the job? I mean, he was a deputy when we were in grammar school."

"He's been a deputy longer than most people have lived here. The permanence gives people a sense of stability. People wave and smile when he's awake and leave him be when he's taking a nap. Peace."

A woman in a dirty white apron and sweaty white shirt with no sleeves brought the food. She put the first plate in front of the sheriff.

Thomas pointed at the plate. "Nope. That one is hers." Pointing at the other plate, "I ordered the one with the extra spit on my eggs."

If a face could growl. The woman switched the plates. "You need a better group of people to hang out with."

"I soak and drink with your brother and husband..."

She looked back over her shoulder as she walked away. "Like I said..."

Nash pushed her plate toward him. "I'm fine. It wouldn't be the first woman I've swapped spit with..."

He shivered his head. "It's fine. Doris probably didn't make it past the idea. And she's not the dullest crayon in the box or the most broken." He shoveled a fork load of scrambled eggs into his mouth. His left hand rolled his finger in the air.

Nash nodded as she swallowed. "We think we found out who the skeleton was. They'll need dental records to confirm, but it appears it was an airman from down Modesto way."

"That's a reach."

"Not really." She took a sip of coffee while she mulled over how much to tell him. "There were reports of an airman from the base who went missing up this way last spring, so I had D.C. do some digging for missing persons' reports and hit a match."

"And you came up with my crazy aunt Millie..."

"Try a young man named Curtis Ghoulish. Attached to Castle Air Base... or what used to be Castle Air Base. Now it's a mishmash of a lot of things, including training for air traffic controllers."

He poked his fork at his steak. Turning with a curious frown. "Modesto is almost three hundred miles from here. How do you place him here?"

She pushed the bite of her steak into her cheek. "The last charge on his credit card was at the Arco station in Drift. He filled up and got a coffee and a burrito. He should have stuck with just the gas and kept on driving."

"Hmm..." He looked at the uneaten half of a steak and hash browns. Drawing a breath through his nose, he pushed the plate away. Standing, he took some bills from his wallet and threw them on the bar. "Breakfast is on me. I'll await the official report from Sacramento."

She bobbed her head as she chewed.

A few minutes later, she felt something at her foot. Looking down, Powder looked up. She could feel the guilty smile as the next stool got pulled out. She looked at the knee-high rubber boots and then looked up at Uncle as he settled in.

"I liked to think the kid would never leave." He waved his hand at the man behind the bar. "Jeez... and it had to be St. Paul of the dead soul."

Nash almost choked on her snort. "Doris seemed pleasant..."

"Doris is the reason I eat at home."

They both watched Paul move away after he put the coffee in front of Uncle and refilled Nash's.

Nash fixed her coffee. "How did you know I was here?"

Uncle paused with the cup near his mouth. "Old Indian instincts and superior tracking skill."

Nash rolled her eyes as she picked up the last of the steak and dangled her arm. Powder inhaled, and the evidence was gone. "Yeah, the discrete unmarked car with a cute bitch in it."

Uncle put down the mug and reached for the meat left on the

sheriff's plate. Powder obliged. Uncle straightened and leaned in. "So where you been?"

Nash looked over with one eye. "I think the real question here is, where have you been? I get home, and Powder looks half-starved and is licking the glass door like it's a water dish."

"Nah… she's just strange that way. Or maybe Daisy went back to washing her windows with an old steak or something."

Nash growled. "And you…?"

He pulled himself back up and smiled proudly. "Been bone fishing."

"Did you limit?"

He smiled. "Not to sound funny, but I have five humeri." He paused to let the quantity sink in.

Nash closed her eyes and took a slow breath. *This is getting out of hand.* "What else?"

He washed the last of his coffee in the mug's bottom. Thinking the better, he placed it on the counter and pushed it away. The grounds were too close to what he had spent the week doing.

His lips furled as he swung his legs around, preparing to stand. "Along with almost three hundred pounds of wheel weights and three unmatching feet …" He gave her a stern look. "I can either tell you the list, or you can come look."

"Coming with or following?"

"Better follow."

16

UNDERCOVER

THE LARGE BARN looked like it had started blowing down early in the last century. If there had been any paint on the wood, it had long faded, scorched, and peeled off. The gray, dark brown, and black looked more like a brindle dog than a color scheme.

Nash parked next to Uncle's battered truck in front of the large door. As she got out, the door slid open enough for a man to slip out. She recognized the electronic tool in his hand. She had used many of the snooper detectors at Quantico. The unit in his hand had a triple wand. He was hunting for listening bugs, trackers, and GPS recorders.

She stood watching the man work until Uncle waved her into the barn.

The inside was not what she expected. Four vehicles lined one wall of the large modern interior. Someone had built a garage and more inside the shell of the old barn. An armored dune buggy squatted on a low car hoist—missing its engine. She recognized the mounting rack secured to the roll cage from her time in the marines. She couldn't imagine what they needed a dune buggy with a sixty-caliber machine gun for. But she was sure she didn't want to know.

Uncle directed them to an extensive set of stainless-steel tables. Evidence bags lined up along four of the five tables. A crate full of bags sat next to the fifth table.

Nash and Uncle looked up at the sound of a dirt bike approaching. A moment later, it drove off as the man slipped back into the garage. He placed the snooper on a shelf and came over.

"Nash, this is Peter. Peter, Agent Nash Running Bear."

They shook. "I've heard some great things about you, Nash. Some from D.C. and more from Mike in San Francisco. I think I was his student a few years before you. Later today, I'll be taking this load down to him. I hear he has some new help he wants to break in right."

Nash's eyebrow rose. "That was fast."

Peter chuckled. "I heard. It seems your recommendation was kind of stalled on a desk somewhere until I called the FBI and then emailed the tally from Wednesday. Things kind of moved fast after that. I understand one was even a volunteer who wanted to work closely with her partner."

Nash snorted. "Does she wear a hijab but still believes pork rinds are halal?"

He laughed. "I don't know about the pork rinds, but the rest fits. I guess I should pick up a bag or two on the way down."

"Get the hottest ones you can find, and if I remember right, Mike likes them too." She rolled her eyes.

Uncle frowned. "I take it you're not a fan?"

"With this body? I'd gain five pounds just by touching the bag. No, not a fan." She pointed back at the snooper. "Anything?"

He glanced back and then looked at Uncle then Nash. "You had an infestation problem. Four audios were inside, two standard trackers in the wheel wells, and one with a GPS recorder as a backup. Someone who didn't understand heat and electronics hid it in the engine compartment. There's a reason they call it a firewall. But Felix will find new homes for them all. The trackers will probably end on long-route trucks, and the audios will end in bathrooms. He likes ladies' restrooms in sleazy honky-tonks. The language usually burns up the circuits."

She looked around, taking in the vehicles, the large garage space, and the doors leading to other spaces. "DEA has some kind of budget."

Uncle snorted. "Close, but no cigar, Indian. We only kick in some funds and toys. Peter is on the ATF side, and Felix, out there on the motorcycle, is Homeland. This is, and always has been, a down-the-dark-black-rabbit's-hole combined operation."

Peter pointed at the garage area. "When we first got here, Uncle was running his old truck into the ground. The Green Triangle had gone far beyond the hippies in the hills, growing some pot. The cartels moved in and brought their armed farmer mentality. A single agent with a back pocket peashooter and a hundred-year-old lever action with iron sights was outgunned and out-manned."

Uncle bounced his eyebrows once. "By the end of Clinton, we knew this was no longer a domestic thing. And then came 9-11, and the world changed. When they first cobbled together Homeland, they robbed agents from all over and stirred in an outhouse dump of incompetent military with bigger hard-ons than brains. Too many people in charge wanted to prove themselves, and it was a shit show for a few years. But with the lack of sexy headline-grabbing actions out west, we got passed over in the shit show, and we finally settled down into a team of friends spread about the area."

Nash gently rocked her head forward and back as she thought. She spread her hands over the multitude of evidence bags. "Which brings us up to bones and why I'm here. What all do we have?" She looked down at the three tables.

Uncle furled his mouth. "Short story is, we have three and a half bodies, but one guy has two left hands. Wheel weight wise, we have our three combined weights in lead."

Nash shook her head. "I doubt it. I had a bad slice of pie yester-day, and I'm sure I added a few pounds." She picked up a smaller bag and looked at the three coins. "And with the extra hand already

down in San Francisco... we know we've got at least five bodies."
She looked at the two men. "Either we have a mass grave, or we
have a long-term serial body dump."

The two nodded. "We're leaning on the latter. And it's not
selective."

Nash frowned. "Selective?"

Uncle shifted a few of the larger bags. He held up a large bag
with what Nash recognized as pelvic bones. "Based on the rib count
and how this pelvis goes together, we have a female... and she
might have been pregnant."

"So we're not just looking at a certain type of victim, but more."
Her one eye squinted hard. "Could this be a community dump
site?"

"We're not sure. Certainly, nobody was suspecting anything like
this."

She waved her finger at all the bags. "And you got all of this out
of the one pool?"

Uncle looked at Peter with a hesitant look.

Nash leaned on her hand on the table. A tactic that only occasionally worked with her wife. "What?"

Peter shifted. "None of us dive. So we don't have any SCUBA
gear, and we didn't want to overstep your position..."

Uncle nudged him with his arm. "What the chickenshit is trying
to say is this all came from what I could reach with the water only
up to my belly. We didn't even work the northwest side of the pool.
And I probed it with an avalanche probe. It's about twenty feet
deep."

Nash hung her head to one side and closed her right eye. "You
don't have any dive gear, but you have an avalanche probe?" She
swung around wildly as if searching. "Where do you get the
avalanches? In the bar?"

Her pocket vibrated.

She noted the caller and put it on speakerphone. "Go ahead
Mike. You're on speaker... and I think you know who all is here."

The voice was hesitant and female. "Um... Agent Running Bear?"

Nash rolled her eyes. "Muna, meet Uncle and Peter. Guys, this is Special Agent Muna al-Faragi. What's up?"

"Mike heard you were bringing down some more bones... Well, he asked me to find out how much room we needed. We just got some Ostia evidence from San Jose, and they kind of have a rush..."

"Tell Mike he has the day to rush San Jose's lab work, but by tomorrow midnight, every table he has will be full, and then some. And tell him I need a full rig from triple tanks to skins to flippers. His bribery is on the way. As if he doesn't already owe me. How many bodies did you bring with you from D.C.?"

"None. But we have two on the way from Quantico. They'll be here tomorrow."

Nash hung her head. "Rookies?"

"One is. But he just finished six months with the body farm."

Nash's one open eye studied the rafters as she thought. "Who's the other agent?"

"No agent. He was a teacher at the farm."

In the background, Nash could hear the distinctive sound of Mike's metal feet on the floor. "Ol' Oz himself, Nash. He requested the transfer."

Nash's enlarged eyes locked on Uncle. "Now I wish I was coming down. Hey Mike?"

"Yeah, I'm here. Muna put you on speaker."

"I need a full dive rig with... better make it two sets of triple tanks. Thin skins, but I want hood to flippers."

"I have a summer rig with a hard helmet. It'll give you about a hundred sixty degrees of vision with built-in lights. It's one of those full-face rigs you were using down in the Keys when we did the coral theft investigation."

"Perfect. But I don't know where I'll be refilling around here, so I'll need at least two full rigs of tanks and regulators."

"I'll borrow a recharge unit from the Coasties. Triples are a beast, so I'll just send some singles. Even with shallow diving, if you're doing any work, you don't want to be down for over four hours in twenty-four."

"Okay mommy. Get on the San Jose thing. Your lab is about to be full, even with the Wizard of Oz himself."

"Okay, we'll talk to you later."

Nash turned to Alex as the call cut off. "Let's get you loaded and on your way."

"You know, if we both went, you can try on the suit there and share the driving."

Uncle rolled his eyes and smiled at Nash. "White boy hate driving long trail."

"What about old Indian?"

Uncle shrugged and grumped. "Sit on stool or drive big truck. All the same to cast iron butt."

Alex shrugged. "It doesn't matter to me." Pointing at Nash. "You can't dive until the suit and stuff are here, and the old man is afraid of deep water."

"Not afraid. Just don't swim."

Nash smacked her lips wetly in boredom. "This won't all fit in the Challenger, and his truck wouldn't make it halfway to the city. So what are we taking?"

Alex laughed. "Oh, his truck would make it to Washington, D.C. and back faster than you could drive your red flash to Chicago. Don't let the Rodeo Ready look fool you. We stuffed over five hundred horses under the hood. But you're right. Neither is the rig to take all this down to the city." He crooked his finger in the air as he walked deeper into the extensive building.

Nash frowned at Uncle. "Rodeo Ready?"

The man laughed. "Beat to shit, but ready to run all day."

They came to a stop in front of an RV. It looked like it had its best days on the road in the last century. The faded light green paint was showing signs of peeling. The golden tan was more sand and rust.

Alex smiled like a proud parent. "Meet Pepe. The burro of the fleet."

"Burro?"

"Hard worker, carries a lot, runs all day, and eats modestly. Well, okay, I lied. She sucks a gallon of fuel every five miles. But she can run those same five in under three minutes if you need to. She's got sixteen hundred horses with a ten-speed automatic. She'll climb the Grapevine doing a hundred or eighty if you're pulling a twenty-eight-foot sport fisher. Or so I've been told."

Nash shook her head. "But you couldn't have started with a newer body?"

Alex smiled. "Your red cherry bomb out there is the same year as this body. The paint is special and hides the extra bulk of the armor plating. The glass will handle an AK-47, but if you're up against a Barrett or more... run."

He walked along the side and opened one of the lower hatches. "These bays will handle four times what you'll be hauling."

They turned at the sound of Uncle pulling his truck in. A moment later, he approached with a small knapsack. "While you have my truck, you might look at the lifters. Not always, but when it's cold, I can hear a ticking. She's also ready for an oil change, lube, and tire rotation."

Alex snapped to attention. "Oh, yes, sir. We'll get right on that."

Nash turned on her heel and headed for her car. "Boys..." And as she looked at the vehicles with a new understanding, she added in her mind *and their toys*.

17

DIG DEEPER

THE TWO LARGE bags of Jalapeño Pepper Tex-Mex BBQ that will burn the inside of your mouth and fried pork rinds landed on the slick table and slid to the other end. They meant for the cartoon logo of a cactus person swinging a flamethrower to be a joke. But Nash knew it was more of a true warning.

The dark face of the young woman lit up. "Allah is wise. She has sent me a true understanding friend and savior."

Mike peeked over her shoulder and started to reach out. Two more bags slid down the table. The general motif was Jamaican. He laughed. "I bet you had to search long and hard to find jerked rinds."

Nash shrugged. "We ran out of steam and spent the night in the truck stop in Vacaville. If there ever was a supermarket of all weirdly edible, it's a truck stop."

Mike leaned toward Muna. "I don't think you'll be able to get those at the little market you found."

Muna rolled her eyes. "The Little Shikhar? Yeah, not hardly. But they do have all the spices I like to cook with."

They all turned as the four security guards pushed in the lock cages. They lined them along two of the tables.

Mike's eyes grew as he glanced at Nash. "Man, you weren't kidding about a large load..."

The one security guard winked at Nash. "The other three guys just got back from their break, so we'll bring up the rest of the load."

Nash smiled in a grimace to not laugh. "Thanks."

She turned to Mike and his shocked face. "You also get about a hundred and fifty kilos more of wheel weights. For all the good it will do. But something I want you to focus on is this..." She transferred evidence bags from the trolly to the table.

She held up the large bag with the pelvis. Muna frowned at it. "Is this a female?"

"What was your first clue?"

She held her hands in a cradle shape. "The pelvis isn't up and down as much as it is cradling. Male pelvises are up and down for more productive walking or running."

Mike smiled at the lesson time. "And what causes the bones to open and spread like this?"

Muna squinted at the bones and then at Nash. "She was pregnant?"

Nash slowly blinked as she nodded her head to one side. "That's our thinking. And your job is to figure out which skull is hers and how she died."

Mike's eyes opened wide, and he held up a finger as he spun on his one prosthetic. "Speaking of which..." He strode to one bench and picked up a small piece of plastic.

He handed the plastic to Nash. "We used to take molds of the skull and then make a series of casts. Now we use the laser scanner and then print it with the 3-D printer. A lot less waste and leaves the skull or whatever ready to go to court. Any ideas?"

She turned it over several times as she listened to the sound of quiet walking boots and the untrimmed nails of a dog. She held it up near her shoulder. "What do you think, Uncle?"

He took the piece of plastic the size and shape of a serving spoon. "I think I would want more than just this little bit of the egg for breakfast."

Muna glanced down at the dog sniffing her leg. "Who is this?"

Nash smirked to one side. "Very Special Agent Powder. You must have been at the shooting range this morning." She remembered the junior agent's penchant for starting her mornings with a prayer and a bang.

The enormous eyes were Nash's reward. "How did you know?"

Nash pointed at the dog. "She knew the moment she walked into the room. She also could smell the bones in the water from the shore. I'm skeptical, but she led Uncle straight to the stuff we brought down before."

Mike squinted one eye and frowned. "Usually, a dog gets trained for explosives or cadavers, not both."

Uncle grabbed at his ponytail and gently pulled it to his front. "Those would be white man dogs. Powder is an Indian dog. She knows more tricks than just explosives and bodies. She sees things beforehand as well. If I didn't know better, I would think she was a reincarnated shaman."

Mike's one eye ratcheted up a notch. "We're getting into tall tale territory here."

Uncle fluttered his cheeks and lips in a snort. Looking down at the dog, he snapped his fingers. "Powder, where does Mike hide his treats? Show us where the treats are."

The dog bounced, turned, and ran along the cabinets, desk, tables, and chests. Finally, reversing and carefully walking to one of the filing cabinets, she sat down.

The man was flustered. "Okay, enough of the games. We have work to do…"

Nash chuckled. "Oh no. Let's see what she found." She held her arm out, stopping the man. She pointed at the floor. "Stay. This is her work."

"It's just something I brought in a few days—"

Nash stopped him with her outreached hand. She opened the lower drawer. Powder didn't move but kept watching Mike.

She opened the top drawer, and still no response. The same with the next drawer down. But she put her hand on the drawer's handle above the bottom. Powder stood and looked at the drawer.

Nash rummaged through the drawer. She held up the still-sealed bag of chocolate chip cookies. She held it to her nose. "Sealed, and I can't smell a thing."

Mike looked at Uncle. Uncle shrugged and tossed his ponytail back around to his back. "Yup. Indian dog. Scary how they know stuff." He held up the plastic piece. "What is this?"

"A 3-D print of the dent in what we think is Curtis Ghoulish's skull. The first skeleton you found."

Mike took the piece from Uncle. "We just need to figure out what the rest of the bludgeon looks like."

Uncle worried his tongue against the side of his teeth. "It didn't go deep, so I'm guessing it weighs less than a hammer or pipe."

Mike looked at Muna. "There's a start. Let's figure out the weight and striking energy of the blow. From there, we can extrapolate closer to the weapon by cutting out the feathers and wrecking balls." Turning, he gazed at the piles of bags and bones. "Then, too, let's find the skulls."

Uncle smiled. "Well, we'd like to help, but we have some other business to deal with across the bridge."

Nash frowned curiously at the man. "We do? What business?"

The man rolled his eyes. "Secret Squirrel shit. Okay, DEA stuff."

She nodded at the piles of work. "And you need me...?"

"You and Powder are involved."

She shrugged at Muna. "We'll check in. Also, you might look deeper into missing females in the area for, say, the last five or six years. And check with the Bureau of Indian Affairs as well. The reservation doesn't always report things they should. Or it's just that the usual authorities don't report or file things with any diligence regarding the first nations." She noticed the slight nod from Uncle.

NASH GAZED AROUND THE GIANT DECK WITH MANY tables. The one arm in denim raised with an outspread hand for a flag.

Uncle leaned back as Nash pulled out her chair, and the young waiter set two large mugs of coffee on the table.

The waiter stood waiting as Uncle grabbed the menus and handed them over. "Please tell the chef to just surprise us. I helped build the original deck for this place, and they've never done me wrong since."

"Very good, sir." The waiter vaporized like a mist in the morning.

Uncle glanced at Nash as he adulterated his coffee. "How's your wife?"

"Probably starving."

He harrumphed softly. "Or ordering delivery. You know, in the cities, you can order a month of frozen dinners geared for any dietary needs. They ship them by the week, right to your door. Just throw them in the freezer and pull out what you want. A few minutes in the microwave, and bingo, you have dinner."

Nash scowled at him with only one eye open. "What do you do in the country?"

"Oh, we just drive around on the back roads looking for whatever got hit. You know, the same as when you were a kid."

Nash stirred her coffee and then glanced over at the woman, who was shifting uneasily from eavesdropping on a conversation not as delicate or as salacious as she was used to. "I remember a lot more oatmeal and potatoes than I do fine dining on roadkill. But maybe things were different on your reservation than ours."

He leaned back into his chair with his mug to his lips as he gazed across the San Francisco Bay. "Growing up... I remember more flatbread than anything else. At the first of the month, we might even have Skippy peanut butter on it. Not much. But just enough to change the flavor." He sipped as he watched a sleek catamaran slide past. "The seasons would change the flour from nuts to corn, wheat, or even barley and oats, but the strangest part was it always tasted like the inside of the barrel the women cooked it on. I hated it when the sap was surging in the creosote brush. It made the fire hotter, but the flat bread tasted like burned tires."

Nash watched the older man.

"What?"

Nash shrugged her eyes. "Nothing, really. I've never had this kind of talk about food or lack thereof with anybody else. Everyone I know has memories of the meal that reminds them of their grandma or how their dad used to get up early on Sundays and cook pancakes with chocolate chips in a smiley face. We joke about eating roadkill, but we also know it was some of the better meat we got."

He grumped. "What do you mean got? I have at least a hundred pounds of roadkill jerky in the teepee. If it's still warm, it's still good. Two years ago, the truck in front of me hit a doe and her two fawns. He never even slowed down. I had been headed down to Sacramento. I went two days later. Still, some of the best jerky I've made in years. How did Mina grow up?"

Nash chuckled as the lunch arrived. She pointed at the lobster sandwich on a croissant. "Like this. Her father is a face surgeon, and her mother was a marriage and family counselor in one of the tonier neighborhoods in Virginia. Now she runs an NGO working with PTSD for rape and molestation victims."

Uncle smiled at the sandwich. "So no roadkill there."

The woman at the other table finally pulled out her purse and threw some money at the table and left with an ugly look back at the two.

Nash snorted softly as she lifted her sandwich. "Good thing she left before we got into talking about dead bodies, skeletons, and missing girls."

"What are the chances of finding a missing girl from the area?"

Nash peeked one eye over the sandwich. Hundreds of girls go missing from reservations every year, and she knew this was the statistic they were talking about. She pondered as she chewed. Washing the food down with coffee, she dabbed at her lips. "Muna is good, but you know the system."

He cleared his throat. "Both systems. The one ignoring what goes on at the reservation, and what the reservation is not reporting, and the system of the reservations not wanting to talk about their problems."

Her head bobbed. "We'll let Muna take the first crack at it, but then when we head back up, I think we should plan on a dinner stop at Tucker's and talk to Three Toes' daughter, Tracy. Even having grown up off the res, she might have some insight or know something. I think the Three Toes connection was still a strong connection. She's the one who pointed me at Travis Air Base and the Airman Desai."

18

NOT QUITE RIGHT

UNCLE GAZED down at his boots. They weren't filthy, but they also weren't clean.

"What?"

He glanced up at Nash. "My boots. Should I take them off?"

Nash called over her shoulder. "Pi, he's worried his boots aren't clean enough for the lab. Should he take them off and just walk around in his socks?"

Uncle cleared his throat and groused—embarrassed. "I don't wear socks."

Nash chuckled and repeated. "Sorry, he doesn't wear socks."

A dark something lobbed through the air and splatted on the floor in front of them. "Are his boots cleaner than the cow turd?"

Nash shrugged at the man now turning red. "Well? Are they?"

Uncle turned. "I'll wait in the RV."

The short man came around the edge of the large table. "Hey. Aren't you Agent Yazzie?"

Uncle turned back with one eye squinted.

Pi kept approaching and sidestepped the turd. "The official file says you drink like a fish but run like a scared chicken."

Uncle glared at Nash. "Is this your doing?"

123

Pi stopped in the man's shadow. He extended his hand. "Hi, I'm Pi. Just like the mathematical equation. You must be Oceal Yazzie."

Uncle extended his hand gingerly while he kept glaring at Nash. "People call me Uncle."

Pi snickered. "I'm half your size, and you give up so easily?"

Uncle let go of the hand and turned back toward the hall. "I'll be in the truck."

Pi laughed and turned back to the lab. "Okay, but we have doughnuts."

Uncle stopped. "What kind?"

"Tasty ones. Even ones that look like a sickly cow patty."

Uncle turned. "Apple fritters. How old?"

The dwarf turned at the table. "Better if you dip them in some good Tanzania double-berry coffee."

The grumpy man strode through the door. Sidestepping the turd. "Okay, I'm in."

Pi called down the lab. "Four for coffee and doughnuts, Mandy. And a cow shit in the entry again."

A minute later, the assistant came out of the break room, pushing a lab cart. The carafe stood braced by four mugs. The pink box was recognizable in twenty-seven countries. She stopped and glanced at the turd.

Walking over, she stooped and picked up the rubber gag turd. She Frisbee'd it at a refrigerated unit. It splatted flat on the door and stuck. It was obviously one of the lab jokes.

Nash noticed a tint of red on Uncle's neck. She finished the introductions. "Mandy, this is Uncle. Not your uncle or my uncle or anyone's uncle—just everyone's uncle. You might say he's kind of slutty in an uncle sort of way. But I sure wouldn't."

Uncle stopped at the cart, peeked in the pink box, and fixed his coffee. He retreated behind a lab table with his coffee and fritter.

As he listened to Pi and Mandy go over the chemicals in the creek's water, he fingered the plastic printout of the dent in the skull. The piece was about a half-inch thick but crudely shaped like a goose egg. He kept thinking something was missing.

He finished his fritter and stood. "Can I use your phone? I need to call San Francisco."

Mandy walked over to the desk and punched in the numbers. She held out the handset. "Sorry about the cow turd. Some people have a hard time with our humor."

He took the phone. "Wait until we get up to speed about making dinner out of roadkill."

"Jeez. Is it dinnertime already?"

Uncle laughed. "No. Sorry Mike. Just finishing a long conversation. Listen, I've been toying with this piece of plastic you printed up... How much would this need to weigh to make the kind of dent in a skull we're looking at?"

"About a pound should do it, but you would have to swing it hard. What are you thinking?"

Uncle examined the serving spoonful of plastic. "If you put two of these together, would lead do the trick?"

He could hear the guy on the other end of the phone bend to do something. "The computer says we're a few grams short, but sure."

"Can you cast them up for me? I think I left some lead lying around over there."

Mike snorted. "At least a pound or two."

Uncle looked across the lab at Nash. "We'll figure out the handle when we get back. Oh. And the skulls...?"

Uncle could hear Mike clear his throat. "Yeah... all but one have the same dent and are in the same location. So we have a serial killer. But the one without... well, we think it might be your pelvis. The girl. But there are a couple of other things. I'll show you when you two get back."

"Okay. I'll fill Nash in, and we should be back tomorrow or the next day. I think she wants to track down this guy from Travis Air Base, but... jeez, this is getting out of control fast. How are we going to figure out the rest of the bodies?"

The sigh was deep on the other end of the phone. "Let's see what her diving turns up."

Uncle snapped his fingers. "Oh, thanks for jogging my memory. Do you have access to an underwater camera with lights and all?"

"I'll talk to the Coast Guard. They're supposed to bring the recharger over tomorrow morning."

Uncle softly kicked at the large rubber tire on the table caster. "I just wish they had a camera that would give us a picture of this killer." His lips furled as he looked up.

Pi and Mandy had also noticed Nash's sudden drain of color.

Uncle hesitated a moment. "I got to go." And hung up.

He watched Nash as the other two hovered about her. Her eyes were on Uncle, but she wasn't seeing him. Uncle could feel her holding her breath. Afraid to breathe. There was something there. Just outside of her sight.

Mandy reached out. "Nash...?"

As her finger touched Nash's elbow, they both jumped as if shocked. Mandy gave a sharp whimper as Nash looked at her. "It's the town drunk."

"What is the town drunk?" Pi echoed Uncle.

Nash turned to look at him as if she were just waking up. Her face cleared and then turned dark in confusion. "I don't know." She frowned at Uncle. "What did you just say...?"

He thought, but it was gone. "I don't remember. We were talking about getting more gear from the Coast Guard." He glanced back at the phone. "It was something about getting an underwater camera." He turned back.

Nash peeked at her watch. "We need to get you some food. It's your blood sugar."

Pi pointed at the pink box. "We have doughnuts..."

Uncle twitched his head. "Nah. That's probably what happened. They jack me up but drop me further. I need protein and balance."

"We can stop at the truck stop."

Uncle nodded as he took Nash's lead.

She turned to Mandy. "That's great work on the chemistry. Keep me posted. We need to know who we should be looking at and what they do."

The young woman nodded. "We'll keep on it. In a few more days, we should have all the fine spectrometer readings from San Francisco as well as our own. Then we can start marrying them together to get exactly what we're looking at."

Nash gave Uncle a side-eye. "Let's get you fed."

THE RV EASED OUT OF THE PARKING LOT AND ONTO THE back road through cattle, grass, and open sky. Nash kept watching the rearview mirrors. Uncle sat stewing in the passenger seat. Powder sat on the engine cover, watching the road. It surprised Nash that the dog wasn't watching the cows—being technically a cow dog.

Uncle scrunched down in the seat and put his boot up against the dashboard.

Nash glanced over. "Have some respect. Put your filthy boots where they belong."

He glanced over at the woman. Thought better about saying anything and pulled his boot back and crossed it over his knee. He thought about which way they were driving. His finger pointed behind them, and his mouth opened.

His finger retracted and hovered down to his lap as his mouth closed.

An hour of silence later, Nash steered the large RV into the enormous parking lot full of trucks and trailers. She pulled to the open pump and stopped. Turning, she looked at Uncle. "Yazzie?"

He glared through the side of his eye.

"I get Oceal. It's a Mexican name. But how do you get Uncle from Oceal or Yazzie?"

"It's from my first name." He watched a trucker thumping his tires with a large hammer.

"Oceal."

His head twitched slowly. "Nope. Mateo."

Nash turned and looked across the lot at what the man was watching. "Oh yes. Mat is easy to turn—"

"It was my baby sister. She couldn't pronounce the first syllable. She could only say Teo. But with a little girl, it sounds more like Tío. And in Spanish…"

"Uncle."

He nodded.

He looked over. "What are we doing here?"

"Getting fuel. We're at a half tank."

"Well, it wouldn't have anything to do with you driving in a wild circle through every cow pasture and alfalfa field."

She glared at him.

"So we get fuel… And then?"

She pointed out across the parking lot at a large airplane slowly rising above the tree line. "The plane is a C-17. It just left Travis Air Base. We have questions."

"I thought you said you were going to feed me?"

She looked over. "What did you say back there?"

"Mike and I were talking about borrowing the gear from the Coasties, and I asked if they had an underwater camera. He said he'd check. And I said…" He stopped to think. "I said something like I'd like to see a clear picture of the killer." He looked over. "And you kind of cried out about a drunk."

Her eyes narrowed as she rocked—thinking. Frustrated, she stood. "I'll get the fuel." She paused at the bottom of the slide-out step. "And then we eat."

NASH CRUMBLED MORE SALTINE CRACKERS ON HER chili. As she stirred it all together, she stared out the window and across the large parking lot. Trucks with license plates of every color and state sat or moved about the truck stop. Which explained the store stocking the wild array of pork rinds.

"Last September, an airman named Nilesh Desai went AWOL. They extended no special effort to find him. I want to know why. And if he has dental records, San Francisco could use them to help identify a skeleton." She gazed at Uncle.

The man was scowling as he stirred his coffee. His lower lip twitched gently, as if he was speaking to himself.

"You're working on something..."

He peeked up, slightly startled. "You do that to your wife?"

Her eyes narrow to dark slits.

His chest bounced with the soft chuff. "Yeah. No wonder you two aren't getting along."

Her one eye eased open. The black showed more wet dark brown bracketing the black pupil. "What makes you think we're in a rough patch?"

He laid the spoon on the table and picked up his fork. "You talk to her every day. You get at least two or three texts from her. But it never lights up your face." He shoveled a bit of the Cob salad into his mouth, but shoved it into his cheek. He pointed the fork at Nash. "When we were raking up the bones, your face looked like you were ten years old again. This morning your face looked like Mina had just read you the shopping list."

"It's hard. I'm on the road and she's going through chemo-therapy and still trying to work and..."

He swallowed. "Yeah, yeah, yeah. And, and, and... with you two, there will always be another and another. It's not hard. Are you strapped for money?"

"No..."

His hand waved the air between them. "No. It was a yes or no question. I didn't want to hear the stories. So it's not like you're living from paycheck to paycheck. So take some months off. Take some compassion leave. Be with her. Hold her hand when she's sitting there with the chemo machine."

"She does it alone. In a private room."

He shoved more salad into his mouth and pointed with the fork. "Let me guess. The private room is so she can sit with her laptop and do work."

She nodded.

"Bullshit. Nobody is that mercenary. She does it because it gives her a sense of normalcy. Same as you out here running around the wild west chasing skeletons and missing airmen. It's just easier to do what you know how to do and work than learn how to talk with your wife and just be there for her."

"We work."

He gently laid the fork on the edge of the plate. He dabbed at his lips. "And at her funeral… will you also take your laptop so you can get some work done?"

"You're disgusting."

He sat back with his hands in his lap. Old damage softened his voice. "Nope. Just already been there."

He glanced out the window. "When my little sister was dying of Hodgkin's lymphoma, I was working a case in Missouri. The long-time mayor and his two sons were trafficking the local drugs, with girls on the side and the occasional gambling. At best, they would go away for five to seven years. They were peanuts in the larger shell game. But, because I didn't know what to say to my sister, I called, and we talked about how hot it was and who had stopped by to say hi."

He stabbed at the salad but laid his fork down. "I kept working because I was afraid to figure out how to be with the woman I only remembered as a gawky little girl. I even put in lots of overtime. And when it was time to go to her funeral, I was arresting three men who spent a total of twenty-seven months between the three of them. Not in prison, not in jail, but under house arrest. Which, in the backwater of the world, means the whole damn town."

He leaned back in the booth. His hands lay in his lap. "Nothing changed—except me. I had lost the last of my family, and all I knew was how hot it had been in Albuquerque. Years later, I found out she died on the day she was supposed to get married."

He leaned forward and angrily stabbed at the salad. His eyes were wet as he stared out the window and silently chewed.

19

HOT WATER

NASH WALKED in just the booties. The flippers were for the vast open ocean. Two kicks would have taken her across the creek. Three or four to cross the large pool. This trip, she was only taking the camera and a sediment broom. Even with the large dive knife strapped to her right leg, she somehow felt naked without her weapon.

When the water was to her elbows, she squatted and started swimming slowly. The large pool slowed the flow of the water, which was never rapid anyway.

She could see where Uncle had raked. There were small spots where the marks showed he had missed.

Watching for bones, she thought about what Tracy had told her.

The girl's eyes grew wet as she thought back to her good friend. "Betsy had it all. Most of the semesters she at least squeaked her way into the Honor Society. Chemistry and math were her air and water. But she was just the girl. Her brother was the star. He was the running back who was always good for a lot of yards. I think at home, he got to sit at the head of the table. He drove the car, even when he didn't have a license. She walked."

Nash glanced at the few booths down where Uncle sat. He

wasn't in the club. He didn't know how things were on this reservation. And he wasn't one of them, or a female.

"Did you know she was pregnant?"

The young woman nodded. "Well, we had all guessed. It wasn't like they had won the lottery and started eating a lot. But she was growing out of her pants." She gazed up at Nash. "When a girl start safety pinning her pants closed, and wearing her father's flannel shirt—everyone, well, us girls, can guess."

"Who was the boy?"

The girl drew in a large breath through her nose as she stared out the window. "Take your pick. She wanted to be popular or at least feel like she fit in. We all did." She looked back at Nash. Her mouth drew back in a one-sided frown, along with her shrug. "I don't think there was any single boy. Pick any on the football team. I wouldn't even put it past Hank, her brother. Us girls knew better than to get caught anywhere alone with him. We called him the gunslinger. Not because he shot a gun, but because he had fast hands."

Nash furled her lips. Generations to generations, some things never seemed to change. "So there wouldn't be any way to know who..."

Tracy squinted one eye hard as her head tilted. "Even she probably didn't know. I'm not saying she was loose, but I had heard more than a few boys refer to her as a six-pack."

Nash's eyes narrowed in confusion. "Six-pack? As in beer?"

Tracy turned away, embarrassed. "Take one for you and pass it around."

Their silence hung as an exclamation point on the crude assessment of the girl's life.

Tracy shook slightly and looked back. "Can I ask if they know how she died?"

Nash nodded. "Evidence leads us to believe they strangled her."

The girl shuttered. "She deserved better. Anyone deserves..." A tear squeezed out of her closed eye.

Nash grimaced. The single tear encased her entire world. Nash wasn't there unless someone had deserved better.

The warm water was murky, but Nash could see lumps on the bottom, hidden by tufts of algae and silt. She swam down to where she could see where Uncle had disturbed the bottom.

Pulling the plastic silt broom out of its holster, she waved it around a small mound. As the silt swirled away, the rounded form showed through. The dent, now that she knew what she was looking for, was, if not clear, at least evident.

She swept the broom over the surrounding masses. More bones. She cleared at least an area as wide as she thought would be one side of a ten-foot by ten-foot grid. By tilting the broom, she swept the water to take the silt away from the cleared swath.

The tinny beeping on her wrist told her to check her air level. She pulled the meter to her mask. She was under the green area, and almost at the bottom of the yellow. Even in the pool, she knew her time was up.

She holstered the broom and pulled the camera from its holster on her belt. She quartered the exposed area and shot images from all four directions. She knew the digital imaging would mitigate the filtered light.

Holstering the camera, she paddled to the surface.

Uncle stood on the bank. The sheriff was standing next to him. Gun drawn.

"You can't run in the creek, Nash." He waved the gun. "Just come on out."

She walked to the edge and climbed out. Unlocking the helmet, she pulled it off. "So I'm guessing you didn't want us digging up your little burial site. Care to tell me how long you've been killing kids and sinking them in the pool?" She squinted into the sunshine at the man.

Thomas bit on his lower lip. "They're not mine. I knew about the skeletons, but they're not mine."

Nash undid the buoyancy and utility belt and let it fall to the ground. Pivoting on one knuckle, she cautiously rose. "Then if they aren't yours, why are you holding a gun on two federal agents?"

"Only one."

She shook her head. "Nope. Two. But then, I'm guessing you came alone and didn't check if we had a lookout."

His head twitched before his eyes narrowed. "I'm not stupid. I'm not falling for some bullshit line."

She pushed out her lower lip. "Okay. We'll simply go on with the questions. Like, why the gun?"

"I told you to leave it. But no... you had to keep at it. You stuck your nose where it didn't belong when we were kids. And now, it's just like the feds to come sticking their noses into our business where they don't belong."

She nodded toward the creek. "Federal water. It's not local. So the bureau has jurisdiction."

"Bullshit. The water comes out of the ground three thousand yards up yonder. And goes back into the ground down south. It's all in Harkin County. Local. No feds."

Nash grimaced a smile as her head twitched to one side. "Nope. According to the spectrograph, the rain and snow land somewhere north in British Columbia. The underground aquifer runs deep through Washington and starts taking up the minerals and lime before it passes under the Oregon border. Under Mount Hood, it picks up some of the schist giving it the greenish tone, and feels so good on the muscles. As it wanders east about mid-state, it picks up the salts of dolomite and starts its way to the geothermal beds about eighty miles north by northwest of here. The heat stews it all together, and we get water that feels good to soak in but not so good to soak for two to three months in. So, in a nutshell, the water crosses an international border and three state lines. Making it Federal."

Watching his eyes, she took the three small steps. "Which brings us back to the DEA and FBI agents you're holding at gunpoint. And the ATF agent with the sniper rifle who has his laser dot on your forehead." She sidestepped. And pointed her finger at his forehead and moved it to his chest. The red dot followed. "Which brings us to the real question. Which do you want? Dog bites, or a single ventilation hole in your chest?"

Powder growled behind him as a red truck slowly made its way up the road.

The sheriff didn't move as Uncle turned.

The long arm with perfectly manicured fingers waved from the open window of the truck. "Who's ready for lunch?"

Thomas looked down at the red dot and back up at Nash.

Nash smiled. "Sheriff, I'd say your timing sucks. This isn't as simple as football, but we'll get back to it when the civilian leaves." She turned and made a chop sign across her throat as she snapped her fingers at Powder. "Personally, I'm getting chilly in this wet suit, and I'm definitely ready for lunch."

The sheriff holstered his pistol and turned toward Uncle. "DEA...?"

Uncle twitched his head with a toothy smile. "Yup." He jerked his thumb out toward the distant trees. "ATF is out there. But they won't be coming in for lunch. They have over watch."

Nash held out half an egg salad sandwich to the sheriff. "Now that you know who plays for what team, are you in, or will you draw on me again?"

The former spoiled jock showed through as he twisted his face and squinted at her. "Twenty years, and he never identified himself to the local authorities."

Uncle picked up the can of soda. "Not true. Your former boss knew the day I set up shop. He was the one who wanted someone else to do the ugly work. So he invited me."

"Did you tell anyone else?"

Uncle swallowed. "Only other person in the sheriff's office back then was Otis." He held up his hand. "Now, before you ask the next question, I want you to think long and hard about everything it entails." His eyebrows raised as he smirked and nodded his head. "Yeah, think about what you kids thought of the deputy back then."

"Not much." He glanced up at Nash. "Why did you ask Cindy not to stay? I mean…" He pointed at the food. "She made lunch."

Nash sat. "Because I asked her to make us lunch. I told her we would be at the large pool. But I didn't say which large pool." She watched his face.

"But we already got the samples from the other pool…"

"But she didn't go there. She came here."

Thomas screwed his face up and shook his head. "You couldn't know that. She went there, but you weren't there, so she came here."

She nodded to Uncle. He pulled a walkie-talkie from his belt and spoke into it. "Felix?"

The answer was squawk and tin. "Go."

He put the radio to his mouth as he watched the sheriff. "Did the sheriff's wife, or anybody, come to the flat pool today?"

"A couple of kids drove past in a late nineties Toyota Corolla. Color was primer spots over maybe white. It was nine forty-eight this morning. No wife."

Uncle smiled. "Ten-four." He shook his head. "Something tells me your wife doesn't want to be connected to the lower pool. Care to tell us why, Sheriff?"

Thomas's eyes narrowed. "What are you implying?"

Nash cleared her throat. "Not implying anything, merely observing and asking. You're the local authority, as you so forcefully pointed out. Which means you should be the one who knows what's going on in your county. Especially in the creek you frequently soak in with your friends."

"I know enough."

Uncle sat to be less threatening. "You knew the skeletons were there but said nothing until the kids found the first one. How long have you known, and how many?"

The sheriff winced and whined in protest. "There have always been bones. It's why it's named Bone Creek."

Nash rolled her eyes. "It's not named Bone Creek. Only ignorant locals call it that." She leaned in. "They also say things like there were always bones in the creek."

His eyes narrowed. "Are you calling me ignorant?"

Uncle snorted softly. "No, just stupid... or complicit." He raised the side of his face and eyebrow. "Which is it?"

"Complicit in WHAT?"

Nash relaxed and sat back on the ice chest. "Murder."

His eyes snapped to hers. "What murder?"

"How do you think the first skeleton got there? Just shed its skin and muscles and walked on in?"

"It's just bones. How do you know it's murder?"

Uncle grumbled. "There's still evidence as clear as a bullet hole through the skull."

"They were shot?"

Nash put her hand out toward Uncle. "That's not what he said. But yes, there is evidence of foul play on all of them."

The sheriff peeked over at the pool and then back at Nash. "The diving gear." His chest lost its bravado as he looked back at the pool. "How many?"

"We have three skulls, and I just uncovered four more."

His head ground slowly back around. Pausing at Uncle's eyes. "All the same? How long do you think they've been there?"

Nash shrugged. "One down there is so encrusted with the lime, at first, I passed it over as a rock. But then I exposed the spine. I'm no expert, but I'd say more than a decade. But not twenty years. I think by then, it would be another rock."

Thomas's hands lay lifeless in his lap. "That's a long time..." He looked up at Uncle. "Remember the shooting out at Mel Blankenship's place?"

Uncle frowned down to one side. "About eight years ago. Two

tuffs broke into their house. Mel hit one with his shotgun... liked to cut him in half."

The sheriff rocked softly. "A twelve-gauge full of dimes will mess things up a bit at point-blank range. The doc even found the wadding in his guts."

"But the other guy got away..."

"He left a trail of blood. We tracked him for a mile or so. He came here to the creek." The sheriff pointed upstream. "Months later, I finally found his body at the next horseshoe bend. His foot was sticking out of the manzanita. He'd been there with his one hand and forearm in the water the whole time. That's when I figured out why it was called Bone Creek."

Nash leaned her head to one side. "Wonderful story, but you said you had found other bones. Skeletons."

He pointed north. "And it's still there. There's a boulder in the middle of the stream as it straightens after the snake bends. It's wedged under the rock. I think the current drove it in there."

Uncle rumbled. "But you didn't want to tell anyone?"

Thomas's head twitched to one side. "The lime has welded the ribs to the rock. I figured it was too much of a cold case to even think about. I never counted on the nightmares."

Nash and Uncle both nodded minutely. *The nightmares will always get you.*

20

CHEMICALLY SPEAKING

"HEY, PI?" Mandy walked out into the wet section of the lab. She squinted at the bright sunshine streaming down through the open skylights. She held up the sheaf of papers. "You're not going to like this."

The large-faced respirator, over the rubber suit, swung around. Mandy could see the face laughing. And then the stench hit her.

She backed out of the large room as her face folded into a pained crumple. The door couldn't close and seal fast enough.

She turned to hit the air evacuation button. The meter above it already showed the giant fans working at maximum speed. The air in the large room exchanged every thirty-two seconds. *No wonder the open skylights*.

Leaning in, she looked at the methane meter. The air in the chamber stood at fourteen percent. Running some fast math, she realized if the chamber weren't open and aired, the methane level could easily reach an explosive level.

She had forgotten he turned his new digestion microbes loose in the manure tank last night. She looked through the window in the door. The small man stirred the manure with his gloved hand. The paddle she would have used still leaned against the side of the tank.

Blinking with a bright look on her face, she turned back to her work on the other side of the laboratory. "He's as happy as a little piggy in his own wallow."

She knocked the red slapper button with her elbow. The phone stopped beeping, and she could hear traffic in the background. "Mandy."

"Mandy, it's Nash."

The young technician snorted. "Were your ears burning?"

"Should they be?" The sound of a turn signal punctuated the background noise.

"I just got the final compilation of your water."

"And...?"

"I need to run it over with Pi, but you've definitely got serious pollution there."

The sound of the large car engine rumbled as it accelerated. "Care to talk a bit about generalized specifics?"

"We already figured you had a drug lab involved, but it's more like what now. The usual suspects we would expect to find out there in the backwoods appear to be a lot more sophisticated."

"Tell me like I was a freshman?"

Mandy chuckled at her mother's favorite saying. "They made your hot dog from finely ground asparagus, eggplant blossoms, Iguana livers, ocular orbs of salamanders, left wings of night flying rodents, and the hair of a left-handed lesser Sloth living in a honey mango tree on the western slopes of the Amazon headwaters."

Nash groaned. "Please tell me you're lying about the eggplant."

"No worries. It's just the blossoms. The taste is similar to roasted dandelion roots."

The car slipped out of traffic, and Nash looked for somewhere to park. "So it's more complicated than what you were expecting."

Mandy glanced at a couple of the sheets. "I expected to find a base of ephedrine because what we see these days is people cooking pseudoephedrine to get methedrine. But this looks more like the old-school boil and bubble chemistry to get LSD or speed. Maybe both."

Nash sat in the quiet of the idling car. "I thought we left the LSD in the seventies…"

Mandy leaned against the stainless-steel bench. "It would have been nice. But it's gaining popularity along with black tar heroin, mushrooms, and ecstasy. The kids didn't learn from their parents."

Nash hummed. "Or grandparents."

"When can we expect you?" Mandy looked across the lab at the red-light cycling to green. It would take Pi at least twenty minutes to decontaminate and then probably take a long shower.

"We have more work to do here. I cleared a grid, and there were four more skulls. I think it's time to call in the cavalry, but having an invasion of federal agents scrambling around the woods would spook whoever is running the drug lab and they would end up shutting down and going dark. If not for the drugs, at least for the toxic pollutants, we need to shut them down."

Mandy laid the sheaf of papers on the counter. "Okay. Well, when you've solved your bones, we'll be here for the chemicals."

"Just a thought, and I know it's not like crude oil or something, but is there a way to mitigate the pollution?"

"I'll talk to Pi when he gets out of decontamination. For now, we can work on that angle. And for you, good hunting, Agent."

"Thanks, Mandy. We found this hunting already. We just need to figure out how big it is. But I'll take you up on the other when it's time."

The connection snicked off.

Mandy crossed her arms as she recalled some of her chemistry classes. Most of the time, the goal was to do the experiment and not blow up the lab. Most of the time. Nobody was teaching what to do after someone released the chemistry on Mother Nature.

She turned toward the computer and typed. She slowly scrolled through the listings of departments within the Environmental Protection Agency.

Pɪ CROSS-CHECKED THE FIGURES BETWEEN THE TWO screens. He lightly made a note on the paper printouts.

Mandy gathered her purse and lunch bag from her desk. As she walked past Pi, she leaned over and stuck three yellow notes and a pink note on the bezel of his right monitor.

He looked up. "And...?"

She pointed at each note as she qualified them. "We took a few chem classes together. He's working at Exxon labs, and I think he might help us with the petrochemical traces. We worked a few cleanups together."

She pointed at the third yellow sticky. "She heads up the interface office for the EPA. I think she could help us find some people. She went to the same school as my mom, and I think sorority sisters." She wavered her hand in the air. "Any allusion to connection is still a connection in a war."

Her finger jumped to the pink sticker. "He remembers you. Said you were one of the laziest students in his classes. I guess he didn't flunk you because you took three classes from him."

"Five." He looked up with a smile. "And he sat lead council on my doctoral board. I'll reach out to his wife. She and I lab buddied often." He glanced at his watch. "Ouch. I'll reach out tomorrow." He grimaced at Mandy as he pointed at the screens. "This is what we do month after month. And you've been a real trooper with this... but would you be interested in doing this full-time? I know your first interest is microbiology... but..."

She rested her hand on his shoulder. "Let me finish my doctoral first, and then I'll let you know." She pointed at the time in the bottom corner of the screen. "I set the self-destruct for midnight. Make sure you're out of the building by then. You had an extremely physical day with the poop bugs, and you'll feel it tomorrow. Get some rest."

Pi looked back at the retreating woman. His voice was too soft for her to hear. "Yes, mommy." But as he leaned forward toward the monitor to ensure he saw the numbers right, a faint smile hovered at the corner of his mouth.

21

CHECKING IN

NASH STARED at the laptop screen. Nothing had changed since the connection. The picture behind the deputy director's chair was still a quarter-inch low on the right side. His father-in-law had taught history, and the picture of Washington Crossing the Delaware had always hung in his living room over the faux fireplace. When the AD finally got into an office, his mother-in-law had taken it off her wall and handed it to him. She asked him to please hide the thing in his office where she would never see it again.

It had probably hung crooked since then.

Nash could hear someone enter the room. The white starched shirt cinched into the Welch-slate gray pants belonged to the office owner. She could see he had just arrived. The prominent bulge in the small of his back hadn't been stowed. She cleared her throat.

The man froze. By the twist of his torso, she could tell he was looking back at his office door.

She caught his attention. "I guess Danial forgot to tell you of our face-time report."

The man sat. "Agent, Running Bear."

"Deputy Director."

"Sorry. He mentioned it. I've just been... distracted this morning. A lot going on today." He grimaced and leaned forward as he pulled his weapon out of his belt. "Sorry."

He leaned back as his eyes rolled to one side. "I saw something a couple of days ago… more skeletons. And Agent al-Faragi sent in a requisition for some specialized machinery and more people. Are you dredging a little creek out there or digging up a city's cemetery?"

"Yes, sir. I wasn't aware of the requisition, but it also doesn't surprise me. This case is starting to look like the lab's annual workload when it comes to skeletons."

"And yet, you haven't kicked your investigation up to major crimes or asked for a recovery team… Why?"

Nash paused and furled her lips as she sorted what she needed to get across. "First, it seems we have more than just a single serial killer conducting their crimes for over ten years. We also have a female who died of strangulation. We have reason to believe it is a member of the local Indigenous tribe who went missing a few years ago. I'll be reaching out to my contact later today."

His eyes narrowed. "So she's an outlier to the primary investigation."

"We're assuming so."

"We?"

She chewed on her lower lip for a moment. "It appears there has been an agent for the DEA in place for a couple of decades. The secondary investigation is where he comes in."

"The girl."

"No, sir. She's in the bones of the investigation, and the bones provide cover for a secondary investigation into criminal polluting we uncovered during the preliminary."

The man drew up his hands and buried his face in them. "Okay. So how bad?"

"Skeleton count is up to nine males and one female so far. Once we have what we need to find the perpetrator and narrow in on the polluter, we can call in a team to dive and drag the entire two miles of the creek. At least about a half mile bracketing where we are now."

He spread his fingers and looked at the screen. "What kind of pollution? Tire dumping, old furniture, restaurant grease, what?"

"Drug manufacturing. Old-fashioned methedrine. Not the recooking of pseudoephedrine, but all the chemistry of cooking speed from the ground up with the residual ethyl ketones, acetone, ether, and you name it. But my source lab also is looking at cross-contamination with some other petrochemical markers. It may be throw-off from a legitimate cover business or another dumper."

He rubbed his face. "I need some coffee. Anything else?"

Nash shook her head. "I'd ask for a different rental car, but I'm afraid of what they would give me. Thanks for assigning Agent al-Faragi and the others. I'll be diving in the creek for the next three days, but I'm not sure we've seen the end of this."

"Any ideas on the killer?"

"The DEA agent and his partner with the ATF are working on the weapon. It doesn't leave a mark we can readily place, and the killer was consistent as to the placement."

The assistant director rolled his eyes as he muttered, "Great. Now we have ATF in the mix as well." He grimaced a smile and signed off.

Nash closed her laptop and looked out through the forest.

The wet nose on her calf reminded her that she only wore panties below the shirt. She dropped her hand to the fur. "Okay, girl. You take the backyard, and I get the bathroom."

SMELLING THE DAMPNESS OF HER BRAID AS SHE TURNED the corner, she stopped. Uncle sat at the dining table.

"Powder came looking for breakfast. I figured you were taking a shower, so I brought you some real coffee. I don't think Daisy has anything but the canned stuff she picked up a few years ago."

Nash stood at the table and lifted the mug to her nose while she watched Uncle. The aroma was pungent and comfortable. She took a small sip. "Where did you get Tanzania Pea berry?"

His one eyebrow rose as his lower lip pushed out. "I'm impressed. You not only knew the flavor but the proper name."

"My wife does a bit of lobbying for fair-traded coffees from several places. But we went to Tanzania to meet with a consortium of women. The landowners, the pickers, the workers, and even the truckers who drive the bags of beans to the docks are all women. The Civil War orphaned or widowed most of them in Rwanda." She decided not to mention the small scarification tattoo she shared with her wife at the base of their spines. The two scars looked like the twin beans of coffee.

She sat as she sipped more of the coffee. "We must dive the pool's north end and work up the stream. But I need to see Tracy this evening. She wouldn't tell me who, but there is someone she said I need to talk to around seven-ish."

He rocked in thought. "Depending on what we find, I would take the RV to San Francisco. Some supplies are waiting at the Presidio. I don't think you should dive alone. So you can either come with or do something else. But whoever you're meeting, I think it's woman stuff, so Powder and I can wait in the RV."

"THAT BRINGS THE TOTAL TO..."

Nash pushed the SCUBA tanks into the compartment. "Seventeen and a half." Her fists were buried in the small of her back as she leaned back. "I stopped raking in all the wheel weights. When we bring in a dive team, I figure they can use metal detectors to find the weights. That will tell them the location of the skeletons."

"Metal detectors don't see lead. Just ferrous metal."

She grabbed a weight out of the small box. Holding it up, she pointed to the steel clip. It holds the weight to the wheel rim. "What is this? Plastic?"

Uncle slid the last plastic tote into the front compartment as he muttered. "Kids. They think they have all the answers."

He straightened and looked around. "Did you swim up to the boulder the sheriff was talking about?"

She grimaced with a nod. "I checked the skull. Whoever it was didn't meet our killer. And he was right about the rib cage getting welded to the boulder. Age and pressure have been crushing the ribs. The spine is only about two inches from also welding to the stone. Another fifty years, it will all be just a strange, shaped boulder. No use disturbing those bones. But the left hand was missing. It may be part of our half in the count."

Uncle stood at the door. "Until we have names to put with all the bones, the harvest is more than overkill."

She paused and looked around before closing the side doors. "Where's Powder?"

Uncle chuckled, pointing into the RV. "Asleep on the engine cover."

Nash latched the doors. "Smart girl."

22

OLD HISTORY

WHEN THE WOMAN walked into the diner, Uncle rose. He knew the woman but had never spoken to her. "I'll take Powder for a walk. Take your time. We can park tonight at the truck stop."

Nash didn't have to turn around. She could feel the change in the air.

The woman and Uncle nodded as they passed. At the booth, she turned to look at Nash.

Nash smiled softly. The woman had been close friends with her mother. The gray hair and long braids hadn't changed her much. "Dorcas." Nash held out her hand at the empty seat.

The woman carefully set her worn purse on the edge of the booth table. Nash noted the fuzzy edges of her jacket's collar and how she moved into the booth. The woman had changed little, and Nash may have remembered the clothes from when she taught her sixth, seventh, and eighth-grade classes on the reservation. Schools never paid a living wage and paid teachers of Indigenous heritage and students even less. Every penny must stretch around a dollar and past the end of the month.

The woman checked herself and looked up. "Well, it's been quite a while."

Nash had a twinge of sitting in a pocketknife graffitied school desk. "I lived in the mountains of Afghanistan when my mother died. We operated under a communication blackout."

The woman's stare turned from stone to hardened steel. "I made no judgment."

Nash only allowed herself to squirm where the woman couldn't see. "I know you two were close."

"I understood this meeting was not about our relationships but missing children."

Nash carefully sucked on her upper inner lip and rubbed it back between her teeth once. "The greater Indigenous tribes community remains painfully aware of the girls who go missing every year."

The woman delicately adjusted her purse to line up with the corner of the table. "They aren't a pair of glasses. They don't get misplaced. They're either runaways or kidnapped."

Nash rocked and nodded her head. "Yes… but…"

The woman's eyes snapped to teacher mode. "We never know what happened to them unless they come home or turn up somewhere else. It is the rest who are of concern. That is the FBI's department."

Nash stiffened as her jaw flexed. She hadn't ground her teeth since high school. "If they aren't reported, we have no way of knowing. There are channels the tribal leaders need to follow. The Bureau of Indian Affairs has long had an open communication policy. They automatically share any reporting with the FBI. Most of the local sheriff's departments also have no way of keeping track of children if people won't talk to them. Just because a young girl stops going to school, she isn't automatically assumed to be a runaway or kidnapped. That is the responsibility of the parents to the tribe or community."

She realized her voice had raised and become strident with her former teacher. She looked down at her hand, nervously rotating her coffee mug back and forth. Looking up, she continued in a calmer voice. "The FBI only gets involved if someone identified the child as kidnapped. We investigate only in cases of or may involve the movement of money across state jurisdictions. We aren't called if it's confined to local. If the girl had a boyfriend down here in Taylor, they would investigate it as a runaway or domestic kidnapping. The sheriff would investigate the boy and anywhere they may live. The FBI would receive notification only if the boy and family check out."

The woman waved her hand across the air in dismissal. "Well, you're here now. And Tracy said they had found a body..."

"Skeleton. There's a difference."

Her one eye narrowed. "Then how do you expect to identify her?"

"Mostly, we would use dental records. But with medical the way they are on reservations, it's more circumstantial. Deposits on the bones indicate three years in the creek. The cheekbone structure rides higher than on a white person. The spread of the pelvic bones suggests active pregnancy. She stood five-foot-nine. Ten in shoes. So it wasn't like she didn't stand out. Two breaks on her right arm were never treated, and the medical examiner said the nodule in the hip joint would cause her to walk with a limp or rocking motion."

The woman's face melted as her shoulders sagged. Her voice was little more than a whisper. "Betsy Singer." She reached for her purse and took out a few sheets of paper.

Pushing the paper across the table, she explained. "These seven girls... missing since I started teaching. The five others we know either came back or are living someplace else now."

As Nash scanned the list, the woman continued. "This is all the general data about them I could gather. School records might also provide you with their yearly class photographs. Few of the families could afford the packages the photographers sold. But the schools kept copies for their records." She squeezed her lips together. "They might also have some kind of dental or medical records. Be that as they may. Usually, the school nurse was the closest the children ever saw for any kind of medical help."

Nash looked up. "This is an enormous help, Mrs. Dunforth."

She blinked softly. "Please. Dorcas. Your mother and I were close friends."

Nash slightly twisted her head. "But not Daisy?"

The woman stiffened. "Different times, different generations."

Nash searched the face for more. Her addition was soft but not accusatory. "Different religion?"

The woman sighed. "She doesn't teach at the same school."

For the first time, Nash realized her sister taught at a public school with mostly white kids. The woman could see the light of recognition go on in her eyes.

"You didn't realize by her teaching down here…"

Nash furled her lips and twitched her head once to the side. "Nope. I did not. I never spoke to Daisy about her teaching." She looked at the woman with new respect. "I never thought about where you teach is a choice."

"She teaches at a private Christian school."

Nash's head rocked lightly as her eyes wandered to one side. "Makes sense."

The older teacher slid to the edge of the booth. "It goes only part way to explain the bible and pistol in her purse." She looked hard at Nash and held for a moment. "I hope this helps you with your investigation."

Nash held up her finger. "Betsy's family…?"

The woman shook her head as she stood. "There was only her father. Her disappearing did him in. He was gone before the end of the year. She was his world after her mother died."

"Thanks."

The woman held out her hand. "Don't get up. I'll see myself out."

Nash nodded.

Powder stood in the doorway of the RV.

Nash laughed. "What? You think you need my permission to go pee?"

The voice grumbled from the dining area. "She wants to know what treats you brought us."

Nash looked at Powder. "None. But you can go pee." She swung her arm and pointed to the grass at the side of the parking lot. Powder hesitated and finally stepped down and walked over to the grass.

"Any other dog would jump out and run. But no. She saunters." Nash climbed into the RV.

Uncle looked up from his book. "The old schoolteacher from the reservation?"

Nash pushed the sheet of paper across the table. "Evidently, she's been keeping track of those who've disappeared."

Uncle gave out a low whistle. "For a small tribe, seven is a large group of girls."

Nash pointed at one. "Holly was in my grade. I think I remember her. Quiet and a loner."

Uncle squinted up at Nash. "I think you would find that description would fit all these girls. It's who disappears. The cheer squad or socially athletic aren't the ones to slip from the attention."

She picked up the dog-eared and scuffed paperback. Weighing the thickness in her hand, she looked at Uncle. "Nominated for a Pulitzer..."

He dodged his head to one side. "It's better than it sounds. You might get something from it."

She looked up from reading the blurb. "Because he's a marine?"

He shrugged his face. "Many people in there, not just the marine. But it rings true about finding where home is."

She reverently laid the book down. "I have a home."

His head bounced up. The face still stoic. "Yes. I see how much you're there."

Her middle finger rubbed along the side of her nose.

"Did you talk to your wife today?"

She leaned out of the door. "Powder. We're leaving."

23

OUT OF THE PAST

UNCLE GLANCED BACK at the four large boxes in the middle of the RV. "Don't you think you bought just a little much?"

Nash glanced over her shoulder. "No."

He stared at the boxes for a minute. "I'm not a lesbian..."

She snorted. "That's for damn sure."

"What I started to say... before you so rudely interrupted me, I'm not a lesbian, nor do I understand the dating rituals. But don't four cases of Jet Fuel Pork Rinds qualify as... um...?"

She glanced over. "Prelude to renting a U-Haul? Boy, you have a screwed-up mind."

"Then do you care to explain?"

She chewed her lip as she made the wide left turn. She noticed the wide eyes on the city bus driver as she prepped to make her own left. Nash brought the RV within a couple of feet of the bus but slid on by.

"The day I came here, I ripped the assignment from under her feet. The deputy director intended to send her to do this job. I'm not saying she can't dive with her hijab, but I don't think her attire or color would get far in Harkin County." She grimaced as she pulled to a stop at the light. "I was less than tactful about the point as I made my exit."

"So the ninety-six family-size bags of pig skin are an apology?"

"Not exactly." She looked over as the RV rolled forward. "I don't apologize." She looked forward. "But I've been known to reward and encourage jobs performed above and beyond expectations on occasions. And more importantly, she must share with Mike."

Uncle rolled his finger in the air. "And the reward for job performance is for...?"

"Thinking to talk the Wizard of Oz into visiting Dorothy in Kansas."

Uncle laughed. "Yeah, and a truckload of skeletons had nothing to do with his decision."

She eyed the GPS and turned right. "I think she might have mentioned something about more sailboats in the bay than all of Delaware and New Jersey combined. Not to mention the better crab and fisheries supplying the fresh fish market daily."

"I take it the guy loves seafood."

She pulled to the curb. "No, I think he's a vegetarian. But his wife came with a fifty-gallon crab pot."

She looked at the GPS and out the window at the large store. "Doctor Ripper's Toy Parlor?"

Uncle smiled and looked out the window. "Yup. It's been a minute."

The interior looked like an over-stuffed pawn shop married to an army-navy surplus store with touches of old police equipment owned and adapted by Marquise de' Sade. Nash eyed the antique-looking torture rack. She lifted the heavy iron chains, only to find them lightweight and plastic.

Uncle leaned over her shoulder. "Looking for a special anniversary gift?"

Nash gave him the glare she usually reserved for unknowing Congressional aids loosely attached to a Congressperson Mina had schmoozed at a party. Uncle backed up a bit.

"Somebody call the morgue; they're missing an uncle."

Uncle chuckled as he walked to the counter. He reached for his back pocket and produced the two castings glued to a popsicle stick. He dropped it on the counter. "I have a problem, Mo." He glanced over at Nash. "Oh, and Nash. Nash, Mo, the oldest San Francisco police officer ever." He turned with a frown. "You're still on the job, right?"

Mo nodded. "Nice to meet you, Nash. I'm assuming you're only attached to this reprobate under duress?"

She rolled her eyes. The wonky smirk said it all.

Mo gathered the cobbled-together weapon representation. "I don't know how many licks you've invested in this, but you'll never get to the center."

Uncle ignored the usual tired humor of the octogenarian. "It's a weapon of some sort. These castings' halves are from the skull bashed in by it. We can't figure out what did the damage."

The man held the weapon out at eye level. Examining, he carefully turned the collage in his hand. Hefting the weight, he knocked it on the counter a few times. "The contraption you've rigged up could never dent a skull. First, you need to get through the skin layers. Skin's about three-eighths of an inch thick and absorbs a lot of energy. Then you must have enough kinetic energy left to crack the circumference and still punch the center. But even if you had a five-pound one of these, you'd never get it done."

Nash stepped in. "Why?"

The old street cop smiled. "I'm going to love this." He fished the air with his hand. "Give me your right hand."

Her eyes slowly narrowed.

Mo snorted. "Come on. Trust me. You're going to love it." He nodded at Uncle. "He won't, but you will. Give me your hand and make a fist."

She did what he asked.

He struggled to move her hand around. "Loosen up. Just let me position it." He moved her fist to one side of his other flat hand resting against Uncle's shoulder. "Now, without pulling back or adjusting, hit his arm as hard as you can."

She pushed out and mushed her fist into the man's arm.

"Not very satisfying, was it?" Mo wiggled his eyebrows. "Before you haul off and wildly swing... adjust your feet, body, and swing."

Uncle sidestepped as Nash laughed. "Chicken."

Mo laughed. "Now, come over here and bring the toy."

He walked to the Formica part of the counter. "Just a minute." He went into the back and returned with a small cutting board. Flipping the board face down on the Formica, he nodded at it. "Go ahead. Hit the board as hard as you can with that thing."

Nash picked up the collage and struck the board. The piece exploded in two ways as the stick broke.

Mo leaned over and looked along the board as he rubbed the area she had struck. "Wow, massive damage, huh?" He peeked up at her with a smile.

He straightened up leisurely. "Now, a kid like you, I can forgive. But Uncle here is old enough to at least know the term from growing up watching old black-and-white talkies on the reservation." He fished something out of his pocket and set it down on the board, concealed by his hand. "Now have a go with this good old-fashioned Beavertail blackjack."

He withdrew his hand. Neither Nash nor Uncle needed to try it out. They both knew they were looking at the weapon.

Nash turned on Uncle with a squinted eye. "Shit. Time for both of us to go back to kindergarten."

Uncle picked it up and weighed the heft. "About a pound?"

"The lead only weighs about fourteen ounces in the Beavertail." He reached into his other pocket and pulled out a larger version. "This is called The Don. Still the same fourteen ounces of lead filings, but there's also another two ounces of spring steel shank running most of the ten-inch length. Judging by how narrow your toy was, I'd say the sap or blackjack used was a Don."

Mo nodded at the board. "Go ahead."

Uncle took a swing. The board jumped, but the dent was shallow.

Nash put her hand out. She hefted the weight and then raised her hand above her head and swung hard at the board.

The dent was barely deeper.

Mo put his hand out to stop her from swinging again. "Excuse my misogyny, but you're swinging like a girl." He picked up the Beavertail. "This is two inches shorter and two ounces lighter." He turned the board around, found the two dents, and snapped a quick hit.

He turned the board back around. His dent was almost as deep as the ones in the skulls.

"The swing is a slight backhand, so you can pull with your body as the arm pulls with the gravity." He held his arm across his face in an exaggerated move of what he had just done.

Nash took the position.

Mo put his hand out to stop her. "Yes, but you don't start there. You're going to gain another twenty percent of energy by starting down here near your hip and then snapping up and then down. All in one movement."

The board jumped. The dent was the deepest.

She closed her eyes and thought about the vision she had seen. As the mists swirled in from where she couldn't see, the arm was wrong. It was high. It was wrong. It replayed again. The arm quickly raised and then snapped down in a side sweep.

Her arm jerked in the mirroring. The board jumped as it split in two. Half of it rattled on the floor, and the other was in Uncle's hand where he had caught it. As Nash opened her eyes, Uncle's shocked look was from looking at half of the dent.

"Yeah. I would say that blow would dent the cranium." Mo stood with wide, appreciative eyes. He wiped his hand over his bald head.

Nash turned and held out the blackjack. "How much?"

The merchant warred with the police officer. The tip of his

tongue slid gently along his lip. "If you put away the killer, you keep it on your trophy wall."

She rocked her head and upper body. "It was an important missing piece to a complicated puzzle. Thanks."

She grabbed at her hip. The phone didn't stop vibrating.

She glanced at the screen as she brought it up. D.C. "Running Bear."

"No, sir."

"No, sir. Not this morning. I didn't expect her to call before noon. But…"

She stood silently listening. Her eyes locked on a US Marshal's badge with a bullet hole through it. The frame was rubbed and dented, but the belled glass was whole.

"Yes, sir. DEA Agent Uncle can do what needs to be done here. There is also an ATF agent or two in the woods. We've made arrangements, and now it's just a waiting game."

"Yes, sir. Thank you, sir. First available flight. I'll work up the reports on the flight. Thank you for calling, sir." She thumbed off the phone—thinking.

She speed-dialed a number and then hung up. She dialed another number and turned to lean back against the counter.

"Muna, we're about thirty minutes away. We have about five cart loads, but I need your magic computer skills. Find me a seat on the first flight to D.C. after, say, two this afternoon. Anything will do, but I need to get some work done."

"Thanks. We'll see you in about a half-hour."

Uncle slowly pushed his chin up to one side as he watched her.

She froze, and then her shoulders slumped slightly. "Mina. They took her in this morning for emergency surgery. He tried, but they wouldn't tell him what. He's not family." Her lip furled tightly as her cheeks reflected the clenched jaw. "I can call, but they operate on the same old shit protocol. I'm her wife—but only if I'm physically there. We have magical phones, but we still live in the Dark Ages."

Uncle nodded. "Let's get you home."

She turned to Mo and pointed at the Marshal's star. "Is there a story to go with the badge?"

Mo blinked leisurely a few times. "I can find out. It was here when I took this over thirty years ago. I have files on most things of importance." He swept his arm around. "Most of all, this used to be collecting dust in evidence lockers. Now, as they move to digitize everything, I get boxes of old stuff. Usually, the old paper records come with the boxes."

"If there's a story to go with it, I'd like to buy it."

She turned to Uncle. "Let's saddle up." She snapped the end of the blackjack into her palm.

24

MINA STOP

NASH PULLED her roll-on out of the overhead bin. The redeye had been almost empty. She had plenty of space for her laptop in the front row and an empty seat next to her for the extra folders. Mina would have scolded her for having airplane coffee, but even if the tanks weren't clean, the coffee hadn't killed her yet.

"Did you get it all done?"

She looked up at the flight attendant and smiled. They weren't friends, but she had recognized the man from a few flights before. "Yes mommy. I got all my homework done."

The man slightly swiveled his hip. "Just making sure us taxpayers get our money's worth, Agent."

She snapped the briefcase to the arms of the extended handle. "When did you move over to domestic, James?"

"After they canceled Brazil runs. I rode it out for a while with London, but eventually, it all got shut down. I'd just forgotten how fun domestic could be."

She stood and moved out of the aisle. The other seven passengers filed past. Bloodshot eyes set in zombie faces. Her one eyebrow raised as she watched James saying goodnight at the door from the galley.

He glanced over and laughed. "Oh, don't give me that eyeball, girl. You know this is the quietest flip on the planet. Now I'm home for three days and get to be the Funcle. At my age, I don't need the hard jams. I've seen the videos and heard the stories. I just want to get my forty-year pin and spoil the kids."

Nash glanced back. The next passenger fought their bags at the twentieth row. "Well, good to see a friendly face. Hopefully, you'll be working when I head back."

James pulled out his work phone and checked something. "I've got plenty of room on the eight-forty heading to SFO on Thursday. I'll slip you in, and you can let me know if you cancel." He pointed at her phone pinging.

She frowned and pulled out her phone. There was an Airdrop available. She allowed, and it lit up the screen. Reservation and an addition to her contacts. She glanced up at the impish smile and the wiggling eyebrows.

"Have a great week, Agent."

She was still chuckling as she approached the only two rental car desks open in the early morning. Her phone vibrated, and she stopped to pull it out.

"Deputy Director, you're up early."

"I'm always up at four-thirty. Old habits die hard. I got your email. When did you land?"

"I just did. The flight attendant gave me access to their net. I compressed and encrypted, so it was a small package."

"How are you getting home?"

"I'm renting a car now. For this brief stay, it will work out best."

"Well, put it on the company, but keep it discreet. I know you're heading to the hospital, but stop by in a couple of days for a debrief."

"Yes, sir. Same car as I've had in California, sir. I should be in to see you on Wednesday morning. There's a lot to cover, and more is needed going forward. This is a very complicated case and more than likely three or four cases."

She could tell by the distracted tone of his voice; he was still going over her report. "Yes, see you Wednesday, Agent."

She knew the man had hung up. She looked at the woman still working on the large coffee on the back counter. Nash laid her credentials on the counter. "I still have a car out in San Francisco. I'd like the same here. I'm kind of getting used to it."

The woman stared at the computer as she typed. She paused and peeked over at the FBI agent. "Um... It says here you have a..."

"Red Hell Cat. Yes."

The woman blinked and snuck another peek at the dark-skinned agent with the long braid of black hair. "I have a black Hell Cat and a white standard Challenger. Or I have a silver-gray Malibu."

"I'll take the Hell Cat. We'll leave the other two for some belters on a budget."

The woman smirked slightly at the disrespect for the usual punching bags in D.C.

NASH PULLED UP TO THE FRONT DOOR OF THEIR apartment. Chester, the doorman, laughed.

"Did they give ya the sack, Ms. Running Bear?"

With a pull on her jacket, she flashed her holster, weapon, and badge. "No, Chester. Still armed and dangerous unless you call me by my proper name."

The gray-haired man smiled. "My granddaughter just turned forty. Until you catch up with her, you'll be Missy or Punkin."

She stood as she pulled the roll-on bag out of her trunk. "Punkin or Nash. You chose. But I can't wait for you to call me Punkin in front of my wife."

The man blushed among his freckles. "The Princess? Never. She'd have me strung up from the floor above you so she could admire me swinging in the morning sunshine while she enjoys her morning tea."

Nash leaned in as she slipped the man a ten. "I'll let you in on a secret. She likes her morning tea the same as she likes her men."

The man winked at the same old joke. "Not at all."

"I need to get down to the hospital, Chester. Can you see to the bag sometime this morning?"

"Done." He pointed at the car. "I like the new car. But, for some reason, I had you pegged for more of a red than black."

She paused at the driver's door and looked back over the top of the car. "My Hell Cat in California is red. Do you really think it's my color?"

He pulled his hat off and ran his hand and hat over his forehead and hair. "Who chose the color for your dining room?"

"You."

"Who told you where to take your wife for your tenth anniversary?"

"And we had a wonderful time."

"Who told you where to order your food?"

She nodded softly. "So red."

His head twitched to one side as he winked. "It's your power color, Punkin."

She pointed her finger gun at him and snapped the thumb.

She nosed the powerful car out of the driveway and roared up the street.

Chester chuckled as he lifted the bag and carried it inside.

Nash snapped her fingers as she sat at the light. "Dang. I forgot to ask him about the dog policy."

She poked the green icon.

"You miss me already?"

She laughed. "We're good on red. But what's the building's dog policy? I've only seen little fluff dogs and the tan one on the ninth floor."

"Forty-five pounds unless it's a service dog. What are you thinking about? You two travel a lot, and I'm not getting any younger."

"I think she's called a blue heeler or cattle dog."

"She better be a service dog."

"I've been working with her for the last few weeks. She's great at sniffing out skeletons."

He laughed. "Sounds like something your wife could put to good use."

Nash chuckled. "I'll investigate her getting a badge. But I don't think she'd look good in one of those vests. She's kind of a country girl."

NASH HAD BEEN IN TOO MANY HOSPITALS TO FEEL comfortable visiting. There always seemed to be a bed with her name on it.

She stopped at the front desk. "Excuse me. Can you direct me to the room Mina Walsh is in?"

The woman frowned at her computer as she typed. "There's no Myna Walsh." She shook her head and peered over at Nash.

"Try spelling it M-i-n-a. Like the city."

Slow shake. "Nope. I have a Mina first name. But not a Walsh."

"Last name Lee?"

The woman glanced up. "And you are…?"

"Wife." To drive the point home, she slipped the clip on her badge and held it up.

"Five twenty-nine. Take the elevators down this hall, and then turn left when you come out on five."

Nash's eyes slid to one side as she turned, slipping her badge back on her belt.

NASH STOOD IN THE DOORWAY OF THE PRIVATE ROOM. She didn't know what she had expected, but the Asian woman with a pen in her mouth, legal pads stacked to one side as she furiously typed on her laptop, was not one of them.

Nash leaned against the doorjamb. Her wife's focus had always amazed her. Even on a rough road while Nash drove, Mina's eyes were glued to her laptop while she worked up a last email before they started their vacation in Belize. Even though it was their third day in the country. The large pothole had only elicited a pleading glance for a smoother ride. When the battery ran out, they had four glorious days with no power and no phone service.

"I heard there was a dead body up here..."

The woman looked up, squinting in irritation. Her face flared with recognition. "What are you doing here?"

Nash stepped in. "The deputy director called me last night saying they had rushed you to the hospital. I didn't hear from you, so I wandered over."

She sat on the edge of the bed and leaned over. The kiss was distracted, but she also registered the wince as Mina leaned over. "What's going on?"

Mina bristled and then leaned back into the raised bed. "A tedious Blue Duck dinner, but we were sealing the deal on the new water quality regulations."

"Bad food?"

She shrugged her eyes and one shoulder. "It's what I thought. So I kept pushing to get it done. I can be sick after, is what I kept telling myself. Right up until I passed out."

"What was it?"

"My appendix ruptured. Next thing I know, they are loading me on a gurney. I grabbed Paul Jenkin's jacket and hauled him down to me. I was so mad. So close. I told him if I died, he would be off the hook. But if I lived, I owned his soul, and he better make it right."

"Senator Jenkin?"

She nodded and pointed at the laptop. "I have him by the short-hairs, and it's time for him to make his donors clean up their acts in the gulf."

Nash snorted softly. "Good. We'll need the trade-off."

Mina narrowed her eyes. "How bad?"

"I'm thinking about a new car." She watched the one eyebrow twitch. "It's not exactly eco-friendly." The one eye rolled to look at the ceiling.

"As long as it's not a Hummer. We aren't driving any GM iron this year."

"Dodge."

The eyes turned into her mother's pencil lines. Nash knew she could still see.

"Probably red." One eye shut as the other opened. Nash was comfortable with this path. "Even Chester suggested red."

The other eye opened into the resolved head tilt. "He's never wrong."

"He's also finding out about our new dog."

Mina's eyes returned to the computer screen. But the tip of her tongue was showing a tiny pink dot between her lips.

Nash sat watching her wife, trying to ignore the subject. "And so the appendix exploded, spewing names, dates, and other information about the restaurant."

Mina sighed and closed the laptop as she laid back. "Surgery went three hours. The ultrasound showed the gall about to go as well." Her head rolled to look at her wife. "I hate being sick."

Nash nodded. "But when you need help, you need to let them help you. You're not superwoman, except to me."

Nash rolled over onto the bed. Mina snuggled into her arm and chest. Nash smoothed the new soft fuzzy hair.

The voice was more of a child. "How long are you here for?"

Nash thought about everything up in the air. "As long as you want me here." She lied.

Mina's head rubbed with a nod. Their relationship was two liars with professional complications. "What time is your flight?"

"Thursday. But it can get pushed. I have nine weeks of personal and sick time."

"Are you staying here tonight?"

"My folding toothbrush is in my pocket."

"I'd like that."

"Me too."

25

THE MADNESS IS IN THE DETAILS

"WHICH PAGE?"

Nash reflexively looked for a page number. "Um, the one with the spectrograph chart at the top."

The deputy director peeked over his glasses. "You have those kinds of charts throughout all of these files."

The junior agent with his tie pulled askew leaned over. He spread the small pile out and pulled a stapled file. "This one. The chart is the gross or mass analysis and only covers the top half of a page." He glanced at Nash.

Nash nodded. She hadn't thought of it in those terms.

The deputy director scanned down the chart and then found the conclusion near the bottom of the page. "And... this leads us where?"

Nash gently placed her papers on the table. "I need to loop in the EPA, but we think what we have is an old-style drug lab making meth. Unlike the new cooks who set up in a bathroom or kitchen and cook down pseudoephedrine, these guys start with the raw chemicals and cook it up in staged builds. But it produces toxic waste. And that is what we're looking at in the water." She pushed the files apart and found the one she had tick-marked in red in the upper left corner. She showed the deputy director the mark. Turning it back around. "Not only are they killing fish, but combined with the petrochemicals, the combined chemistry has created a toxic herbicide for aquatic plants." She looked up. "Think of it as Agent Orange cruising down the creek."

She laid the report down and folded her fingers over the paper. "Three-quarters of a mile downstream, it stops being Harkin County's problem. The entire creek disappears down into the ground, but we don't know where it goes. For all we know, this could pop up as far away as the Las Vegas's aquifer. Which services only two and a half million population, but that's before you add the forty million tourists. Most drink bottled water, which, because of economic pressures, is bottled locally from the same aquifer. But everyone bathes and cooks from the same aquifer. So every year, a sixth of the nation's population is exposed to the water."

The deputy director raised his head from the second paper. "Are we talking about a super fund site...?"

"No. But we need every tooth biting into this to first stop the pollution and then get it cleaned up. The problem with this is the stopping will also kill the legitimate business, and unless they carry a large enough umbrella policy, it won't cover the cleanup. So the EPA will have to tap some general funds to get it done."

"They've done it before..."

"Yes. Yes, they have. But places like Los Angeles, Denver, the riverfront of St. Louis, or the East River are sexy places. Millions of people enjoy those locations monthly or each year. But Harkin County has a population of fewer than twenty thousand, with no real recreation to attract tourists. So we're talking about a sinkhole on Main Street Disney versus a hole in the ground in the middle of the Nevada desert. The latter would barely get a yawn, much less the needed funds."

He removed his glasses and leaned back in his chair. "Unless it's affecting Las Vegas."

She gently nodded. "I would so advise."

The slight smile tugged at his left cheek. "Is this something your wife might be able to help us with?"

The last thing Nash had ever wanted was for her wife mixed in with her work. It was worse than bringing work home to do on the weekends—something they were both guilty of. "Her plate is kind of full at the moment, but I'll give her a heads-up. It's probably coming."

He nodded. "But first, we have…" He looked for the report. "How many bodies?"

Nash didn't need to look. "Right now. We have seventeen. But one skeleton seems unconnected." She pointed at the thin file in its own folder. "It comes under missing persons, but of a tribal nature. It's one we will need to handle delicately."

He turned his head slightly, but still watched her. "Which tribe?"

"Mine. Paiute. Dental records would be conclusive if there were any. But I think we have as close to an identification through healed, broken bones."

"So you've identified the remains. Have you notified the family?"

"There is no more family. But when the time is right, I'll go over it with the tribal leaders." She grimaced. "It's complicated."

He rocked slightly as he thought about the unique position the agent was in to handle it. He glanced at his aid and down at the large spread of files. "Is that it?"

"One more…" She passed the single sheet form over.

He glanced at the form. "A request for a service dog?" He looked up. "What kind?"

"Her name is Powder, and she has proved in the field to be a multipurpose dog."

"Powder?"

She nodded. "Yes. As in explosives or black powder. As in sniffing bombs and weapons, she also proved herself finding the skeletons."

"A cadaver dog..." He screwed up his face around one closed eye. "I thought these skeletons were underwater."

She smiled. "Yes, sir. As I said, she exhibited some extraordinary skill sets."

"And you want to recruit her?"

Nash furled her lips for a second. "It's more like the other way around. She recruited me... So to speak."

The man stared back at the form. "And you want clearance for her to travel with you." He looked up.

"I believe she will prove to be an asset. Yes."

He peeked at his assistant and shrugged. His pen clicked, and he signed the form. Passing the form to his assistant, he smiled. "Has your wife signed off?"

Nash nodded. "Last night. Right after the building called with the green light if she has the needed credentials and badge." They both knew where the power was, and authority rested.

The deputy director rubbed his palms together as he looked at the pile of paperwork. "Looks good. We'll rush the credentials and get everything sent out to you in California."

Nash stood. "Probably the best place to send them is the lab in San Francisco. Special Agent al-Faragi can receive it all and hold it for us to come down."

"How is she working out?"

Nash twitched her head with a smile. "I think she found her niche. She likes the lab work, and is used to the long hours. I think San Francisco is also a good fit for her."

"And the lab...?"

She let all her teeth show as she nodded. "Mike is extremely happy with her. They have a special bond, so to speak, and her having robbed the body farm of their wizard has secured her place walking on water."

He smiled. "You were the lead on this. Can you knock out a review before...?" He frowned. "When do you leave?"

"Eight forty tomorrow night."

"I didn't see any paperwork."

She smiled. "There wasn't any. I think the term is called non-revenue. It's usually for a family member. The flight crew booked my flight. I'm their guest on this flight."

He laughed. "It must be nice to have friends in high places."

She smiled. "At least thirty-seven thousand feet. As long as I keep bringing the premium chocolates."

His eyebrow rose. "So that's the secret?"

Nash leaned in. "The way to a man's heart is usually between the third and fourth rib. But the way to enroll friends' hearts and minds is through their stomachs. Find what stimulates their happy place, and feed it."

"And yours?"

She stood. "Is my wife. Try not to piss her off next week at lunch."

He frowned at his aide. "I have a lunch appointment next week?"

"Yes, sir. It's part of the Ways and Means council. I'll remind you to take chocolates next week, sir."

Nash laughed as she turned. "It's not so easy. And she despises chocolate." She turned at the door. "I'll call you next week from California. Loop me in with someone in the field with the EPA; someone I can actually work with. Preferably someone who can say horse shit without it sounding like their mouth is full of it."

The deputy director leaned back in his chair with a smile. He gave her the two-finger cub scout salute from the side of his head. "Happy hunting."

***

"You told him I despise chocolate? Did he believe you?"

Nash stared out the window at the ramp rats working the jetway. There was always a last-minute rush in the stowing of oversized luggage, baby strollers, and a wheelchair. "It didn't matter. I'll never tell him how to get on your good side."

"He's not always the enemy."

Nash sipped the scotch. "He played for Notre Dame."

"Well, it's not like I went to Michigan. And I seriously doubt if he has ever heard of Deep Springs."

Nash hummed in agreement. "How's your gut doing?"

"Tender, but they'll probably let me stay in the cloister as long as I want."

"And the luncheon...?"

"It's a week away."

Nash could hear a nurse, or somebody, enter and talk. "Is the warden telling you your day is done?"

"Yeah, she's here to give me a sponge bath, a rubdown, and a shot of sleepy juice. I better comply, or I might not get the rubdown."

Nash watched James do the last count and gave her the nod. "Yeah, I'm getting the same directive here, too. They are ready to push back. I love you, and I'll call tomorrow."

"Same." The phone clicked.

Nash put her phone away.

James stopped next to her seat. "I wasn't going to make you hang up yet." His hands went through the safety demonstration for the man already asleep in the fifth row.

"It's okay. My wife was getting called to her spa date."

He frowned down at her. "I thought she was in the hospital."

Nash shrugged. "Sponge bath, rub down. It's all the same as a spa, isn't it?"

His eyes grew wild behind his Clark Kent glasses. "Oh gawd, I wish. When they did my knee, the best I got was the PT tech didn't beat me with a stick." He took the life vest off. "How's the scotch doing?"

She held up the last sip.

"I'll be all over it." He rolled up the bag of demonstration items. "Dinner is in an hour."

Her phone pinged. She pulled it out.

The text was from Muna. "I'll be your chauffeur tonight. See you when you land."

James stood with a fresh glass and two small bottles of scotch. "Are you driving when we land?"

She laughed and showed him the text.

"As long as you have a babysitter."

It's beginning to feel that way.

26

SORTING

AS THEY SETTLED into the third lane of the freeway, Muna pointed at the glove box. "The boys sent you a gift."

Nash opened the hatch. Her forehead creased at the blister package. "What's a trail cam?"

The junior agent scoffed softly. "I know you have a laptop. Do you ever open it just for fun?"

"Like games? No."

Muna peeked over. "Games aren't the full definition of fun. I like Mega Crossword, but I'd hardly call it fun. But it does make me exercise the gray matter. No, I'm talking about watching mindless videos just for the relaxing fun of it."

Nash growled. "Cutesy kitten videos?"

Muna stuck her finger in her gagging mouth. "More like cooking shows, how to do something videos, or..."—she pointed at the package—"photos and videos in the forest where animals trigger an infrared light and camera. This is an extra one Mike had lying around. He has a couple up and transmitting down in the breakwater to catch seals and otters. And the occasional poacher. Apparently, the ocean is brutal, and they don't last long when the high surf runs a log into the plastic body."

Nash turned it over to read the back as she looked for a reading light. "And I need this... why?"

Muna triggered the blinkers as she changed lanes. "You don't. And there are no working reading lights while the car is moving."

Nash slumped back in the seat as she realized they were getting off the freeway. "Where are we going?"

"Casablanca. It serves dinner until three in the morning." Muna glanced over. "Sorry, but you missed the belly dancing. They only dance until eight on Thursdays. The dancers all have school in the morning."

Nash frowned as Muna looked over with a smile.

"Thursdays are family night. The families come to watch their children, the student dancers, dance for the patrons. I guess it's a lot of fun when the kids are six to ten years old."

Nash held up the camera.

"Uncle is up in Harkin playing with the better ones. I guess they're hoping to capture faces, license plate numbers, and anything else, but in high definition." She waved her hand at the camera in Nash's hand. "That's just a cheap one. About a hundred bucks or so. The boys are playing with a few up in the few thousand-dollar range. So don't break them, or if you do, make sure they charge them to the DEA or ATF. They seem to have a bigger budget for this than we do."

Nash looked out as the city moved by. She did not know where she was. "If Uncle already went back, how do I get up there? The bus?"

Muna turned left and nosed the car to the curb. "The consensus thinking is you don't for a while. Evidently, they hid your red car, so the general population thinks you have flown the coop, so to speak. So stay gone long enough, and the people of interest return to their old ways."

"I'd rather the killer not return to their old ways."

Muna cracked her door as she looked in the mirror. "Not the person we are setting the traps for."

They walked to the middle of the block. Nash waved her hand at the neon sign with an old tri-engine airplane on top. "Rick's Café American? What happened to Casablanca?"

Muna turned a single fluttering eye on her. "Please do not tell me you never watched the movie..."

"What movie?"

The younger Black woman rolled her eyes and jerked the door open. Jamming her finger through the doorway, she growled. "In."

Nash lowered her menu. "This isn't Moroccan food. This is like what a suburban housewife thinks they would have served in Morocco."

The other menu lowered until only two black pupils showed. "Did you notice the part after it says Rick's café?"

The waiter slid quietly up to the table. "Do we know what we want?"

Nash looked at the young man as her eyes narrowed. "Are your grandmothers still alive?"

The man gawped like a guppy.

Muna dropped her menu. "What kind of question is that?"

Nash held out her hand as in a stop. "Well, are they?"

"My nana is..."

Nash turned her hard eyes toward her partner. "Would she eat here?"

"She has..."

Nash looked back at the still-flustered young man. "More than once? So she came back?"

His mouth pursed. "Yes."

She handed him her menu. "Whatever she would have."

"I don't know what she would have."

Nash looked up with one eye. "Then call her." She pointed at Muna. "Her too."

The junior agent objected. "I know what I want."

Nash gave her a stern look.

Muna looked up and handed over the menu. "I'll have the second dish your nana would have."

The waiter adjusted the two menus as he looked at the hijab. "Anything to drink?"

The women chorused. "Water."

The man spun and was gone.

Muna paused as she readjusted to the senior agent's attitude. "What if Nana is a picky eater?"

Nash leaned forward and searched the towel in the basket for flatbread. Tearing off half of the warm bread, she offered the other half to the younger woman. "As you spend more and more time in the field, you will come to understand human nature. Grandmothers are picky eaters. Spinster Aunt Evelyn runs to fussy eaters, but Nana not only cooks like a maniac but eats anything on a plate. She doesn't suffer dreadful cooking. In a short life, you don't eat terrible food. Trust me. He might have to call her, but dinner will be worth it."

"What if I don't like it?"

Nash scoffed softly. "And this just fell out of the mouth that was snacking on Napalm-drenched pig belly this afternoon?"

Muna bit into the bread, and her eyes opened wide.

Nash nodded. "It's good, but the nan in the Medina of Marrakesh is better. It's not about the bread, but the spices they throw against the red-hot walls of the oil barrel they are cooking in."

"Why not put the spices in the dough?"

"Because it will stay there. You only want the ash of seared spices to provide the scent and taste, but it also makes the bread peel off when it's done."

"And you've seen this...?"

Nash nodded. "A SEAL team dragged me along with them. They figured I looked dark enough to get us past the tourist traps. What we never figured was, in the Medina, the tourists never go to the scary old section of the city, anyway. Once one guy started talking

Hebrew to a merchant, we were golden. The man's son took us to a local café. Think more like standing around a street vendor, but then we were all invited to sit on their private garden veranda."

"Hebrew?"

Nash pushed out her lower lip as she nodded. "Turns out the medinas of all the great cities in the Muslim world were the Jewish ghettos or enclaves, dating back to the Dark Ages." She tore off a small bite of the bread and chewed. "When the king started Marrakesh, he invited many Jewish merchants and bankers to come and help him establish his city. It's still there today. If you get a chance, go. You can stay at the Club Med right off their Grand Bazaar."

"Club Med? Like the swinging singles, Club Med?"

"The very same. We saw many young girl tourists wearing crop tops or bikini tops. No mullahs were coming around to beat them. It's a very progressive country, and English is a common language."

The young man returned with a large tray filled with many dishes. As he laid out the table, he explained. "Nana said we were to serve you this. All communal, so you share." He looked sternly at Nash. "And don't hog all the nan. We make plenty more if you run low. Enjoy."

Nash smiled at the varied dishes. "Thank Nana for us. Now, which are not halal?"

The man blushed but smiled. "My sister says I'm a pig sometimes. So I'm the only thing not halal. Nana keeps kosher. We don't know why, but she does, and these are her choices."

THE YOUNG MAN, STEPHAN, STOOD AT THE DOOR AND waved good night as they got in the car.

Nash laughed as Muna hauled the car around in a U-turn, and they drove away. "Well, there you go. Now you know he's available and as halal as your pig bellies."

Muna fished in her jacket pocket and handed the check to Nash. The phone number, email address, as well as his nana's phone number and address, were carefully printed in perfect form. "I think he's studying engineering. My brother prints in the same font."

Nash leaned the seat back and popped the button on her jeans. "A great meal. And now we can talk. What do I do while I'm not in Harkin County?"

Muna glanced at the top button and back up at the relieved face. "You mean besides sorting through seventeen skeletons in forty-eight tubs and working up the gravimetric analysis of the lime deposits for each so that we have a timeline?"

Nash snickered. "You thought you could slip gravimetric analysis in there and hope I didn't know what it was? You should have your mass spectrometer license revoked."

The woman snickered and hit the turn signal before turning left.

"Not the most fun crayon in the box, but it will keep you busy. Even I'm camping out in the dorm upstairs. Talk about mind numbing. But the wizard is in heaven and working up some new algorithm logs to run once we have the data."

"What sort of algorithms?"

Muna pulled into the compound and waved at the guard, waving them through the gate. "Once we have the timeline, we can run it against all the male missing person reports in the region. The FBI may have done nothing with the reports when they occurred, but they kept them filed, and eventually, the records became digitized. So we can access them for cross-referencing."

Nash pulled her bags out of the trunk. "These algorithms could give new life to a lot of cold cases. Not just here. Thanks again for talking the wizard out of his hole in the woods."

"Are you kidding? Without him to certify all this, I'd be working on those bones from now to retirement. Besides, he's looking at sailboats for sale."

Nash thought about the last time she was out on open water

that got rough. "You can have my share. I'll take planes, fast cars, and submarines."

"But you SCUBA dive."

Nash turned at the large door. "Yes, but it's just as easy to dive from a sub. Trust me. It's also more fun getting to the dive site. Ask Mike."

27

BAD TO THE BONE

THE WARM GLOW of the late afternoon through the windows had long passed to a glittering of city lights below a field of a cloudy night. The printer spat out the labels as Nash stared at the dark windows. She felt alone. Mina was a phone call away, but not in the bed she would be in tonight.

Nash plucked the label out of the printer and turned to what was once a large office stuffed with secretaries hunched over typewriters. Clickety-clacking away in the process of copying forms or letters or reports in triplicate or worse. She peeled the carrier sheet from the adhesive and smoothed the legibly printed label. She had seen too many evidence boxes with crab scratching or faded ink. Even when opened, the folder on top took time to decipher, as too many agents or law enforcement officials didn't take the time to use a typewriter. Or use proper spelling and grammar.

She stared at the spaces left blank. Hopefully, the Wizard of Oz's algorithm would at least fill in the blanks.

The appointment she would need to make when the cases closed weighed heavily on her. But she knew, as a woman of First Nation, she was responsible for not only her own tribe but eventually many others.

She peeled the second label and attached it to the adjunct tub. The cross-referenced tub was smaller but was to be stored with other non-organic evidence, such as tools, pipes, or stakes used in crimes. Guns, swords, knives, or cannons were held in the weapons lockers until they melted them down.

She stacked the tubs on their respective carts. *Another one bites the dust.*

She turned to the next tub on the stack. As she sat with weight on the stool, her phone pinged and then vibrated.

Uncle.

She thumbed the green icon. "Please tell me Powder misses me, and she wants to show mommy something exciting."

"I just sent you a video."

She checked her phone. There was no text message. "Nope. Nada."

"Check the interlink on your computer."

She crab-walked the rolling stool over to the computer. Shaking the mouse, the screen lit up. She typed in her password.

The screen cleared the FBI logo graphic and replaced it with the standard communications screen with a pulsing icon in the upper right corner. She clicked on it and chose the link marked *Urgent*.

The screen was mostly dark. Leaning in and squinting, she could make out the creek. It was darker than the dirt beyond. She knew now from watching dozens of trail cam videos of deer, bears, and cougars that patience had its rewards. But a deer on this camera wasn't why Uncle would flag it as urgent.

She noted the timestamps on the bottom. "What am I watching?"

"The flat pool."

As the truck entered the view and backed up, she realized how much better the quality of this camera was than what she had been watching on the internet. The license plate was crisp and clear. Even blown up on a large screen in a court of law, even a half-blind jurist could read it.

"Fine quality picture." As the brake lights flared, she realized she was watching it in color.

Uncle's comment sounded distracted and distant. "For five grand, it better be. But in this case, there are no do-overs."

She sniffed. "Buck's truck is kind of distinctive, anyway."

The man's voice was soft. Nash could almost sense they were in a deer blind or stalking. "Wrong Crawford."

The driver's door opened. And true to Uncle's word, the driver stepping out wasn't Buck. They walked to the back of the truck full of barrels. Nash recognized the paint on the barrels from her time in Oklahoma.

"Holy crap."

As the passenger door opened. Uncle's voice was more of a whisper. "Wait for it."

The shadow moved to the end of the truck as the driver dropped the tailgate. The passenger pulled on gloves and looked out across the pool. Nash watched the face. She knew the face intimately.

"Oh, jeez."

She froze the screen. Leaning back on the stool, she flexed her back and thought.

As she drew a deep breath through her nose, Uncle sensed she had stopped the video. "There's more here than we thought."

Nash jacked her eyes further open. "Ya think?"

He cleared his throat. "How deep are you and junior still buried?"

She turned on the stool to the stack of tubs. "We're down to the last three on the grunt work. What are you thinking about?"

"I think we looked at the wrong financials."

Her furled lips hardened as she looked at the frozen video. It was explicit as a bloody bunny hanging limp from the jaws of a wolf. "I'll show this to Muna, and we'll get back to you in the morning."

"Morning is the weekend."

Shit. She thought about the sailboat that they'd be on. "You guys get a weekend?"

He snorted. "Powder and I are going up the mountain to look at deer."

She thought about deer hunting. "When does the season start?"

The chuckle was soft. "Ask Powder."

Her snort was short, knowing the laws vs. rules of life on the reservation. "Monday."

"Monday."

NASH STUDIED THE MUTED IRIDESCENT BLUES, REDS, and purples of the hijab. The woman hardly wore the subdued dark gray anymore. It was as if the new city and cultures were drawing her out of her shell. What few meals they had eaten out were usually after an online search for someplace new or had come recommended by one of the other local staff. Most were sensitive to halal or kosher, but only a few had them settling for a salad.

Nash leaned forward and stopped the video. Only once had she played the video in its entirety. The last of the video did not weigh on the identification of the criminals or the crime.

Muna turned around. "Wow. I would say that is pretty damning."

Nash twitched her head. "But success in court doesn't rely on just eleven minutes of video. They could have been dumping rainwater for all we know."

"I think those gas masks convincingly prove it wasn't rainwater. Are they gathering samples?"

"Already done. They're coming down by Felix's express."

"You mean FedEx?"

"Nope. When it has to be there as fast as possible, you send it with Felix. He'll be here by the morning."

"But we'll be..."

Nash snorted. "Relaxed, fed, and rested when we return to them on Monday. Yes, the other guys could have done the job, but it would have busted the chain of possession. Even if the chain transfers from DEA to ATF to Homeland to us, it's still solid."

Muna's hand and finger drifted back toward the frozen video on the monitor. "And the deep dive on..."

"Yes. Both and any connections it leads to. That will be you're your lighthouse."

The small face scrunched in pain. "Wheelhouse."

Nash growled. "Nope. Lighthouse. I want you to turn the brightest light on those two." She reached forward and moved the arrow to the slider on the video. She moved the slider to the spot she wanted but didn't click on play. The frozen image was enough.

Muna sat looking at the image and all the implications it meant.

28
WHAT NOW?

JAMES STOOD with his hands clasped behind his back. He bounced lightly on the balls of his feet. It was a rare flight when he knew exactly how to prepare a seat, the overhead, and greeting.

He smiled as the legs, boots, and the dragged bag came into view down the jetway. Outbound from D.C., people are somewhat predictable. Suits, nice shoes, sometimes a dress, more often slacks, and always the ubiquitous computer bag. Outbound from San Francisco, the epitome of the central west coast, it could range from the overtly casual of Southern California to the cargo shorts and any kind of footwear of the grunge capitals of Seattle and now Portland. But his favorite passenger was, if anything, predictable.

"I have your office all set up, Agent."

Nash looked up as she stepped over the threshold. "I didn't have time to find your usual, so I'm hoping some skanky airport junk will do."

James feigned an offended face. "Oh gawd. Don't even pull it out of the bag. Oh wait, we have some new girls in the back. I can hide it back there."

Nash laughed as she followed his hand to the first row on the aisle. The scotch stood, poured, and waited on the window seat tray. She pushed her bags up into the overhead. "Don't tell my wife we're seeing each other so much. She gets jealous easily."

James stood watching the jetway. "Something tells me she trusts you more than most. After all, she's been letting you roam around in the wild country all this summer."

Nash glanced over with a smirk. "Why, James, is that an Indian territory joke?"

He ducked his head to look at something farther up the jetway. "If the war bonnet fits, honey."

He turned and started arranging the seats across from her. "We have a dog coming." He looked back at her. "I hope you're okay with dogs."

She sat as she raised her one eyebrow. "So does my dog, Powder."

He stood and stepped back to the door. "What kind of dog?"

"Bombs, bodies, criminals, errant little boys, and anything else I want her to do."

"Service dog?"

"She's getting used to the harness. Until now, she hasn't even worn a collar."

James did his slight bounce. "Good evening. How is Apollo tonight?"

Nash heard a low female's voice.

"Well, you're right here in row one, D and F, on the left."

Nash watched as the woman walked haltingly into the airplane. The large black dog seemed attached to her prosthetic leg. At the sight of the uniform, Nash popped her seatbelt and stood. "Let me help with your bags, Captain."

The woman studied Nash, and the smile was slow. "Which service?"

"Marines, sir. Lieutenant retired. FBI now, sir." She put her hand out. "Agent Running Bear, Nash, sir."

The officer took her hand. "Thank you for your continuing service, Nash." She turned and sat as the dog found his floor space by the window. "I'm assuming you were Jag?"

Nash took the bags from James. "Enforcement." She glanced down and smiled. "And a little extra. Good practice for this job." She closed the hatch covers and sat. "I'm unattached to any specific division. So I pick up the unusual investigations."

The captain struggled to crouch the question correctly. "Delicate...?"

Nash shook her head. "Not usually. Just the odd collection of bones. Cases that need to be investigated but don't easily slip into a pigeonhole."

James stepped back into his galley as the crowds crushed through the door.

Nash leaned away from the stray bag, arm, or hip and sipped on her scotch as she flipped through the copy of Travel Today laying on the tray table. She flipped back to the cover to read the mailing label. She smiled—James' personal copy. She wondered if he had ever taken any of the cruises. A cruise out to sea sounded relaxing if the water was calm.

MINA WAS STILL ASLEEP, SO NASH SLIPPED DOWN around the block. A coffee shop. Her rare indulgence. She hoped the extra calories and solid load of pancakes would settle her stomach and calm the feeling she wasn't going to like the emergency meeting they had pulled her back to Washington for. She couldn't shake the old sensation of being called to the principal's office.

D.C. started work after the third cup of office coffee or lunch. A nine o'clock meeting with the deputy director was on the marginal cusp of useless to what now. Her hard-soled boot strikes ricocheted off the granite floors and marble walls. The three security guards peeked and became busy with something on their desk. At eight-thirty, nobody wanted to become involved.

Nash stood at parade rest six inches from the polished stainless steel of the elevator doors. The sudden slowing and then the pause never settled her stomach. The opening doors revealed nothing but an empty hallway.

Nash pushed open the door and stuck her head in.

The junior agent at the desk shook his head. "Still in a meeting."

She nodded. "I'll go get some coffee. Want anything?"

The young man lifted a clear tumbler half filled with green slime. She never understood the appeal. She furled her lips and withdrew.

Coffee at hand, she sat at her assigned but rarely used desk. She pulled up her emails.

Delete, delete, delete, archive, delete... *Where the heck is the SPAM filter on the government server?* Delete. She leaned in and read the report from Muna.

The passenger's shallow dive read as to be expected. The driver showed similar for the last eleven years and then turned to blanks. When she ran CODIS, it also came up with a blank trimmed in red. Someone had flagged her search.

Nash went back and pulled up the shared file. Harkin County National Credit Union showed money in and out. Nothing stood out. Even the house value and payments were what Nash expected. The average home value in Harkin was less than a decent purchase payment on a similar home in a poorer neighborhood of D.C. You couldn't even get a one-bedroom Alexandria condo for the cost of a home and five acres around Harkin. Even the truck still had three more years on a seven-year loan. She leaned back in her chair and sipped on the coffee. *I should have stopped for a Vente.*

She glanced at her watch and dashed off a quick note, directing

Muna to keep digging on the driver. Nash hated enigmas. She got up and started for the hall. Pausing, she set the office coffee on an unused desk. She knew the janitors would clear it, or it would turn into a deep carpet of green mold.

The deputy didn't bother to stand as Nash entered his office. He nodded at the couch behind her.

"Agent Running Bear, this is United States Marshal Smith."

She turned and nodded at the man, who also didn't stand.

Turning back to the deputy, she took the stance of parade rest. "What's this about, sir?"

He leaned back in his chair. "Evidently, you are digging where you shouldn't be."

She could feel the eyes behind her burning between her shoulders. "The seventeen murdered skeletons, or the four hundred gallons of deadly toxic waste dumping, sir? Because I know you wouldn't give a rat's ass about a murdered pregnant First Nation girl of sixteen, sir. Much less pull me from a critical time in the investigation to fly across the country for an early morning meeting."

The deputy carefully rolled forward and tented his elbows on his desk. "Stand down, Agent. Before you step to thinner ice than you're on."

"I just want to be clear about why I've been called to the principal's office, sir."

"Where are you on the skeletons?"

"We're a few days away from having all the timeline parameters, so we can feed it into the new algorithm matching missing persons in a three-hundred-mile range. The algorithm will sort by height and approximate weight and weigh the analysis for broken bones. It's very exciting, and if it works even marginally, we could put it to use nationwide."

"So a week or so?"

"For the identifications? More than less, but yes, sir."

"Any luck on the murderer?"

"We think we have identified the weapon."

"I thought they had drowned?"

"Yes, sir. But they were first knocked out, weighted down, and placed in the creek."

"And the weapon...?"

She glanced back at the still-silent other man. "An ongoing investigation, sir."

"And the toxic dumping?"

She glanced back at the man on the couch, now leaning forward.

"The list of the chemicals covers about two hundred pages of the MSDS reports. But the top five toxins are as we expected and are showing up in the aquifer of Inyo County and as far away as Las Vegas. I would look at Phoenix but doing so would mean it somehow has gone under lake Powell and would be a wild stretch. So we'll just stick with the thirty-six-million population using the water in Las Vegas, sir."

"Which brings us to the good Marshal, here." He opened a thin folder. The protective seal on the front of the file didn't escape Nash. He turned the file around. The photo was a more flattering picture of the driver than the high-end trail cam had taken.

Nash looked at the deputy. "They were the driver of the truck and instrumental in dumping the toxic waste, sir."

He flipped the file closed. "They're off limits. The EPA can figure out something else, but they are a ghost. They never existed. If they show up on Main Street, you change course and use another street. Do I make myself clear?"

She glared down at him. "Besides the charges of manufacturing a class one drug with the intent to sell, we have them on no less than seven controlled substances being dumped in a toxic stew. It's not like they didn't mean to hit the cow, and we'll let it slide this time. Kids being kids and all. These carry fifteen to twenty sentences for each offense. And that's before we look at collusion and conspiracy to commit federal crimes."

"Are you done?"

She opened her mouth and let it shut.

He peered over the white knuckles of his interwoven fingers. "What did I say?"

"Stand down, sir."

He nodded. "We're done here. Have a nice flight back."

She raised her right boot, toed into the left heel, and snapped an about-face. She stepped to the door and left. Not once acknowledging the man on the couch.

THE TABLE WAS A MESS OF LITTLE WHITE BOXES. THE chopsticks never left their hands.

"Did the guy have a bad comb-over? Maybe touches up the dark with a dauber?"

Nash snorted softly around the pot sticker. "Yeah. From his appearance, his high school nickname was probably weasel."

Mina grimaced. "Deputy director to deputy director. The sleaziest of all premier power moves. You can't win this one. Whoever the witness is, they were probably part of something more important than a penny-ante Mob rollover. This kind of protection would go more toward domestic terrorism or selling Top Secret information or technology."

Nash leaned back with the box of double mushroom chicken. "Something more to do with Homeland?"

Mina nodded as she searched the boxes for the dim sum. "More Homeland than ATF. Although, if it was domestic terror, ATF would probably have had the lead." She looked up and frowned. "It's not like you to give up a bone. What are you thinking?"

Her smile was toothy and sinister. She missed their Chinese lunches. "I'm thinking of my new friends in low places and wondering how much weight they can carry on the high grounds of Washington."

Her wife smiled as she sat back with her hand and the chopsticks resting over her other arm.

"What?"

"I just realized how much I've rubbed off on you. You were smiling, thinking about pulling strings to get this done."

Nash growled. "I don't care who the drug seller is or what good they may have done in the past. Drugs and killing people don't get a pass."

"And yet, here we are with marijuana legal in almost half of the nation."

Nash's eyes narrowed as she stabbed at the slices of bamboo shoots in the box. "Only because everyone still believes grass doesn't kill anyone. Just like guns don't kill people, people kill people. Drugs are drugs, and they all kill."

Mina put the box on the table and sat back. "When do you head back?"

Nash pulled out her phone. "I don't know. I didn't check with James because I didn't know what this was all about." She typed in the phone and set it on the table.

The phone vibrated with a ping. She picked it up and read the message. "He says he's off for four days, but he'll grab me a seat and send me the info."

Mina batted her eyelashes. "Wow, four days. Well, sailor, what would you like to do?"

Nash rubbed the sides of her tummy as she stared wide-eyed at the food. "After all that, I think I'd like a long nap."

Mina stood. "I'll help put this all away. You're reading my mind on the nap." She leaned over and kissed the top of Nash's head. "Mmm, I like the new shampoo. It smells like the forest or something."

Nash rose. "Two types of sagebrush. One is called bitterbrush, and the other is rabbitbrush. It's Powder's favorite shampoo. Well, almost shampoo. The soap is just plain Ivory with no scent. The brush petals I rub in as I'm drying my hair."

Mina turned back as she stuffed the boxes in the refrigerator. "Should I be jealous of this Powder?"

Nash pushed the last two boxes in as she hugged her wife. "I don't think we have to share our bed. She's more of an on-the-floor-standing-guard kind of dog."

"Mmm, I like this girl more and more."

29
REGROUP

UNCLE STUCK his arm out of the window and then turned the truck left. The BMW braked hard and blew its horn.

"Sounds like someone squeezed his seal."

Nash closed her eyes. "You have turn signals, don't you?"

"Sure." He stuck his arm out and bent it at the elbow. At the corner, he nosed the truck up the alley. "See. It works just fine." He turned with a toothy smile.

"Millennials never drove Model Ts. They don't know what arm signals mean."

He pulled to the curb. Turning off the truck, he leaned forward, his arms crossed over the steering wheel. "What do you want to do now?"

Nash rolled her head to look at the man over her shoulder. "Are we talking about lunch or the assholes?"

His head bobbed softly. "Both, I reckon."

She pointed to the other side of the street. "Dos Pollo. We can talk assholes over beers, chips, and salsa. Not necessarily in the same order."

They rolled up the windows and got out. Uncle thumbed the fob, and the truck chirped softly.

Uncle glanced back over his shoulder down the alley. "Any guidance?"

She shook her head. "Pretty adamant about it all. We walked through all the aspects of the investigation, and then they told me to grab a trash can full of shut up and stand down. I don't think he had a choice. The driver is Wit Sec and from the looks on man's face, in worrisomely deep."

"But after eleven or some years...?" He pulled the door open.

She stood quietly next to him as they waited their turn. "Know anybody who can get us around the roadblock?"

He flashed two fingers to the hostess. "Let me kiva. I might know somebody from back in the day."

They followed the hostess. Nash kept her voice soft. "Military back in the day?"

As he sat, he shook his head. "More like back in the day on my reservation."

"Bureau of Indian Affairs...?"

Uncle wobbled his hand in the air. "Kind of. He was supposed to take over as chief or shaman. I don't remember which."

"What happened?"

"He was smart. The bureau hired him and sent him to school. Last I heard, he had his law degree, and the DOJ called. He's undoubtedly buried in some dark bear's cave in D.C. somewhere."

Nash was positive she knew more about the obfuscation of D.C. than he did. "How do you plan to track him?"

Uncle gazed out the window with a smirk. "Like a good cowboy, he left breadcrumbs."

She snorted. "Breadcrumbs get eaten by birds or turn stale."

Uncle shrugged as the chips & salsa arrived. "Then I'll call his momma."

NASH LEANED OVER THE JUNIOR AGENT'S SHOULDER AND watched the slender finger jump about the large screen.

"I think this is who they turned state's evidence against and got Wit Sec." She scrolled down. "So the money enters here in Columbia. This account is their shell. Then it drops out and heads for the Cayman Islands. It lands in this account with Georgetown National. They're a large bank and can manage full-bore transfers. But then the split happens and heads to Scotia and Butterfield. Here and here." She glanced up with a smile. "Someone got creative."

She pulled up another form on the wing monitor. "Butterfield breaks it into four transfers but takes a ten-per-cent shave for their cut." Her finger drops to the next page. "These two go to Switzerland, but these two route to—"

"Argentina." Nash stood.

Muna turned. "How did you know?"

Her eye's narrowed. "I've seen the same routing number before. I just can't remember where… at the moment." Furling her lips, Nash looked around.

Muna waved her hand in the air. "It's just us. I swept the entire room an hour ago. Why…?"

"I'll tell you at dinner. What about the driver?"

Muna furled her lips into two pencil lines. "You aren't going to like it. They're co-mingling. As far as I can tell, the funds making it back here are in only one account in Los Angeles."

"Bank?"

"Private. Merchant's Bank of Beverly Hills. Two branches and meticulously tight on security. We can only guess at their customer list. But I'm guessing they pay dearly for more tight-lipped discretion than a Swiss whore."

Nash shot her a look of consternation.

"Or so I've been told…"

Nash rolled her eyes. "So it stops there?"

"As far as I could get. Like I said, legally, their security is unbreachable."

"Let's not go off the reservation on this."

Muna gave her a stern look.

Nash yawned and moved to the other seat. "When it's time, we'll need a federal warrant anyway. So the funds are there, or they left, but we'll be able to find out where and if they split." She twitched. "Oh, can you find out if both names are on the account?"

Muna grimaced. "Not without that warrant. But they split the funds in Georgetown. And at that time, they are going out to single accounts at single banks. So we can assume they are still joint unless the split was to split them instead of just diversification."

"Any way to go through Interpol and find out if they were sent as split or joint?"

Muna saw the clock and then Googled the time in Zurich. She thought a moment and then clicked on an app on the work bar. A form came up, and she started filling it in. "Nobody will do anything until after their espresso and biscotti are done. So you might as well go up to bed. That's where I'm headed once I get this sent. It's nine in the morning there." She glanced up over her shoulder. "If we're lucky, we might have an inquiry back in the morning."

The jet lag suddenly caught up with Nash, and she yawned. Stirring, she stood and put her hand on the small shoulder. "You're right. But do what you said. Get some sleep as well."

The slender, dark hand swirled in the air. "Yeah, yeah, yeah…"

THE COFFEE SHOP WAS A MILE FROM THE COMPOUND. But by looping through some of the lushest parts of Golden Gate Park, Nash had mapped out a three-mile walk to clear her head. The mile would be for the after-breakfast stroll.

The morning glow was a factor of the sunlight being filtered through the haze of the East Bay and the last of the fall fog hovering over the bay. It gave the air a certain edge of verisimilitude that fall was coming, but the last of the heat wasn't gone. The day could go either way by noon.

Her phone pinged as she pulled out the chair at the window counter. The view of the distant ocean was what she had come for. The tops of the houses on the next block were almost two stories below the street in front of the café. Just the unobstructed ocean view was worth the walk and the cost of breakfast.

The text was their simple shorthand: "Up."

She texted back a shocked face along with "Breakfast with Jerry (EPA) and Willis (US Marshals). Will share." She closed with a purple heart.

Nash replied with her three purple hearts and, not for the first time, wished there was a rainbow heart.

Perusing the menu, she sipped on her coffee.

There was movement out of the corner of her eye. She turned and watched. In the next block, part of the roof had moved. Two large wings opened, slowly folded in half, and stacked on each side.

The waiter stood next to her. "I love this part."

Two men rose from the roof, seated at a small table draped with a rainbow tablecloth. As the platform stopped, one poured from a carafe as the other served the food from silver chafing dishes. The entire tableau had the sense of refined dining in an exotic place, like a rooftop restaurant in Paris.

Nash looked up at the young man. "Do they do this often?"

He twitched, still obviously wrapped up in his own fantasy. "Not if it snows or rains. But otherwise, daily."

Nash looked back at the rooftop dining. "The opening roof and lift must have been a pretty penny to build."

The waiter elevated his chin in thought. "Cheaper and more logical than having a vacation home somewhere else. Besides, why travel when you have a million-dollar view every morning? Every year, millions of tourists travel around the world to come here. Few ever get this view, and nobody gets their kind of experience." He shifted and looked down. "Did we decide what we wanted to eat?"

Nash chuckled and tilted her head with a smirk as she passed him the menu. "I don't know what you're having, but if it has a side of those buckwheat cakes, I'm having the same. Unless the chef wants to surprise me."

He smiled. "I'll tell the wife. She was down at the fish market yesterday…"

She turned back to the two eating on the rooftop as he left. She raised her coffee to her lips and froze. What the waiter had said replayed in her head.

She picked up her phone and scrolled for Uncle. Her thumbs hit the key icons.

"Does Buck Crawford have a second home or a hunting cabin?"

An old saying played through her head. The professor had taught Social Criminal Justification. But even more powerful than the statistics and standard coursework were the illustrative stories and saying he shared from his Rabbinical day job. The two that stood out were: *Don't shit where you eat* and *Soil someone else's bed.*

She glanced back over her shoulder to where she thought the waiter was. She smiled. *Why travel when it's all at home?*

"THERE'S A PACKAGE ON THE DESK FOR YOU."

Nash wiggled the mouse to wake up the terminal. She turned the medium box around to read the label. The monitor lit up, and the seal appeared with the log-in box. She typed in her passcode and hit return.

She picked up the box and leaned back into the chair. The return address was the office of the deputy director. The package had come by priority mail. She smiled.

Muna's face rose behind the large monitor. Her hijab was a subdued swirl of iridescent reds. Her face was childlike in happy curiosity. "What did big daddy Santa send from home office?"

Nash smiled and glanced around. She whistled a sharp, beckoning note through her teeth and lip.

"I think Uncle took her out for a—"

The soft sound of nails on the linoleum begged to differ.

Nash smiled as she turned. "Uncle is out in the loading dock, spreading the macho bull manure with Mike and the two security guards."

Nash showed the package to Powder. The dog sniffed and then sat but kept nosing one corner of the box.

"Is this the place to open it?"

Nash fished in her front pocket and brought out a small knife. Flicking it open, she slit the seals on the box. Returning the knife to her pocket, she opened the box. In the corner was a baggy of dog treats. Nash examined them through transparent plastic. The treats appeared hand-cut. She guessed they were homemade. She didn't remember the deputy director as a dog person, but it wouldn't have affected his job or those who worked under him.

Under the official harness, she saw a large envelope. Opening the fastener, she slid out the shield, ID, and certificate. There was also a small note.

My wife says the treats are all-natural, and our mastiffs approve. Welcome Agent Powder for me. Anthony.

Nash opened the baggie and took out a treat, offering it to Powder. The sniffing lasted for less than a second. The chewing reminded her of the first time she had tried calamari. It was a slow chew to make a judgment. The dog swallowed and looked at the bag.

Nash laughed as she fished out a few more. "They'll do in a pinch, huh?"

Muna blinked and smiled. "Wow, who knew the tin woodsman had a heart under all his layers of cast iron?"

Nash thought about the times she had interacted with the man away from the bureau. She knew the young teens who fell in love with their high school sweethearts were still mutually in love. She just hadn't known about the dogs.

"He has a warm and caring wife. And a couple of large kids." She handed over the note.

Turning, she pulled out the new harness. "Let's see how this fits."

Removing the borrowed old generic harness, Nash installed the new official harness. She let out the chest bands a small amount, and the buckles clicked home. "Wow. Who knew you were such an athlete?" She installed the badge in the breastplate holder. "Now you can fly home with me."

Powder curled her head around and impatiently sidestepped. She looked back at Nash and then at the baggie in the box.

"Uh oh. We have a treat hound."

Nash gave Muna a sorrowful look. "Are you talking about her or me?"

Muna turned her head into the air and walked away. "If the feedbag fits..."

Nash fed Powder a couple more treats as she thought about some of the extensive tactical harnesses she had seen in the marines. "I've seen worse rigs, girl. Heck, I've worn worse."

30

NEW LIVER, SAME OLD EAGLE

UNCLE RUBBED his face with his hands. "I think I'd rather be sitting on my stool in the bar."

The female voice floated from across the large room. "You kids don't know how easy you have it. In my day, we had to play with rocks."

Nash snickered from her laptop near the window where Powder was sleeping in the sun. "Whole rocks or broken and ground down to dust like ours?"

Muna stood with a shocked look on her face. "You had DUST? We had to make ours the old-fashioned way with a mortar and pestle."

Uncle laid his head on the desk and let his arms hang from the edge. "Oh, my gods and spirit animals, she had a real pestle like the rich folks."

Mike stepped into the room from the hall. "Quit your bellyaching. We had to fly kites in the rain to get electricity."

The three sat up with shocked faces and chorused. "You had kites?"

Mike rolled his eyes as the other three laughed. "All right, all right. There's a pizza guy waiting downstairs."

Nash snorted as she looked over at the culprit. "Okay, Muna. Whose turn to go pay?"

The diminutive woman stood and looked at Uncle. "Rock paper scissors."

Uncle held up his index finger. "Light saber. I win. Nash gets the door. How much is the bill?" He leaned forward and fished out his wallet.

"It's three garbage can lids, so close to eighty."

Uncle held out a hundred. "Tip him well so he survives San Francisco and the pandemic."

Nash snatched the bill from his hand. "Keep the change; it is."

Muna sat down and leaned back in her chair with her arms outspread. "Finally." She leaned in and read the email. "Bingo. Interpol for the win."

Uncle walked over, followed by Mike. "What did they find out?"

Muna tapped on the screen. "The transfers left Zurich still co-mingled. Both parties are equally signatory. They are all joint accounts."

"Did they find anything about Buck Crawford?"

She shook her head. "I can ask, but we had to send the names and transfer accounts to get this information. But if they are in this deep, what's a little more?"

"Pizza." Nash walked in with the three large boxes.

Mike leaned back to look out into the hall. "And nobody followed you?"

Nash tossed her head. "He's bringing the salads. One of us ordered sensible food."

Muna flipped open the first box. "Nope." The second brought a smile. She turned and shouted at the archway into the hall. "Oz. Veggies are here." She folded two slices in half for a sandwich and returned to her desk.

The ping was audible across the room. Muna clicked on the pulsing icon as she took a bite of pizza. "Hee mumba."

The screen ballooned to show the lab at UC Davis. Mandy did a double-take and started laughing. "And how is your lunch?"

Muna snapped her fingers five times and gave her a thumbs up.

"Ooh, five snaps up. Must be the veggie."

Muna put her finger on the end of her nose and nodded. Nash planted her feet and pushed. The rolling chair shot across the room as she turned to slow down and stop. She overshot and ended up slightly past Muna.

"Hey Mandy. What's up?"

"Hi Nash. Just giving you a heads-up. We looped in the DEA and EPA somehow, and they crunched the last samples Uncle dropped off. So we have an idea of what you guys are looking for." She looked down at her monitor and clicked her mouse. "I'm sending it all to you guys. I tried to call Uncle, but I got an out of office." She suddenly looked up behind Nash. "Oh. Hi, Uncle. What are you guys doing? Having a pizza party?"

Nash turned around and then looked down at the man's bare feet. *Sneaky Indian.*

Uncle smiled. "We threw Powder a surprise birthday party."

"Powder?"

Nash rolled her eyes. "The newest member of the team. I'll bring her the next time we're out."

Mandy frowned marginally as she turned her head. "Okay... But we're done with all your work. So why would you come out?"

Uncle rocked his head. "We want to see if the cow dog can do cow dog stuff."

Pi walked by in the background. "Hey guys." But kept on walking.

Mandy explained. "They're switching the cows to feed instead of graze, so it's manure week around here."

Uncle slowly ground his head back and forth as his lips furled. "Don't turn on the huge fan."

Nash grew her eyes large. "Goodbye, Mandy."

"Bye y'all." The connection winked off, leaving a pulsing icon of a pdf and the remains of a game of sudoku.

Muna reached to open the folder but paused to take another bite of pizza.

Uncle rumbled as he turned. "Eat first. You open that, and you will lose the next nine hours of your life."

True to his prophecy, it was dark out before she threw a pencil at her screen. She looked over at the desk where Nash had sat all day. The laptop lay closed.

Standing, she walked through the hall and the laboratory. Mike was on a phone call, and Oz was working intently on something with a lot of numbers. Muna didn't want to know and left.

She went back to shut her computer station down. On the end of Nash's desk was a pink sticky note. *Shooting Range downstairs.*

Muna frowned. "What shooting range?"

She found the two guards at the loading dock. "Where is the shooting range?"

The older one smiled at the younger one's confused look. "Take the elevator, press and hold the 'B.' It will take you to the sub-basement. Follow the noise."

She followed the directions. Sure enough, the elevator had another level hidden in its panel. The door opened to silence. She looked both ways down the long hallway and then noticed the small sign that said: *Noise.* And an arrow pointing toward the right.

At the end of the hall was another sign. Two more turns, and she found a door marked the same.

The man looked up from the counter as she opened the door. "Jeez. Everyone waits for the last hour before shooting their quals."

She snorted softly. "I shot my qualifiers two months ago before I left D.C."

The tall man smiled. "You must be al Foraging."

"Al-Faragi. Muna."

He looked at a sheet. "Yup. Haven't qualified for the field in fifty-three days, seventeen hours, and forty-one minutes. What are you shooting?"

She glanced through the window at the three shooters behind the soundproof glass. "I'm a lab squint."

He pointed at the clipboard. "Not according to the roster. They have you down for infiltration and enforcement. Are you shooting or not?"

She grimaced. "Three-eighty." She pulled her weapon and cleared it as she dropped the clip. She slid the clip to one side as he handed her two empty clips and a box of rounds.

"Bring me a qualifying target, and you get your clip back." He scooped up the clip and bullet. "Glasses and headgear are through the door to your left. Your lane is number three."

She nodded. "I'll be back in a few minutes."

As she pushed through the door, she sized up the seven-alley shooting range. Six and seven were the tense shoot-out between Uncle and Nash. Their shots sounded more like a single shot as they tore the center out of their respective targets. Muna snorted softly as she turned to find the glasses and hearing mufflers.

She smiled as she turned into alley three, next to the white lab coat and two metal legs. Three targets lay on the floor behind him. The centers obliterated in a lace pattern ranging to the edges of the eighth ring. The practice test pattern is not always about qualifying as much as seeing what you can do by choice. Anything with a nine-millimeter would tear up the body mass.

She laid her box of shells on the counter and put on her headset and glasses. Pulling her weapon, she checked the slide and fit of the range master's clips.

As she set down the full clip and filled the second, she noticed the flash coming from Mike's muzzle. The exhaust flared in a set of wings through the Magna-porting on the long barrel. Her eyes narrowed as she realized he was accuracy shooting with a.50 caliber Desert Eagle. She had picked up and shot one—once. Her hand and wrist had hurt for a week. Watching his shooting, she realized he had two hundred-round boxes of bullets. She guessed he shot a lot.

She snapped the first clip into her weapon and snapped the slide. All six bullets flowed through the barrel and into the center in a couple of seconds. She pulled the target back. One hole had touched the line.

She ran out another target. Taking a calming breath, she snapped off the next six. She had left the four serifs of the center X. She pulled the target and started policing her brass.

"There was a lot of anger in that first one."

She turned toward Mike. Her lip furled as she thought. "It happens. That's why they call it practice."

He studied her serious face. "Have you ever just shot for the fun of it?"

She looked down at her weapon and her hands. Years before, they would be shaking. "Not with a Desert Eagle. That was a serious date I never went on a second time."

Mike reached into the shelf and pulled out a padded gun case. Unzipping the case, he pulled out a WWII Luger. He cleared the gun and stepped around the acrylic barrier. "Here. It's a Mauser Luger, nine-mill, oh-eight."

"I'll stick to my three-eighty, thank you."

He smiled. "Don't let the nine millimeters scare you. This was my sister's when she was about your size."

"What does she shoot now?"

He thought for a moment. Realizing she knew nothing about him or his legs. "Daisies. If they don't mow the lawn over her." He waved his one hand at his legs. "She was in the car when I crashed. We didn't wear seatbelts back then."

Muna blushed. "I didn't... I didn't know."

He closed his eyes as he nodded. "I don't talk about her. I just come down and play. My sister and I were as competitive as those two kids." Nodding his head toward Nash and Uncle. "Shooting helps me remember her and the good times we had growing up."

He offered the pistol out. "Try it. If you like it, it's yours. But it's just for fun. It's not your service piece."

Hesitantly, she took the pistol older than her grandfather. She looked it over and inserted the clip. The grip was more forward and fit her hand better than her service weapon. She looked at Mike. "Interesting design."

He nodded. "The slant transfers the punch to the entire hand instead of just your web."

She focused on the sight. The tiny white dot of the unblued steel sat in the saddle of the rear sight. She thought about squeezing the trigger. The pistol jumped a little.

She pulled it back and looked at the weapon. It was a vastly unique feeling.

Mike stood at the back of her cubical. "Now, hold your hand up and point your finger at the center of the target."

She pointed at the target.

"Again."

She put her hand on the counter and then pointed at the target.

"Now. Close your eyes and repeat. Open your eyes when you think you've pointed at the target."

She pointed. Then slowly turned.

His face gently drew into a smile. "Now. Close your eyes and shoot."

She thought a moment as she looked at the target and the pistol on the counter.

"Stop thinking. You know where the target is. Just shoot it with your eyes closed. Trust yourself."

She picked up the gun, pointed it, and fired in one movement. As she opened her eyes, she put the gun down. She reached out and triggered the return for the target. The hole was hiding in the black, just to the right of the white cross of the X.

Mike turned on his one foot. "That, my dear, is what we call shooting for the fun of it. Enjoy May Bell."

Muna looked up and turned. "Mabel?"

The man stowed his weapon and boxes of empty shells in the hard case. "No. As in May 1945. My father shot the bell in a church tower. The German sniper dropped his rifle over the parapet and almost lost his hearing, but he gave my father the Luger in surrender."

31
TEAMWORK

"OKAY, we'll see you Thursday in Taylor. Nice talking to you, Robert." She hung up and turned the chair around to address the vultures.

Uncle beat Muna to the punch. "Who's getting lead?"

Muna drew back with a snarl. "Who found the toxic waste?"

He leaned in with a snarl that Nash had watched him try on dogs. "Who found the skeleton?"

Muna's nose almost touched his. His snarl hadn't worked on the dogs either. "The sheriff."

Nash stuck her little fingers in her mouth and blew. The sharp whistle startled both fighters. Powder, in the corner, groaned and rolled over. "Back down. Both of you." She stared them back to sitting down at their respective ends of the table. "For now, the Incident Command Structure is me. Period."

Uncle whined. "But DEA—"

"Will be in there. Trust me. Your work and ATF have been invaluable. And as little as you think of Felix, he is Homeland. And they are the big dog these days. They get forty-five percent of the budget for a reason. Justice gets about twenty-five, and the rest of us divvy up the bones. But we all play our parts. And the LEOs hate all of us." She turned toward Muna and then thought of another point. So turned back to Uncle. "And remember, if you engage in this, your cover will be history, and you can start figuring out how to move your teepee."

She turned and hefted the two inches of printout. She waved it at Muna. "Great job, by the way. I sent copies to the deputy director and the local US district attorney. A Rafael Romulus will come over later this morning to talk. He will be the prosecutor, or at least working closely with whoever is the prosecution for this. By tomorrow afternoon, he needs to loop in. He might be in the huddle Thursday in Taylor. I don't want you back row kibitzing while we're hammering out this takedown. So if he's an idiot, tell me. I'll get his boss sent over, and you can run them both down any of the seven alleys in the sub-basement. Do I make myself clear?"

"Crystal."

Nash's eyes snapped shut as she grimaced. "Just for this case. Please don't use that term."

Muna blushed as she thought about the drug they were raiding. "Roger that."

Nash closed her eyes and waited.

"Clear."

The sound of metallic feet on the linoleum got her attention. She glanced up.

She stared at the Tuesday uniform of a white lab coat over faded surfer's board shorts and a tie-dyed T-shirt. "Yeah, Mike?"

"They're holding a suit at the front desk. He says he has an appointment with someone named Agent Allen Fargo?"

Muna rolled her eyes. "Yaa, you betchya." She stood. "I'm guessing it's my date. And strike one."

Nash looked at Uncle. The weeks of working full speed had built up a head of steam in the brain. Now it was a waiting game while the delicate ends got wrapped up in neat little bows. But the blank hours felt like years. "I need to take Powder for a long walk. Care to go for a drive?"

"Where did you have in mind?"

She stood and pushed her fists into the small of her back. "I heard there are some great oysters in a place called Tamales Bay."

"Oh, sure. It's right next to Taco Bay and south of enchilada."

She feigned a punch to his gut. "Don't be an ass. And just for the bad pun, I'm driving, but you're buying."

He groaned as he rolled off the desk. "So what else is new?"

UNCLE INSPECTED THE LIGHTWEIGHT TECH HARNESS ON the seemingly frozen dog. "I like the fit. And the badge holster is a brilliant touch. The last thing the perp sees before he loses his face is the badge."

"I can see circumstances where it will instantly answer a lot of questions. Like in the airport."

She glanced over at her partner. "Did you ever put a leash on her?"

Powder turned her head and gave Nash an assessing look.

Uncle smirked. "There's your answer. Even as a pup, she never gave me reason to find a leash. She was just always right there."

"Has she always watched the road? Or is it just my driving?"

He harrumphed as he slid down in the seat and scratched her back. "Ever since she could see over the dashboard. For the first year, I thought it was my driving. But then, we rode with a couple of other people driving, and it's always the same. She just watches where we go."

THE LATE AFTERNOON SUN WANLY WARMED THE TWO sitting at one of the picnic tables. The fifty-fifty platter of oysters lay between them. Half sat raw, and the other half cooked Rockefeller style.

Nash swallowed and cleared her mouth with the herb tea. "Are you going to talk or just stew from now until Thursday?"

He shifted on the bench. "I hadn't thought about it."

"Talking?"

He peeked up. "No. About being undercover."

Nash snorted softly with a gentle start. "How many people have you told what you do? I mean, we already know about Sheriff Mushroom."

He shook his head as he chewed. "Nobody, really. Only those undercover for their own agency know about the rest of us."

"Meanwhile, you're just the happy little uncle to everybody in town who has no visible means of making a living?"

"You never asked."

She slurped a raw oyster and chewed. "Loo."

He laughed. "I'll wait for you to clear your mouth and explain whatever you said."

She swallowed. "True. I never thought about it. Probably nobody else did either."

He squirted lemon juice on the Rockefeller and then sucked it into his mouth.

She continued. "All my life, I heard how the government sent every Indian a subsistence or compensation check. It was always fatter than the talker's paycheck. But I never remember ever seeing one."

He nodded as he washed his mouth with his coffee. "There are some. Not everyone, but some. Back in the sixties. But they were always compensation for something like land rights-of-way or timber. Never just because it was the right thing to do. The fantasy never happens. The casino splits probably come the closest."

Her head bobbed. "Or the pueblos would have running clean water and electricity." She watched his mouth tighten. "Yeah, I ran across it a few years back. So what are you going to do?"

He grumped as he sprayed the last three oysters with the lemon. "I think I need to kiva on the possibilities tomorrow. At least going into Thursday, I need to know if I'm part of the raid or part of the shocked townspeople."

"Sheriff knows who you are..."

"Which doesn't make it any easier. And with the raid, it will most likely make my undercover a thing of the past."

Nash poked a small piece of garlic bread in the dish where one of the Rockefeller oysters had rested. Mopping up the juice and spinach. "I don't suppose there would be any need for a bar stool DEA agent back on the Navajo reservation."

He furled his lower lip and vibrated his head. "It's much more active down there. The border collies drive, and the DEA and ATF ride shotgun. Usually, it's a two- or four-SUV team."

"Oh, exactly your kind of job." She snickered.

"Truth is"—he wiped his mouth on the napkin and laid it beside the empty platter—"I've got my thirty in, so I'll get seventy percent, but I'm only ready for a job standing next to Mo at the trinket store. At the range, I punch paper with the best of you, but I couldn't run a mile to save my life."

He turned and straddled the bench seat, staring out across the bay. "I've spent the last twenty-nine in Harkin. I hunt when I want, get up when I want—or need to pee—and I eat what I fix. Nobody disturbs me. The rednecks ignore me, and I'm too fast for any woman except Powder. And now she's yours." He looked over at her. "If I'm in the raid, I'll have to move. If it goes worse than we think, I'll have to move, anyway. But I can't think of any place I want to be."

"So don't come. And see how it plays out."

He lowered his head as he picked at the chip of old paint on the bench. He peeked through the side of his eye. "What about the ICS?"

Nash flashed her eyebrows up and gazed out across the bay. "The Incident Command Structure looks like the Forest Service and DOJ sharing the top knot. With all the rest of us suckling pigs on their teats."

"Why Forest Service? I mean, yeah, the lodge is surrounded by BLM land, but Forest Service? Smokey Bear?"

She snorted. "You've never been part of an Incident Command Structure, have you?"

"There are a lot of letters carved into my stool, but I don't think anyone carved those initials, per se."

"Well, Forest Service has a large arm of enforcement. Do you know the cute little badge Smokey has on his chest? It makes him an officer of the court. And the cabin is on their land. Which means three points of the law in their basket. The DOJ will be there no matter what. Because it's federal crimes, they'll prosecute. Which means the sheriff is out before it starts. And that's fine by me. The last thing I want is to be hauled back here in a year or so to sit through an ugly trial or four. Besides, we investigate, not take down and prosecute."

She squinted at his frowning face. "What?"

His face cleared as he looked up and over. "What? Oh... No, I was thinking about Smokey's badge. I never thought about it, but you're right."

She nodded. It wasn't often a man admitted she was right. "After the initial arrest and the cleanup starts, the structure will shift into your court. The hazmat will be under the EPA, but your Tox Team will take the lead or co-lead because of the drugs. Or at least it's how I've seen it happen in the past. Except for a case we had in the Virgin Islands. What started as coral plundering became drug smuggling when Homeland took over most of the Command Structure."

3 2

TEAM TIME

THE CHAIRS WERE FULL, as some were sitting in the back on tables.

"The borderline runs down along this patch of woods. It jogs a bit here because of the old well. But it continues straight through the backdoor and out the front. The small barn here is the turn point. The barn is outside the National Forest. But from what we can tell, the falling-down nature of the barn is correct. It is empty, besides an old wagon and maybe a car hiding in one corner." Nash circled the cabin with her pointer. "As you can see from this drone photo, there's nothing for fifty feet around the cabin. This is not uncommon in fire country."

She pointed at the blond with the military haircut. "Yes, in the back."

"Do we know they are in there?"

Nash smiled. "Good question, just twenty seconds too early on the trigger. But stick with us, and you'll learn the power of patience." She turned off the pointer. "We've had the property under constant watch for the last four days. Overwatch tells us the count is four people in the cabin. They are actively cooking crystal meth. We know that because we have taken samples of their toxic waste."

"Crystal meth is an old term…"

Nash nodded. "Thank you. You know, that's good news for those of you who have some snow on the roof. But it is also bad news. The toxic nature means we will breach in full hazmat gear. We don't want any cowboys who think they won't be exposed to enough to do any actual harm. It's not true. We don't know how contained their cooking is, but we have observed them coming out on the porch for breaks in the air, and they have full respirators pitched back on their heads."

She looked around. "Questions?"

"Bill Mooney with the DEA out of Sacramento. Looking at the Incident Command Structure handout, we're kind of kissing the hind wind…"

Nash twitched her head to one side. "If you'd like to be the one to take a bullet for the team, I'm sure the Smokeys would be more than happy to hold you out as the cannon fodder. But by Sunday, and the after-action, you'll be co-lead with EPA. I'm sure there will be more than enough opportunity to take some great photos for your get book, Bill." She looked around. "Is anybody else feeling left out on the ICS? Because with this, there's plenty to go around. And if you hadn't noticed, the FBI is behind all of you. I've been here for almost two months, and to quote my boss, ain't no glory in a coffin."

"Okay, we're going to break into the tactical squads, and you can coordinate your lines. The terrible coffee will continue, and we have lunch coming around noon. So take a break, and we'll start the squads in about fifteen minutes."

The group rose in various stages of age and in their careers. Nash raised her eyebrow as she looked over at Uncle, still leaning against the workbench, sipping his coffee. She remembered the young recruits in the Corp. The young marines would run all night to get to a battle first thing in the morning. She also remembered the gunny that slowly peddled a bicycle along the double-timing column. The light sweat gleamed in his steel gray hair in the afternoon sun.

Nash stopped by the six-man squad going over plans for the cabin. The lead she had reached out to personally. Long before their shared time in hell on North Island of San Diego, humping forty-pound packs through mud and night, he had lived through the wars of East L.A.

"Hey, Running Bear." The man leaned back in the chair.

She smiled warmly and stuck out her hand. "Hey, Esper."

He waved aside her hand and stood into a hug. The hug was longer than one of camaraderie. Both knew the first hug was her hauling him out of the swamp and carrying him to the medics a mile away.

He turned. "Guys, this is Nash Running Bear, the best damn marine to save a guy's life."

She side-hugged him to hide her blush. "Come on, under the skin, you're still my little brother. And I kiss that bald spot on the top of your head anytime you blow another gasket." She turned to the small laughing group. "It was only his appendix. I mean, what bozo joins the crazy squad without first leaving their delicates at home?" She made a goofy face.

They laughed in good fun at their commanding officer.

She pushed him to arm's length and looked him up and down. "It seems Smokey's been good for you."

He nodded with a small smile. "It keeps us hopping. This is a pleasant break from the enormous fires we've been having lately."

"So you still fight fires? Not just enforcement?"

They all nodded. The tall blond with the trimmed red beard explained. "Every ranger is a firefighter first, and whatever else we do, second."

Esper nodded. "Sven is a lands architect by day. But he straps in when we jump, either for a fire or enforcement."

Nash waved her finger. "You're all *Hot Shots*?"

"We're part of a larger cadre, but we're the only ones who pack the full badge."

She noticed Muna waving at her. "Well, tomorrow morning, when you breach, we'll be glad to have you guys." She patted Esper on the hard tummy as she turned to leave. "Great to see you, pequeño."

Muna turned to the laptop as Nash approached. "I thought you'd want to see this. One of my deep dive buddies came through."

"What are we looking at?"

Muna turned and leaned against the high workbench. "Remember when Iraq was rolling along, and Afghanistan was blowing up?"

"Two and three. Yeah, I thought I might get shipped out."

She moved the cursor and chose the file. Clicking on it, the icon ballooned into an article in the Times. The photo was of large cubes of money on pallets. The pallets were in a cargo bay that Nash and every deployed leatherneck would recognize as a C-130 Hercules.

"We threw billions of dollars at the problem."

Muna rocked her head as she closed the article and opened another one. "Except the company supplying the distribution of support, services, and anything else they could finagle out of the White House didn't think they were being paid enough."

Nash fluttered one eyelid closed as her face soured. "Yeah, a bunch of hot air and noise, but the connections and hands in back pockets went too deep. And the excessive heat killing people here, especially in Europe and the United Kingdom, took the headlines away long enough for the election to take center stage and made it about 9/11 and soccer moms."

Muna held one eye shut as she spread her face. "Yeah, too bad nobody was listening to Kerry pointing at the killing heat and warning us about global warming. But war and mom's feeling safe and secure was sexier."

Nash growled. "And Columbine was just a couple of whackos. Forget the easy guns."

Muna pulled up another article. It was small and from a local paper in Houston. Nash leaned in and read. The details were sparse only because the writer or publisher was trying to report a critical problem but was skirting an issue of libel. The company could probably buy and sell the entire state every other day, and the newspaper wouldn't even make a snack.

Nash frowned in anger. "Betty Jo Taylor? They doxed her. Is this paper still around?" She looked at the junior agent.

Shaking her head. "Paper's gone, the lawsuit is no longer, and Betty Jo Taylor is now Roxanne Crawford in Wit Sec." She clicked on another icon. The old Texas driver's license had a younger version of the face on the newer California license.

Nash turned and leaned against the bench with her arms crossed tight. "And we can't touch her."

Muna smiled on one side. "But if caught in the middle of a current crime, it makes it the Marshal's problem to either extract her or wash their hands of her. Personally, I think, either way, she stops being our problem."

Nash thought for a moment. With her mouth pulled pursed to one side, she looked around the large room. "Who else…"

"No one here."

"Let's keep it that way. They can armchair quarterback in D.C. on Monday. But for now…" She turned in and hunched over the bench next to the laptop. "This is what I want you to put together for me for tomorrow morning."

Later, as she stood next to the coffee and doughnuts, sipping, Uncle saddled up.

"Some fox has been in the henhouse."

Nash snorted softly in her mug. "Nope. Just us chickens… with teeth."

"What are you up to?"

She looked at him out of the side of her eye. "What time do you think the sheriff gets to breakfast at the Golden State?"

The man sipped on his mug. "They open at six. But I've seen his truck out front at a quarter till. I don't think he sleeps well."

She put down her empty mug and turned. "Just enough time to find out if he's going to be a problem."

The man's face was deadpan, but she could sense the smile of a little boy the night before Disneyland. "Can I help?"

She thought about the video. Uncle, on the other side, with Powder as backup, would be the smartest play. She nodded as she walked away. "Gotta take the little girl for a walk."

33

COUNTERPRODUCTIVE

THE PALE LIGHT of dawn filtered through the sparse trees. Nash nodded toward the south end of town. The headlights crept unhurriedly along the main street. They knew the sheriff, with his jacketed elbow bent out the window, haphazardly viewed his domain.

The white-over-tan SUV nosed into the parking lot and stopped facing the front door. The headlights filled the storm porch with light. The lack of the lock on the hasp suggested the door was open, but the open sign was still dark.

The lights turned dark. The next was the engine. And then the brake lights turned dark. The door cracked open slowly. The boot toe pushed against the lower part of the door where the paint had turned to dull silver metal.

Uncle's voice rumbled quietly. "I don't think he soaked in the creek last night."

Nash watched the man slide out of the door and stand gently. "I think more like this week."

They watched the sheriff elbow the door almost closed. He stood looking at the betrayal by the tin door. His hip swung and pushed it to the latch.

Nash took in a stage breath. "Did he just swear?"

Uncle scratched Powder's back under the tactical harness. "It looks like he doesn't have that much fight in him."

Nash yawned and crossed her arms. Slumping down in the truck's seat, she leaned her head back and closed her eyes. "We'll give him a few to climb up on the stool and get some coffee."

Powder turned and looked as Uncle copied the slump. She went back to watching the front door of the bar restaurant. Someone had to work.

Thomas separated the two sections of the newspaper and folded the front page back over the whole. He leaned hunched as he took another sip and started reading about the new strike in some plant in some state that had nothing to do with him. His eyes only held the place as he listened to the front door quietly open. Two sets of boots and dog claws.

"I saw the beater truck over in the trees."

"Yeah, not as many trees as I remember." Nash slid the laptop onto the bar as she sat.

Uncle's growl countered on the other side. "That happens when people poach the trees for firewood because the law looks the other way."

The sheriff's growl was close to his upset stomach, stirred by small-town politics. "That's what happens when people can't afford the price of fuel or food."

Nash looked up at the cook. She turned her mug right side up. "We'll have what he's having. It's going to be a long day."

Thomas put down his paper and thought for a moment. Turning his head, he looked at Nash in her official blue windbreaker. "Going fishing?"

"We already did all the fishing we need. Now it's hunting season." She opened the laptop and ran her finger along the reader. The screen blinked and then ran a cascade of boot logos. "You want this now or after you've eaten?"

He stared at her and then glanced over his shoulder at the

armored tactical vest on Powder. "Judging by how you dressed your dolly, I don't think I will like it either way."

Uncle harrumphed. "Bet on it. Just don't bet your life."

Thomas frowned at the man in a faded jean shirt and pants. "What's that supposed to mean?"

"It means we're armed today."

The sheriff rolled back on the stool as the breakfasts arrived.

Nash eyed the biscuits and chunky sausage gravy overflowing the three eggs and a handful of bacon. "Good choice." She moved the laptop to one side.

"What were you going to show me?"

Nash talked around a large bite of gravy-ladened biscuit. "Let's talk first. What do you know about Roxanne Crawford?"

"Buck's wife?"

Nash raised one side-eye as she cut her eggs. "Is there another?"

He forked his eggs onto his biscuits and gravy and cut them all up. "Not much. She showed up in Taylor when I had to run the second time."

"What was she doing?"

He frowned as she chewed on a piece of bacon. "She was working the night shift at the Arco minimart. Why?"

"When did she and Buck hook up?"

"Buck uses a lot of fuel. So he was there a lot. Plenty of chance to talk up all the wonderful places for dating and wooing."

Uncle choked and wiped his mouth. Clearing his mouth with some coffee, he turned and looked at the man incredulously. "Like the Golden State nightlife?"

The heavyset cook growled at him as she poured more coffee. "Did you want this in your lap?"

He blushed. "Sorry, Virginia."

She turned and walked away. "Don't let it happen again, squirt."

Nash watched her walk away and then turned back to the sheriff. "What else?"

The man scrunched his face and eyes. "There was something

about an abusive ex-husband who was stalking her or something. Anyway, she was hiding out and needed to keep a low profile, so Harkin fit the bill. As did the flamboyant jet set nature of Buck."

Nash smirked. "Yeah, I saw that flamboyant T-shirt of his scares."

The sheriff nodded. "So I think they dated, or whatever passes for dating in this neck of the woods, for half a year."

"Where did they get married?"

He swallowed the bacon. "Reno. Everyone goes to Reno. It's faster and easier. Hop over to three ninety-five and straight down."

"So she moved in with Buck. Here in Harkin. What did she do for work? Because I don't think Buck's the kind to take kindly to her lying around on the divan eating bonbons and watching daytime soap operas."

"She probably started doing the books and answering the phone for them. I never really thought much about it. What does this all have to do with the bones?"

Nash pushed the half-eaten plate away. "Ah yes, the bones. They may have brought me here, but the toxic dumping kept me here."

"Dumping?"

Nash opened the laptop back up. "Remember us taking samples of the mud from the lower flat pool? The one nobody walks naked in?"

He drew his answer out. "Yeah…"

She moved the cursor to the video icon and double tapped. The screen was dark and looked blurry. But soon, the headlights lit up the road. The truck stopped and then backed up. The shape was distinctive.

"That's Buck."

Nash raised her finger. "Right truck, wrong Crawford."

The truck stopped, and the lights went out. The driver's door opened, and Roxanne slid out. She walked to the back as the passenger door opened and dropped the tailgate.

Nash raised her finger for him to wait. Cheerleader uniform or work clothes. Even through the nightscope, Cindy Brady was obvious. Nash kept her finger up as Cindy came to the back of the truck and closed on Roxanne. The two locked in a deep kiss as they groped each other. Nash felt the man ride back on his hips. The quality of the video wasn't a big-screen movie, but it was good enough for YouTube or a courtroom TV.

The two women finally climbed into the back of the truck, and one by one, they took the tops off the drums and tipped them over to dump the contents into Bone Creek.

"As you can see, each drum is a not full, fifty-five-gallon drum. They dumped plenty onto the shoreline before it entered the creek. We got clean samples of the three hundred plus gallons the next day."

She pulled up the shortlist of chemicals. "What they used these chemicals for is not fixing hydraulic rams. They make good old-fashioned crystal meth, which produces extremely toxic waste, but also some enormous amounts of money."

She pulled up the printout from Zurich, Switzerland. "As you can see, the money isn't split into two accounts. They are in a joint account, like my wife and I." She let that sink in.

She watched the vein over the bridge of his nose. But more telling was the pulsing bump above his left temple. She had always judged his moods by the bump in high school. The faster the pulsing, the madder he was. Nothing got him hotter than when he felt or knew he had been lied to or played the fool. Cindy had cuckolded him in many ways.

His voice was strained. "Now what?"

She glanced at her watch. "In an hour, we will raid their meth lab."

"And you need me."

She twitched her head. "Nope. You have no jurisdiction and are not listed on the Incident Command Structure. You're only an observer this time. You've been benched."

"But I'm the sheriff. You can't—"

"Homeland and the US Forest Service are in command this time. I have my weapon, but I will sit on the same bench as you." She nodded at Uncle. "He's on the same bench, but he's not going. If he did, word would get out, and his job here would end. So he's going to be down in Taylor getting his ball joints adjusted or something."

Thomas looked at Uncle.

Uncle smiled sheepishly. "I'm going to get a massage so I'm rested and ready to hear about the exciting day."

"But it's a drug lab—"

The older man rested his hand on the sheriff's shoulder. "Trust me. There's plenty of representation already up at the cabin."

The sheriff took a long, painful breath through his nose. "Forest Service. It must be Buck's grandpa's place." He turned back to Nash. "And you want me to drive you up there."

She drew back. "It would help."

He wagged his finger at the laptop. "Therefore, none of this was about the bones."

She grimaced. "We'll talk on the way."

34

CABIN FEVER

Nash pointed to the left. Thomas nosed his SUV onto the dirt road. The long grasses were smashed and ground into the dirt. From the jumbled tracks, they could tell many vehicles had come this way recently.

"Did they come up last night or this morning?"

As they rounded a small outcropping of boulders and brush, the vehicles sat spread out. She chuckled. "I think... Yes, would be the right answer."

"Who's all here? This looks more like a Dead Head concert."

"You go to a lot of Dead concerts?" Nash noticed a young woman in tactical gear waving one hand and pointing with the other. "Pay attention to the traffic controller. It looks like she's packing a Sig fifty on her hip."

Thomas's eyes opened wide as he looked at the holstered pistol. "Yes, dear."

They eased up. Nash rolled down her window. "Where do you want us?"

The young woman's face lit up. "Ah, Agent Bear. Agent Ferogi said when you get here, text her. She's behind the small barn. But it would be great if you could park next to the two Humvees. You're the last in."

Nash gave her a passing two-finger salute as Thomas pulled the SUV forward.

As her window sealed, he snickered. "Agent Bear?"

She backslapped his shoulder behind Powder. Powder gave him a side-eye look. "In white America, it technically is my last name. *Bear* is at least correct. She might as well call Muna *El Senor Froggy*."

He turned off the SUV, and they got out.

Nash turned and looked back through the vehicle. "Do you have any tactical gear? It doesn't look good if a stray bullet takes out the local sheriff."

The sheriff walked to the back and opened the top half. Pulling out a vest, he slid it on and reached for his hunting rifle. He turned as he slid a couple of clips into his back pocket. "Just in case the other four hundred Dead Heads can't get the job done."

Nash looked around. "Is this the little lower meadow?"

He pointed out the dished-faced boulder. "That's where we used to make the bonfire." He turned. "The back way around to the barn is this way." He looked at the trampled grass. "Using the new extension of the Five Freeway."

Nash rolled her eyes at the twenty-foot-wide trampled pathway. She texted Muna. The reply was a silent vibration of a thumbs up.

Behind the small barn were only a handful of agents. Nash had given up trying to remember who was wearing what until they turned around, and she could read the letters on their backs.

Muna turned and motioned with a finger ticking on her hand as a clock and then held up four fingers. They would go for breach in four minutes. Each person checked their weapon. Nash looked at Thomas standing calmly with his rifle slung over his shoulder. He slowly wagged his head and mouthed, *observer*.

One officer in all black crawled to the edge of the barn. His hand on his back was in a spread of five fingers. Then they ticked to three, and the first of many gunshots tore the morning air.

Nash could hear the mixed screams of federal agents in pain. The shooting increased.

Thomas touched Nash's arm. "There's a side door." He nodded through the brush and around the other side of the barn. He pushed the tall chaparral away from the barn and slid through the breach.

Nash turned to Muna and waved to follow. "The settlers called it an Indian door. It's hidden on the outside, but it opens from a bedroom."

They dashed along the side of the barn. If anything, the shooting was increasing. Thomas took the rifle off his shoulder as they reached the corner. He pulled the slide and jacked a round into the barrel.

Nash scanned the windowless side of the cabin. The board and batten pattern was unbroken up to the rim or bellyband, running around the house at the same height as the tops of the doors and windows. She drew her sidearm as they approached the cabin. She could feel the soft pressure of the dog hugging her leg.

A section of the wall swung out and slapped against the wall. Cindy jumped two feet to the ground.

Nash stepped to a firing stance. "Freeze! Federal Agents."

Cindy swung the shotgun and fired.

The blast struck Nash in the chest and shoulder—spinning her around. As she watched the ground rising, she heard two gunshots that sounded like one. One loud and deep, the other high and crisp. The world turned dark.

"NASH? NASH?"

"Agent Running Bear?"

For some reason, it was dark. The winter air pressed heavily against her face. She didn't remember last winter being so cold.

"Nash?"

Uncle's voice was wrong. What was he doing in Japan? He wasn't a marine.

"We need that medevac now."

Who were they dusting off? Why was it so cold this winter?

Suddenly, it was light, and the weight on her face was gone. "Nash? It's Uncle. Can you hear me? If you can hear me, squeeze my fingers."

The sore throat still made her throat hurt and her voice raspy. "What are you doing here?"

Uncle looked at the ice pack and back at the three holes in her face where the buckshot had entered. Her shoulder would be a story for another day. As for her mind, he could tell she was hiding somewhere safe. "I came by to see if you and Powder wanted to go fishing?"

"Powder...?"

"She's right here. Your left hand."

Nash felt and realized the dog was lying along her side with her head in her armpit. She petted the dog and then settled for kneading her fingers into the fur.

Nash blinked. The blur looked familiar. "The raid?"

Uncle nodded. She was back and all agent. "Done. Three dead. Seven wounded."

She tried to clear her throat. "Damn, this sore throat. Who are you medevacking?"

He studied her face. The drugs were taking effect. "Powder. She caught some shotgun. But she won't let anyone touch her without us there. So we need you to go with her."

"Sir. The airship is two minutes out."

Uncle leaned in. "I'm going to put the ice pack back on your face. Just rest, and we'll get you in a few minutes." The dark, cold weight returned to her face. Uncle turned to the agent, taking her pulse. "Knock her the hell out, or she'll get up and try to fly the helicopter because it's going too slow."

Nash snorted. "Where's Thomas?"

Uncle turned back as he glared at the medical agent. "Purshia tridentate. If you're going to insist on still running the show, he's over there answering to Homeland. He's already turned over his rifle and badge."

Nash reached up and grabbed the large cold pack. She glared at Uncle. "Did he ever touch the cabin?"

Uncle looked back at the scene and the yellow tarp.

"Did he?"

Uncle turned. "No."

She laid the cold pack on her shoulder. For some reason, it felt good. "Get me Homeland. I'm still in control. And that's bitter-brush. We only have rabbitbrush and sagebrush around here. Now get me Homeland."

A minute later, the agent with the regulation mustache stood over her. "Your helicopter is inbound."

"I'm fine. Give the sheriff his badge and rifle back."

"He wasn't on the—"

"I put him on the ICS this morning after I interviewed and cleared him."

"But he had no—"

"Jurisdiction? More than you or me. The dirt over this side of the cabin is all his land. The forest starts on the inside of the cabin wall. So even if he touched the outside of the wall, it's his jurisdiction. They can do the pissing dance in Washington, D.C., if you want to fight about it. But right now? I have a splitting headache and need to get my dog to a vet. So stick your dick back in your pants and do what I told you. The man has a murderer to catch."

The man pointed at the cabin. "Drug dealers."

She shook her head as the deep-throated bark of rotor blades beating the air overhead matched her growl. "Manufacturers or cooks. But they weren't the ones dealing. Don't question me if you don't have all the facts. This is my show, and I'll be damned if I let you turn it into a shitshow."

Powder tried to rise, but Nash gripped the handle on the armored harness. The man got the picture.

He waved his finger at the four agents holding the bedposts of their makeshift stretcher. "Get her on the helicopter."

Nash held her left hand up. As she listened to the man leave and start barking orders to others.

She turned to the medic. "Can you knock me out?"

The medic swallowed and nodded.

"Let's err on the better side of thinking and do it. I'm not certified to fly them, but I have pilfered a few of them, so I know how to fly whatever silly hopper they sent."

The medic swallowed and smiled as she looked around.

Nash cleared her throat. "It's just us chickens, Marine. Get it done."

The smile broadened into a full, toothy smile. "Semper Fi, sir."

"Hoorah."

The lights went out.

35

SIT REP

THE TALL ASIAN woman stood with her back to the window. The afternoon sun warmed her back and felt good. She looked at the other bed in the room. "They didn't even give you a private room."

Nash tried to turn her head, but the heavy bandage prevented it. "Is there someone in the bed?"

Mina rolled her eyes low into just dark pencil lines. "No..."

"Then it's a private room, and you can kiss me without embarrassment."

"I'm not embarrassed to kiss my wife. This is a free country."

"Says the woman who has been standing there for six minutes and hasn't kissed her wife or tried to climb into bed with her."

Mina's eyes grew round in mock shock. "You're just out of surgery." She leaned over and lightly pecked at Nash's forehead.

"Ow, ow, ow..." Her smile turned into a snicker. "The forehead hurts. Only the lips are safe. And the surgery was last night. If there was dirt around here, I'd rub a little on the wound, and it will stop bleeding... eventually."

Mina's eyes got even wider as she slowly wagged her head. "You are atrocious. Someone should put you out of your misery."

Nash smiled. "Too late. You already said I do."

Mina walked over to the door and quietly closed it. Returning, she hesitated. "Are you sure you're okay?"

Nash wiggled to her right to make room. She patted the bed on her left. She smiled as her wife dropped the five inches of her spike heels. "They must be your Jimmy Choo's."

The woman lifted the thin blanket and sheet as she climbed in. "Damn straight. I'm out here in the land of heathens who shot my wife." She snuggled down into Nash.

Nash wrapped her left arm around her wife. "I like the new wig. It's incredibly Cathy Rigby."

Mina rested her hand on Nash's chest, feeling the soft thump of the heart. "It's my new travel wig. Easy care. Take it in the shower, wash it, and then blow it out in a minute." She smelled her wife's neck. "They must have washed you for the surgery. You don't smell like the new stuff you've been using. I like that earthy forest smell."

The door opened. Nash looked out the corner of her eye but couldn't see the door. "Is there a decrepit old Indian standing in the doorway?"

"He's got a dog."

"That's Powder. My new... our new child."

Uncle cleared his throat. "We can come back later."

Nash tried to snort but only breathed out. "Come on in. Family is family. Uncle, this is my wife, Mina. Sounds like the bird, but named after a female hole in the ground. Honey, this is Uncle."

Mina pushed her finger on Nash's chest. "Your uncle? I thought you only had a sister."

He stuck his hand out. "She does. My name is Oceal, but nobody can say it right, so I'm just Uncle."

Powder jumped up on the bed and settled at Nash's feet. Nash felt Mina tense, so she squeezed her closer. "It turns out Powder is a bed kind of dog."

Uncle nodded. "And she has her own nurse who gave her a shower yesterday and probably any day she sees fit. She had the same doctor take the buckshot out of her that took the buckshot out of you."

Mina rose slightly. "They shot her?" She turned to the dog and stuck out her hand. "Come, show Momma Mina where they shot you."

Powder crept forward on her belly between Nash's legs.

Mina curled down. "Where did they shoot my girl?" She found the bandage and then started fussing with the preening dog. Powder whimpered softly. "Oh, my... oh, honey, you're injured. Momma Mina will make it all better."

Uncle rolled his eyes at Nash. "And with that, a perfectly heroic dog turned into a simpering froufrou dog. Dude, you're on your own here. I'll stop in tomorrow."

Nash stuck her left fist out. They touched knuckles. "Debrief tomorrow. Bring Muna. I have a little work for her."

Uncle furled his lips and gave her a two-finger salute off his forehead.

UNCLE AND MUNA STOOD IN THE DOORWAY.

Mina bent over and kissed Nash. "I'm going to take my new daughter for a walk. You kids have fun." Turning to Uncle, "Where did you put the leash yesterday?"

Three voices answered. "We don't need no stinking leashes."

Nash frowned at Mina. "No work you have to do?"

She laughed. Shaking her head with a knowing smirk. "I didn't even pack my laptop. It's at home. Still plugged into the buffet charger. My day planner is closed and lying on top. Even my phone says I'm out of pocket because of a medical emergency. D.C. can go to hell for all I care."

Nash laughed as she waved the other two in. "D.C. falling apart just means more work for you."

Mina rubbed her thumb and fingers together as she left. She nodded at the other two.

Nash raised the head on the bed. "Grab some chairs. Can I order you two anything?"

Muna snickered. "Hot pork rinds?"

Nash pointed at the small built-in dresser. "Top drawer."

The light sparkled off the iridescent threads in her hijab. She drew out the bag and turned with a shocked face.

"Sometimes my wife can perform miracles. Other times, she just amazes me. I had told her about your fondness for the tongue-searing pigskins. She stopped by your old drug dealer and brought you a bag from home."

Uncle yawned. "Does coffee come out of the water faucet?"

The orderly rolled in a cart. "No, but we try to stay on the right side of the law." He lifted the cover in the center. There was a small assortment of doughnuts.

Nash growled. "There better be an apple fritter in there."

The orderly smacked his mouth wetly with a bored look. "No... but..." He pulled a small cover to expose a bowl of cut-up pieces of fritter. "I figured you would rather have finger food." He moved the bowl to her roll-around side table. And then he added the large sippy cup. "Two creams and one packet of pink sweetener."

Nash smiled up at him. "Thanks, Vlad." She frowned and looked at the clock. "Aren't you off?"

"Buffy is late on Mondays. She drops off her daughter. So I'm just about out of here."

"Thanks again."

He wiggled his fingers as he left, pulling the door behind him.

Nash sipped the coffee and popped a piece of fritter into her mouth. Closing her eyes in ecstasy. "Okay, first. The shooting. Last thing I remember, Thomas had coughed up his rifle and badge. Or something to that effect."

Uncle shifted as Muna opened her mouth to talk. She closed it and looked at Uncle. He offered out his hand.

Nash rumbled. "Get on with it, Uncle. You like telling stories, and Muna can fill in the facts."

He shifted and touched his little finger to the small piece of doughnut at the side of his mouth. "I was over next to the other side of the barn, but from my perspective. Cindy busted out of the Indian door and shot you when you hesitated. Muna and the sheriff fired at the same time and took out Cindy. Moments later, a man and a woman burst out of the front door, and the total brass count was well over eight hundred in the first seconds. They never stood a chance. It looked like the ending scene of Butch and Sundance."

Nash licked her lower lip as she imagined the scene. "The breachers?"

He shook his head. "They never made it to the door. The Crawfords had set up a camera to watch the front. It was show time by the time the breachers were under the window."

"Cindy?"

Uncle wiped his mouth with the napkin. "One in the chest, one in the head." He looked at Muna. "Between the eyes." He lightly tapped his finger on the bridge of his nose.

She cleared her throat with a slight cough. "I didn't want to chance her wearing a vest. There are rarely any second chances."

Nash blinked as she took it all in. "Center mass..."

"He was shooting a thirty-aught-six. It was a full wad-cutter. It removed her back. She was dead before she tipped over."

"Any word on Thomas?"

Uncle furled his lips and then shrugged his face. "They did a field interview and then let him go like you ordered."

Nash scrunched her eyes. "As I ordered?"

Muna chuckled and nodded. "Yeah. Same reason Uncle told the medic to knock you out. You were down but still in charge. You told the head guy with Homeland that if he wanted a pissing match, you'd arrange it in D.C. Or something close to that effect."

Uncle smiled. "The sheriff didn't know you had added him to the ICS, so he had given up his badge and rifle. For all his ignorance about things, he knows the law. But you told Homeland he had a killer to catch."

Nash waved at Muna. "Do you have the info I had you put together?"

The junior agent reached down into her briefcase and pulled out her laptop. Booting it up, she called up the file. "What do you want?"

Nash waved her finger in the air, swiping right. "The last series of phone logs."

Muna moved through the file and then turned the computer around so they all could see. She put it on the rolling side table. "I put them together chronologically, but I wasn't sure how they matched up. The first is from eleven years ago and was on hard copy."

"The one number that has never changed is area code five-zero-three. It's all the northeastern quarter of California."

Muna highlighted it.

"Five lines are coming into Harkin County Sheriff's Office. This number goes to only one desk. This phone belonged to a young man in San Francisco named Zebulon Beaty. He aspired to be a wildlife photographer and drove his motorcycle all over northern California, taking pictures until he disappeared. The last number he called, at the bottom, was to a friend. That friend remembers how excited he was about going up to go camping with an older man he had found. The term was a daddy."

Nash flicked her finger, and Muna changed to the next record. "This was a student named Robert Portman. He was studying at the Truckee Community College in mining and engineering. A quiet young man who had only recently come out to his family."

Muna found the phone number six times. The next to the last number called was one of them.

"He called his sister. The last number. He was going camping with an older man he was becoming involved with. According to her. She never heard from him again."

Uncle leaned his head in. "A pretty damning pattern, considering the results."

Nash looked from the computer to Uncle. She waited.

He shifted and glanced at Muna. "I guess you laid this all out to the sheriff before you two came up."

"Yes. After you left Saturday morning. Once I was confident he was innocent, I told him I had something else for him." She tipped her head at the computer. "I couldn't read his reaction. He wasn't mad or shocked. It was like he knew it was coming. He just didn't know when. The whole way up to the ridge, we only talked about the area. It was as if we were still back in high school, and football was over."

Muna sighed. "When Homeland released him, he drove back to the office. As he walked past the officer, he said he wanted to talk to him in his office. As he got to his office, a single shot rang out. Otis Greely committed suicide at his desk. On the desk was his badge, a well-used blackjack, and a typed letter addressed to the sheriff. He knew it was only a matter of time."

"At his home, they found a box with twenty-seven wallets. Two of the wallets dated back to his fleeting time in the navy. The IDs matched two sailors they believed had fallen overboard and were lost at sea."

Nash looked at Uncle. "Twenty-five. Time to get the team of divers to scour the entire length of Bone Creek."

He wagged his head somberly. "I don't swim."

Nash squared her jaw. "And not a job I'll be doing either."

36

HOME FIRES BURN

THE CAR WAS gray enough for the deputy director to approve. Powder had long since stopped watching the road and laid on the seat with her head on the center console. The engine purred instead of rumbled as Nash lazily guided the car through old memories and newer ones. The car's engine wasn't seven hundred horses of Hemi, but it was close enough.

The forced week in the hospital, and mandatory two weeks of physical rehabilitation, with a week of extra time for occupational therapy, had done her good. Having her wife oversee the entire process while they poked around the Bay Area improved their relationship.

Only once did Mina give in and spend an hour in an internet café on unsecured computers doing generalized snooping. She had asked Nash to drag her out at the end of sixty minutes because the café employee didn't know how to cut off a terminal.

Nash had called the employee an enabler. The guy smiled and called a friend to ask if he knew where to get a custom T-shirt made with the same sentiment.

Mina had indulged Nash in returning the truncheon to Mo and his magical trinket store. Nash was sure there would be future phone calls and special decorations appearing in their condominium.

She nosed the car off the highway and across the parking lot to the window. After a moment, the young woman looked up and smiled and waved.

Nash turned to Powder. "Are you going to behave, or do I need to get the leash?"

The dog groaned and nuzzled her arm.

After a quick walk out to a space of pine needles for a lawn, the two entered the café.

Tracy kneeled. "So this is the famous Powder."

Nash looked down. "It's okay, girl. She's a friend." She moved her finger forward.

Powder ambled forward and sat sideways to be fawned over. Tracy hesitantly scratched her chest and then more vigorously as Powder leaned into the scratching.

Tracy looked up. "I think she likes this."

Nash sat in the booth. "She likes any attention she can get. Just don't wash your hair with the cheap stuff my sister uses."

Tracy smirked. "I make my own from Ivory flakes in squaw tea and sage. Sometimes I splurge and add lavender."

Nash raised her eyebrows. "Do you sell it?"

"Nah, but I do make it for a few friends."

Nash smiled. "My wife would pay you double if you could mail it to us in D.C. Maybe we could help you get a side gig going."

Tracy stood as Powder ducked under the table. "I'd like that. Coffee?"

"And dinner. I think Powder would go for a hamburger patty or a cut-up steak."

A while later, Tracy slid into the other side of the booth as Nash finished her dinner. "I got the night off for Friday. I know many other people will be there."

Nash put her fork on the plate, wiped her mouth with her

napkin, and slid the plate forward an inch. "When was the last tribal funeral you heard about?"

The girl slumped slightly. "Dad's. Kind of." She looked up with moist eyes. "It wasn't a full tribal thing, but many people remembered him from football. But it isn't the same when there are just ashes to spread." Her mouth firmed as she turned to look out the window.

Nash rocked gently. "Sometimes, ashes are the cruel reality they leave us with. Other times, they are the gentlest reminder of whom we, the living, truly are."

Tracy seemed to talk at the window. "Have they said where they will dust her ashes?" She wiped her cheeks and looked back with red-rimmed eyes.

Nash leaned forward and crossed her arms on the table. "No. Not yet. I'll be talking to David Red Feather tomorrow morning."

Tracy nodded. "It's going to be strange going back to the community center without Dad."

"I've never been to the new center. The stick games were always at the VFW hall. They just called it the community center."

Tracy's mouth pulled back on one side as she softly snorted. "Dad used to say the VFW stood for *very fine whiskey*, and the hall was on the res, so the guys didn't have far to walk home."

Nash firmed her lower lip in agreement. "I'm sure it didn't contribute anything to sobriety."

NASH STOOD ON THE SHORE AS SHE WATCHED THE small, red inner tube with the re-breather unit in the middle. She knew the unit's hose was about thirty feet long. The diver was an attached SEAL member on loan to the FBI or a search and rescue diver attached to the FBI directly.

The dive master stepped out from under the larger canopy. He watched the unit for a moment and then looked at Nash. "Ever dive tether?"

She looked at the man. Except for the lines just starting next to the eyes, he could have passed for any of the young guys she had trained with at North Island. She shook her head. "We used re-breather units in the Virgin Islands. But we were too deep for teth-ers, and even with a torpedo scooter, the drag would have been too much if we could."

He smiled as he watched the inner tube. "Torps are fun. I got to use some big boys a few years back. A lot of fun at twenty knots."

She pointed out to the breathing unit in the water. "I would have thought you guys would do the buddy system."

He tossed his chin at the unit. "Three divers are working off that one unit. When the battery pack is down to only twenty percent, I'll get a warning blast up here, but they get a chime every ten seconds until they hit five percent, and then the chime becomes a constant wailing. You can't ignore it."

She glanced at the other tents with the walls down. "Are you finding much?"

He nodded back at the tents. "The first week, we worked two teams out from the pool you worked over. We also re-examined the area you worked. We found some interesting, much older bones, including most of a bear. We're pretty sure it was a black bear from the size and worn teeth."

"But there were more skeletons I missed?"

"Don't beat yourself up, Agent. We found mostly a small bone here and a larger bone there. Just bits and pieces, really. But along with animal skeletons. We bag and tag them, and eventually, they will go down to UC Davis to be cataloged and studied."

Nash twitched her head. "Pi?"

The guy smirked. "Yeah, the brain on tiny legs."

She gave him a hard look.

He put up his hands. "Easy, Agent. My wife is only four foot six. Pi is quite the celebrity in the small world. It's rumored his IQ is over one eighty—enough to have Mensa chasing him and smart enough to keep them at a distance."

"What's your wife do?"

"She runs her own lab. She's an epidemiologist. They're working on vaccines and cures for retroviruses."

"HIV?"

He nodded. "That's one of them. But her hard-on is the common cold and other pulmonary complications. Upper respiratory diseases are a genuinely serious threat to those with dwarfism."

Nash turned back to the creek. "So skeleton count?"

He tipped his head at the other tent. As they entered, the stainless-steel tables and other medical-grade equipment surprised her. He smirked. "Surprised we aren't roughing it out here?"

She licked her lower lip. "Well, it is a two-mile-long autopsy of a creek that needs to be handled scientifically..." She peeks out the side of her eye at the guy laughing. She chuckled. "Yeah, not what I expected. We just found stuff and threw them in body bags and gallon zippers. This is more like something uptown."

He leaned against one table. His face was as serious as the nature of what they were doing. "Several years ago, I was working a body dump in the gold rush country. It was a nothing hole in the mountain called Electra. It sits on the north fork of the Mokelumne River."

He paused and looked along the rows of tables. "We were a young crew. Basically, fresh out of the Q. We should have had an old man running us. But we didn't. So we missed things we shouldn't have. One girl was from a nearby town. Jackson. She had told her mom she was riding her bicycle to Mokelumne Hill to see a school friend."

Nash's mouth firmed. "She never made it."

His head vibrated. "She made it. And if they had stayed there, we wouldn't have had a job to do. But her friend had a crush on a boy at school... The two snuck out, and someone found their bicycles up the river. When they called us in, the case was already three years cold. We got bones and a little more. The teeth and jaws were shattered."

"There went the dental records."

He nodded. "We had little more than card tables set up at the camp. We just heaped the bones as we found them. Figured the squints, whoever they were, would sort them out. But there wasn't anything we could see to use in identifying them…"

Nash winced. "And it was in the middle of the outback, working in the most primitive conditions, where you young bucks didn't want to be…"

He got a hurt look on his face and feigned being stabbed in the heart. "Ouch… But we deserved that." He nodded. "Yup, we missed a tiny gold locket. And by the time the big tubs of bones got back to Los Angeles, they got kicked to one side. We hadn't even taken the time to count the number of hands and feet. There were five."

"A third girl."

"It was a month before someone started washing the bones and sorting them. And by that time, the gold miner had dragged up and headed for Mexico."

She looked at the tables. "Did they ever find him?"

"Not to my knowledge. But later, we discovered he hadn't been around when we were there. It wasn't until he came home that he heard about the big news. Then he fled."

"So from then on, you set it up and process everything the same way you would in a lab."

He pulled a small tablet off the table and booted it. "So far, between your findings and ours, we're only six short of your target of twenty-five." He looked up. "But the crew up north floated down the first eighteen hundred feet and think they have found another dump. We're bringing in a floating magnetometer detection unit. It should help us do a more thorough job. The wheel weights make it an easy target for finding the area, but we would also like to get every possible bone out. You never know when a watch, ring, or necklace could help identify the remains."

She nodded, thinking of what she would do in a few hours. "And getting closure for the family, friends, and maybe a tribe."

"I heard about this evening." His lips furled. "I don't see it as an easy thing to do. Even after all these years."

Her eyes closed as she shook her head. "Someone handed me a list. It goes back twenty years. Hundreds of kids go missing from reservations every year."

"It must be hard on such a small community?"

She bit her lower lip as she held her hand out at the long, bones-filled tables. "It's time to start the conversations. Otherwise, we will keep filling tables with bones."

BONFIRE

TRACY HUGGED Nash and then squatted down to pet Powder. Nash stood watching as dozens and dozens of people she had never met or didn't remember quietly entered the bonfire ring carved in the sports field. Occasionally, a person would stop and shake her hand, along with a mumble of quiet greeting.

The sundown had been spectacular. But as the dark settled down on the overflowing parking lot, and people took their seats on the rings of logs, a man strolled out of the dark. Nash hadn't seen the headdress since high school. She smiled at the meaning it had placed on the evening's event.

He stepped to shake her hand. "Agent Running Bear?"

She nodded with a soft smile. "Chief Red Feather?"

"Let's bring our daughter home."

Nash smiled wider. "Which one?"

The feathers rustled as he rocked his head. "Both. Come. Join me for the lighting ceremony."

They walked to the one end of the inner ring. He extended his hand to the log. She sat.

He turned and nodded at the young boy in tribal attire. The boy stooped, picked up what looked like a bird's nest, and carried it to the stacked wood in the center rock ring. Kneeling, he placed the bird's nest inside the pile of wood. Leaning forward, he blew on the embers secreted in the nest. Soon, a small flame consumed the nest and grew. The flame became larger and sprouted off arms that crawled along the small twigs, the larger branches, and finally, the larger logs.

The chief raised his arms out with open hands. "As we welcome the light of the fire to let us see in the dark, so do will ask for the light from the Great Spirit to guide us in our kiva tonight."

Nash stood as the chief turned. "We welcome one of our daughters, Nash Running Bear, who brings us one of our other daughters."

Nash stepped forward and held out the woven pine needle urn. "Many moons ago, a daughter of the tribe became lost. I return to the tribe, Betsy Singer." She handed the urn to the chief.

He nodded as he took the urn. Turning back to the fire, he stepped close. Holding the urn under his left arm and hand, he removed the lid and held it with his left hand. Reaching behind him, he drew out a fan made from raven feathers.

The congregation stood.

As he tipped the urn, he fanned at the mouth. Ashes drifted into the fire. "We release our daughter Betsy Singer to the spirit of the fire, that her spirit may embrace the smoke that we may breathe in the spirit, and she will live within us."

When the urn was primarily empty, he put the lid back on and set the pine needle jar in the flames.

Stepping back, he raised his arms again. "Great Spirit, look after our daughter, Betsy Singer. As you hear how she was a part of our lives, so shall she become part of our memories." He turned and stepped to the log and sat.

Nash recognized the woman as she stood. The woman clutched her hands in front of her. "Betsy was my student. She loved the color yellow. Her favorite time of the year was spring when the poppies bloom." She nodded and sat back down.

An older man stood with the help of a cane. "I see you, Betsy Singer. You always had a smile and a good morning for me when I walked past you going to school." He wobbled and then sat back down.

A woman stood. "Betsy Singer was a bright star in my life. She liked my dog and always stopped to pet him even when he smelled of skunk."

Tracy Three Toes stood. "Betsy was younger than me. She was the quiet in a storm."

The evening continued. Each person made an observation about the girl. In the end, there could be no doubt that even a shy, quiet girl is an integral part of the community.

As everyone sat in the silence after, the chief turned to Nash and held out his hand for her to speak.

Nash ran her hand over Powder's head and bent forward to kiss her on the head. Standing, she stepped forward and looked around at the faces glowing from the now-waning fire.

"Some of you know me. Some of you know I work for the FBI now. Some... okay, most, know I've been out at Bone Creek these past months. We were called to come to investigate a skeleton that was found. Now, we are looking for the rest of the twenty-five skeletons. Young men. Young men who came to go fishing or camping or just to hang out in the forest. But they never meant to become missing. Nobody ever intends to become missing. And yet, every year, hundreds of tribal girls and some boys go missing."

She looked around at the gently rocking heads of agreement and shared knowledge. "The best way to not go missing is to talk. If you are having a hard time, reach out to your parent or an elder. Even the chief, if that is what will help. If you need to, go to the authorities. If your local authority won't help, I have provided the chief with a page of numbers you can call. There are also websites you can get to. If you don't have a computer, go to the school. You can go see Sheriff Brady if you need to. Or, if you really need to, even my work number is on the list. Just know I spend more time in the field than I do with my boots under my desk. So you will get another special agent, and they will reach out to me wherever I am."

She looked back at Powder. The last of the fire glowed in her eyes. Turning, she firmed her lips in furls. "At one time or another, we all need help. The hardest part should be the easiest. Reaching out to someone else. They may not be the conclusive answer, but they can help you determine who has the answer. But without that communication, we will continue to bury our young people again and again."

Her left hand quietly snapped her fingers. Powder took a few steps and sat next to her leg. "This is Powder. Three months ago, I didn't know I needed her. But she knew, and she saved my life. She pushed me out of the way of most of the shotgun blast. We shared some of the blast, but her vest took most of the damage. And I'm speaking to the elders here. The tribe needs your wisdom. It needs you to take the bullet if need be. And I'm talking not about the lead from a gun but of the pushback that you already know from experience. Nothing will change if you throw up your hands like your elders did. But if you stand by your tribe, the tribe cannot only survive but thrive. Your sheet will have all the same phone numbers, even mine. Use them, or find someone who can."

She turned with Powder and walked back to her seat.

The chief rose with his arm outstretched. "Let us once again remember our daughter."

The collective stood as the young men threw pails of water on the remaining embers. A great cloud of steam and smoke billowed from the center and filled the rings.

As the last members quietly left, the chief turned to a quiet Nash. Taking her hand. "Again, thank you for bringing Betsy home.

And, too, thank you for giving us a path to prevent this from happening again. I will send copies of the guidelines to all the other tribes. They will need to find their own ways, but by talking, we can make a difference."

"Communication is always the key."

38

GOING HOME

NASH KNOCKED on the door in the early morning light. The yard stood brown, mowed but barely. She noticed spots where the house could use paint. She looked along the street. The mailboxes lined a quiet lane bracketed by tall, naked-until-the-top lodgepole pines.

The door cracked but didn't open. She frowned and pushed it open. "Thomas?"

"I'm back here in the bedroom."

She wandered along the blank, short hall. No pictures had ever hung on these walls. There weren't even small holes where nails had been. She remembered his parent's house. Photos of the family, a photo of Mt. Shasta taken by his mother, and a drawing or two by a young Thomas. His mother's home had a sense of pride in the family and the nest she feathered. This hall and the living room only felt like the remnants of a barn-like furniture store.

She sauntered down the hall to the bedrooms. She heard boxes moving in the back room.

The room lay about in disarray. The mattress and box spring leaned against the back wall. The bed-frame parts lay on the floor beside them. Boxes stood stacked next to the long nine-drawer dresser. Next to the closet, three large boxes stood tall with open

257

fronts, exposing the hanging clothes. Thomas stuck the last handful of hangers and clothes in the last box. He turned as he waved his hand at the boxes.

"I'd tell you to take anything you'd like, but I don't think you wore the same size." His eyes ran over the clothes. "Or taste."

Nash blinked. "I noticed stacks of boxes in the living room as well."

"Pete Sorenson is coming over this afternoon. He will take all this down to a women's shelter in Sacramento. I don't think anyone around here would want to wear her clothes. At least down there…" He glanced up. "They'll go to good use."

Nash nodded. "Can I take you to breakfast?"

He gazed around the stripped room. Adrift. "I need to finish this."

She reached out and rested her hand on his arm. Stopping him. "Take a break. How about a cup of coffee?"

His shoulders slumped. "I already packed the kitchen."

"Okay. How about the Golden State? We can get a couple of coffees to go." She studied the sag in his face. "We can stand on the side of the road and drink coffee and throw rocks at every third car or fifth truck."

He smiled with a soft snort. "And we weren't even drunk that day."

Nash shook her head. "Nope. Just an acute case of seniorities, bored with the end of school not coming fast enough."

He rocked with a silent chuckle at the memory. He looked around the room. "Fuck it. I need breakfast."

Nash smiled softly. "I'll buy, Sheriff."

He leaned in. "Damn straight, Secret Squirrel. I paid the last two times."

Thomas stood on the walkway at the front door and stared at the keys in his hand. There wasn't a key to the front door. Looking at the doorknob, he realized for the first time that it never had a keyhole. They had never locked the door, and he had just never thought about it. He turned, blinking.

Nash smiled at Powder standing on the console—watching them.

"We'll take my car. I don't want to eat roadkill at the Golden State. We'll go down to Taylor. It'll give us some private time to talk." He squinted at her as he walked to the passenger side. "What about your dog?"

"She's an official Secret Squirrel and will never talk."

He shrugged and climbed in. Powder sniffed at his ear, so he rubbed her cheek and played with her ear.

The car rumbled softly to life, and Nash pulled out onto the street.

She peered over at him. "I'm assuming, with all the boxes, you're moving away?"

He looked out the front. "Just over to the apartments for now. They're furnished, so I can make a clean start. There are too many memories. Good and bad."

Nash turned at the highway. "I can't even begin to imagine..."

He leaned back in the seat and was silent for a few miles. "Remember the old mangey hunting dog my dad had?"

"A red bone or something. Had long droopy ears."

Thomas grimaced and scraped his lower lip with his upper teeth. "One summer, we were out hunting. The dog got into it with a badger or something. He got torn up a bit. Not much, but some days later, we knew. He wouldn't go near the water bowl. He stopped eating and got testy. Whatever he had fought with had rabies." He glanced over. "That night, Dad took him out in the backyard and shot him. We buried him deep under the catalpa tree. I always remembered Dad that night. We came back inside, and he told me. Even if it's your most loved dog, if it's rabid, your duty is to put it down. You don't cry about it; you just do it. Because by the time you know, they aren't the dog you loved." He reached up and kneaded the fur on Powder.

Nash took in a slow breath through her nose. "So what now?"

He swallowed. "I heard from an officer down in Fresno. Former marine. He's been on the force for six years. He got married a year ago. They want to start a family, but they don't want to raise kids in the city."

Nash glanced over. "For you...? Or Otis?"

He snorted. "Otis. Heck, you know me. I was born out in the pasture near Bone Creek. I've been to other places. Gone to other countries. I'll get past this, but I'm not leaving."

She rocked in understanding. They both knew there would be therapy involved, but it was true. They buried his roots deep in Harkin County. Even his parents were from Harkin County.

"While researching the county and the reservation, I came across an interesting piece of information."

He turned to face her. "Yeah?"

She licked her lips. "Have you ever seen Uncle's teepee?"

He snorted. "I think it's called a yurt. But yeah. What about it?"

"You know the open pasture it sits on the edge of, with a stand of aspens at the end?"

He gazed out his window toward the trees. "I've sat in that grove. A light breeze in the summer, and it sounds like a waterfall."

She glanced over. "It turns out the pasture and grove are mine. Eighty acres."

"What are you going to do with it?"

She cracked her window. "Nothing. I can't sell it to anyone but the tribe. I guess I could rent the pasture out, but then I'd have to fence it. But my guess is a well, septic, and some solar panels wouldn't cost much to make it livable to drop a teepee on. You'd already know your neighbor." She looked over.

He rubbed his fingers over his few days' worth of beard growth. "It sure would be peaceful out there under the aspens."

ALSO BY BAER CHARLTON

The Very Littlest Dragon: NEW Editions
(All-new full-color ebook, a paperback with
coloring pages, and a full-color Collector's Edition hardback)

Stoneheart — Pulitzer Nominee 2015
Angel Flights
What About Marsha?
Pirate's Patch
Flat Surf

I Drink Coffee and Make Shit Up
One Writer's Journey Without Signposts

BAER CHARLTON

ABOUT THE AUTHOR

Bestselling author Baer Charlton graduated from UC Irvine with a degree in Social Anthropology, monkeyed around for a while, and then proceeded onward with a life of global travel, multi-disciplinary adventure, and meeting the memorable array of characters he would come to describe in his writing. He has ridden things with gears, engines, and sails, and made things with wood, leather, and metal. He has been stitched back together more times than the average hockey team; his long-suffering wife and an assortment of cats and dogs have nursed him back to health after each surgery.

Baer knows a lot about many things in this world. History flows through his veins and pours out of him at the slightest provocation. Do not ask him what you may think is a simple question unless you have the time to hear a fascinating story.

You can find more at
www.mordantmedia.com

9 781949 316254